Prai:

"A very funny book about books, about creativity, about a writer's need for isolation vs. the desire for community—these are outsiders among outsiders, and Ian M. Rogers writes with a wit that's as dry and sharp as the best academic satire. But this isn't just a delightful lampoon—it's a book full of heart and charm, with characters seeking meaningful lives, connection, and inspiration."
TIMOTHY SCHAFFERT, AUTHOR OF *THE PERFUME THIEF*

"I just added *MFA Thesis Novel* to my list of personal favorites alongside *Wonder Boys*, *Straight Man*, *After the Workshop*, and *Moo*. Wry, contemplative, heartfelt, and very funny, Ian M. Rogers is a terrific new voice, and his debut novel is a winner. I would recommend this book to any writer, unless I were teaching in an MFA program, in which case I'd require it."
SEAN DOOLITTLE, AUTHOR OF *LAKE COUNTRY*

"A fierce testament to the struggle of fitting into the MFA environment and choosing to blaze your own path. In this true-to-the bones novel, Rogers expertly crafts a plotline that is character rich, absurdly hilarious, and most of all, honest."
S.R. STEWART, MANAGING EDITOR OF *UNSOLICITED PRESS*

"A delicious romp through the smudged halls of academe where pretenders, druggies, hapless romantics, and the slightly talented do battle in fiction workshops trying to invent a book that will save them from the fate of ordinary life. While suffering bad advice, sabotage, regret, sloth, fear, and longing, their brawling over plot, women, and meaning reminds us of John Irving on steroids. This book will make you laugh out loud as it skewers the sacred cows of the graduate writing workshop and the world they mirror. Ian M. Rogers is a heck of a satirist!"
JONIS AGEE, AUTHOR OF *THE BONES OF PARADISE*

"If you have ever wondered what would happen if Joseph Heller had gone to a not particularly distinguished MFA program instead of Italy and World War Two..."
ANNABEL DAVIS-GOFF, AUTHOR OF *WALLED GARDENS*

About the Author

Ian M. Rogers grew up in New Hampshire before studying
literature at Bennington College in Vermont and creative writing
at the University of Nebraska-Lincoln, where he learned to
write short bios like this one. He has worked as a copy editor,
a greenhouse assistant, a school secretary, a grocery clerk, an
online test-grader, a housepainter, a gardener, and a teacher of
English in Japan.

ianmrogersauthor.com

MFA THESIS NOVEL

IAN M. ROGERS

MFA Thesis Novel
Copyright © 2022 Ian M. Rogers

All rights reserved.
Print Edition
ISBN: 978-1-925965-86-5
Published by Vine Leaves Press 2022

Cover design by Jessica Bell
Interior design by Amie McCracken

A catalogue record for this book is available from the National Library of Australia

For my parents.

But perhaps the great work of art has less importance in itself than in the ordeal it demands of a man and the opportunity it provides him of overcoming his phantoms and approaching a little closer to his naked reality.

– Albert Camus, The Myth of Sisyphus

Kendall Warren is a recipient of the Reginald R. Watcomb Fellowship for Short Story Writers, the Gregory P. Alderman Writer's Award, and most recently the Hasenpfeffer-Schweppman-Hildridge Book Prize for his short story collection, Where the Wind Becomes You, *due to be released in the spring. His work has appeared or is forthcoming in* The Journal of Midwestern Literature, The Black Sycamore Review, The New North American Review, White Frost, *and* The Great Plains Literary Review, *among others. He has twice been nominated for a Riverboat Prize, and his short story "Time of Dejection" was the 2016 winner of the Sterling Prize for Fiction. He holds an MFA in creative writing and is currently pursuing his PhD.*

Phillip "Flip" Montcalm is a writer, artist, poet, and occasional musician who went to a small northeastern liberal arts college you probably haven't heard of. He doesn't have any awesome awards or publications yet, but when he does, they're gonna rock your socks.

An Office with a View

a novel by Flip Montcalm

In the evenings I fall victim to a dull foreboding that immobilizes me in my bed, fearful that if I go to sleep I'll have to wake up again and face the void. I feel the same auguries of near-certain doom in the mornings when I lay with my eyes shut not wanting to get up, and in the daytime I feel listless and am prone to pulsating headaches centered around my nasal cavity. People who know me refer to me using words like *detached*, *morose*, *oversensitive*, and *tense*, and I scare easily when I see someone I'm not expecting approach from around a corner. When I'm forced to confront people in power I often stutter and feel unsure of what I know to be true, and I worry what few remnants of dignity I have left are being extinguished one after the other. It astounds and disgusts me that my life has turned out this way because I never thought it would when I was younger. After all, I work in an office.

My job would be infinitely more bearable if it wasn't for the work environment, which forces my coworkers to act in a stiffly unnatural manner when they interact with others (especially me). The work I do itself is not so egregiously awful (just repetitive, pointless, and boring). I might even consider it pleasant if I could do it alone in my room at my parents' house or at one of those cool, progressive West-Coast startups I hear about where the break rooms have foosball tables and employees are entitled to free snacks and massages (sometimes, I imagine, at the same time).

I don't, however, think anyone in my office plays foosball or would ever get a massage during work hours even if one was available—they're under enormous pressure to maintain a strict aura of professionalism so their superiors will think highly of them and give them promotions, even though there are very few promotions to be had now. I've worked here long enough to qualify for a promotion (or at least a raise greater than my 0.8% annual inflation allowance), though because of the segregated nature of our office hierarchy, there don't seem to be any higher positions I'd be qualified for even if someone were to leave or suddenly die. In the unlikely event I were to be promoted (perhaps because someone left or suddenly died) and no longer had to process the never-ending onslaught of orders, payments, cancellations, and cable TV bundle renewals that comes across my desk every day, I'm sure my new job wouldn't be much better. I'm hounded by my awareness that I'm an insignificant part of this company and thus deserving of my current four-and-a-half-by-five-foot work cube (big enough for only my desk and a single chair), though if I were to ever stop processing the never-ending onslaught of orders, payments, cancellations, and cable TV bundle renewals that comes across my desk every day the company would simply lay me off (no one here is ever fired) and bring in someone fresh out of college who's willing to work for less.

The office complex where I work is located beside a parking lot off of an interstate surrounded by dense woods, though I can't see the dense woods from my desk because my cube doesn't have a window. (It's out of fashion now to say *cubicle*, since that word implies that the people inside the cubicles are slaves to their jobs, and people who are slaves to their jobs don't like being reminded of this.) My cube is situated in the corner of a square of other, larger work cubes across from an office inhabited by an older man who leaves his door open and is prone to sudden clearings of his throat (har-UMMPH!). Adjacent to his office is that of a middle-aged woman who seems predisposed against ever saying more than three words to me; our one attempt at conversation occurred during my first few weeks at the company (back when I was still trying to make friends) as she emerged from her office carrying a Tupperware container filled with pasta salad made from tri-color rotini and cherry tomatoes:

Me (*cheerfully*): Headed to lunch?

Her: (*dismissively*): Yes.

Me (*embarrassed*): Have a good one then.

Have a good one. People need stock responses to survive interactions where actual conversation has been replaced by pre-assembled phrases that convey the appearance of interest ("Doing anything fun this weekend?" "No, not much.").

I'm unsure whether people realize this, though it's the best explanation for why so few conversations of substance occur in my workplace—several of my coworkers are avid *America's Got Talent* viewers, and I suspect it's because it gives them something to talk about.

Since there are so few younger people here, most of my coworkers begin what few conversations we do have by asking me where I went to college and what I studied, though when I tell them I double-majored in sculpture and electronic music they tend to pause awkwardly before changing the subject. As a result I've begun bringing a book to read on my lunch breaks.

If I were to stay at this job (which I'll have to if I can't find a better one) I wonder whether I'd eventually become a shallow, passionless, and slightly overweight thirty-something like my coworkers, incapable of any thought more substantial than a complaint about local zoning laws, with my abilities to think critically and creatively withering away until there's nothing left but—

1

"WHEN WE'RE young writers," the balding, middle-aged assistant professor said from his place at the classroom's front table, "we all think we can change the world and write something that's never been seen before." He paused to give his audience time to consider that maybe—just maybe—such boldness could yield effective results before continuing. "But this is just a fantasy we cling to when we haven't yet found our writing voices."

Flip's attention had mounted tremulously at this statement and he now sat upright in a state of nervousness tinged with surprise.

"I would agree," said Kendall, the sallow-cheeked student with the rimless glasses and polo shirt sitting at the other end of the table. "I'd say what this novel is suffering most from is an intense aversion to plot, with no real conflict to hook the reader's interest. What we have instead reads like an arrangement of the main character's thoughts, and while they tell us a lot about who we're dealing with, they never give me any incentive to keep reading."

Hearing his last two years of work dismissed so carelessly made Flip cringe while also balling his hands into fists under the table. Besides Kendall (who'd spoken with the same all-knowing smugness that had sparked Flip's dislike for him) and the professor (whose name was William Stark, though Flip was still uncertain whether to call him *William* or *Will* as he'd done with his undergrad teachers or to use the more formal *Doctor* or *Professor* he'd imagined were standard at midwestern universities. Since he didn't know for sure it seemed safer not to call him anything, though in his own mind, he referred to him as *Stark* for lack of a clearer solution) there were five other grad students sitting around the ring of tables. Between Flip and Stark sat Jackson, a lanky, relaxed individual who'd said little beyond his perfunctory introduction during their first workshop meeting and who'd said even less when Flip had tried talking to him at the English Department mixer the previous weekend. On Flip's right sat Craig, who wore all black despite the heat outside the air-conditioned English building and whose notebook pages were covered in inked spirals and lightning bolts. Beside Craig sat Melvin, whose evenly trimmed hair shone with carefully applied product, then Lawrence, whose vacant eyes wandered glossily around the classroom out of either curiosity or boredom. The final workshop member, Brad, sat straight up in his chair between Stark and Kendall, his fist thrust under his chin in strict attention and a hearty, open-mouthed smile stretched across his face. There were—as Stark had pointed out with nervous laughter during their first meeting—no women in the writing workshop, nor would any of the participants have been justified in checking anything other than Caucasian on their grad school applications.

Stark nodded very slowly in response to Kendall's point, his eyes focused on a space just beneath the ceiling-mounted projector. "Yes," he said, drawing out the word. "I think you've hit on something crucial." He moved to the whiteboard, where he uncapped a dry-erase marker and began writing as a stifling silence enveloped the room:

CONFLICT → PROBLEM → TENSION → PLOT

"As Kendall mentioned," Stark continued, "all novels start with an initial conflict that triggers a larger problem, which in turn leads to tension and creates plot. It's the plot that drives us to keep reading to see how the problem will be resolved."

Flip sensed that he'd done something abhorrently wrong but sat waiting for the best time to address it.

Stark glanced briefly down at his notebook. "What Phillier, Flip's novel seems to be doing is instead assembling a lot of *details*—mostly the main character's thoughts, but also a lot of," he paused, fumbling for the appropriate word, "*episodic* scenes that don't quite create a plot because they aren't linked to a progression of events."

"But there's plenty of conflict there," Flip announced, his words resounding with the same firmness he felt about the novel, "because we know the protagonist is miserable at his job and we're wondering what he's going to do about it."

This statement caused the other students to look at him for the first time. Lawrence's eyes slid awkwardly toward his and then away while Brad maintained oddly direct eye contact and nodded more vigorously than necessary. It was Kendall, though, who actually spoke. "I got that," he said as if this should have been obvious. "Very easily, actually, since it's clear that this guy—at least I assume it's a guy—doesn't like whatever he actually *does* at this office job of his. What's not clear to me is, first, where the novel's going, and second, why I'm supposed to care. There's plenty of people out there who hate their jobs, so I'm not sure what makes this guy so special."

Though the second of these comments struck him with its possible truth, Flip felt well-equipped to argue with the first. "Oh, it's definitely going somewhere," he protested. "We know the narrator doesn't like being trapped in a claustrophobic work cube, so that's why when the corner cube with the window view opens up in chapter six he tries to get it for himself as an arbitrary prize. Having an actual window is less important to him than achieving some sort of victory in the hopeless work environment."

In contrast to Flip's earlier interruption this explanation drove everyone (except Jackson, who still wore an expression of dull detachment) to glance down hesitantly at their clipped packets, with Melvin and Brad turning forward several chapters. Stark, too, looked down and resumed his seat at the front of the ring of tables. Amidst the paper shuffling Flip could hear the steady ticks of the wall clock.

After some seconds Lawrence aimed his blank stare out the window with his brow furrowed as he began to speak. "It's interesting that you say the problem of the new office happens in chapter eight," he said in his languorous southern drawl, "because I also wasn't seeing the importance of that as a turning point. I'm thinking that might be a little late to hook your readers, so instead you're going to want to start with a more pressing problem to draw them in right away." His childlike eyes lit up. "What's that term, the Greek one for starting in the middle of the story, at the moment of conflict, that in medium, or in mediation—"

The tone and speed Kendall used to interject was more arrogant than helpful. "*In medias res.*"

"That's the one!" Lawrence agreed. "I really think this novel would benefit by starting *in medias res* with that new office thing so we'd know right away what the book is about."

"I was thinking that too," Kendall said firmly. "Especially since the opening pages felt so disorganized. If we started with an immediate conflict between the narrator and whatever it is he's up against, we wouldn't need all that back story because we'd be getting to know the narrator through his actions."

"That," Melvin said, "and literary agents are always looking for attention-grabbing openings, so when they read your first page and can't tell where the novel's going they're just going to move on to the next email in their inbox."

Flip wanted to speak again and explain that starting with the new office scene would be impossible because readers needed to feel the anguish and despair of the working world before the new office appeared as a beacon of hope, but as he thought about the best way to say this he heard a distinct but low tapping of a fingernail on the table next to him. The fingernail belonged to Jackson, who still sat with his chin resting on his palm as his tapping finger indicated the words scrawled in the margin of his notebook:

Don't talk during workshop. Sucks, eh?

The pause was broken by Craig, who smashed his fist against the table while jerking his right leg up and down like he was working a sewing machine pedal. "I'm definitely all for starting with the action—we want to have the most things happen in the shortest amount of time so we'll keep reading, like doing a line of coke, but with your book. That's how coke works—it makes you want more, like, right away, but you're the cocaine dealer in this case because you have to give us more throughout the book little by little so we can get our fix. If you keep promising more then we'll keep coming back until your book's finished, and then BAM!—you hit us with a slam-crash ending so we'll want to buy your next book." He waved a hand casually toward the ceiling. "If you can't do that then readers are gonna go find another coke dealer."

"That's a clever way of putting it," Melvin said. He spoke in a business-like tone as he studied the room around him. "If you're looking for some good examples of attention-grabbing openings you might try Dwayne Furlough's *Turpitude* or Bernard Callahugh's collection *I Know the Truth I See*, since all those stories open with really strong conflicts."

"Or anything in Ashton Krantz's *Acreage of the Bedeviled*," Kendall said. "There are a lot of succinct opening lines there that draw you in to keep reading."

Flip hadn't heard of any of these books but had attempted to copy down a snippet of each title to google later. He looked back at Jackson's message as he wrote.

"My advice," Brad said, addressing the room for the first time, "is to scrap the whole office-with-a-view idea. I see where you're going with the Oscar Wilde reference, but you really need a more substantial focal point that leaves your character taking action instead of acting passively. I mean, who wants to read a novel where the main character gets stuck listening to a bunch of arrogant know-it-alls telling him what to do?"

"I'm glad you brought that up," Stark said. "If we're all clear on Phil—Flip's starting immediately at the point of conflict, does anyone have any thoughts on how he could give his main character a more active role?"

Once again, it was Kendall who answered first. "To be frank, I think Phil's novel would benefit from having his character do just about anything, since there doesn't seem to be much tension in his office at all. Instead we start off with this mass of characters all at once, making it impossible to keep track of them all and causing us to get confused."

"Yes," Stark said with a nod. "Instead of throwing out all the characters in one long opening scene, focusing on the main character's interactions with each of them individually would help us get to know them better, especially if you did it in separate chapters."

"I also feel like what we're reading is more a piece of something else," Lawrence said in his slow drawl. "Like the framework for a story without the story itself, or like the writer's just getting to know the character but doesn't know what he wants him to do, if that makes sense?" He extended the question as if afraid someone would cut him off, then stopped without saying anything else.

"It does," Brad said with an almost regal air of authority. "There's nothing about this character that makes me care about him. Not only is he not facing any real conflict, but he comes from a privileged middle-class family, he's college-educated, has a full-time job, and doesn't seem to be under much financial pressure—at one point he even mentions that he's almost saved up enough to move out of his parents' house." He allowed a pause, reminiscent of the one Stark had used to open the discussion, to let this sink in. "That shows me that he feels entitled, and he thinks his problems are the biggest ones out there. I found myself thinking that if this guy hates his job so much, why doesn't he just find a new one?"

Lawrence leaned forward. "I kept thinking that too! If he's that unhappy, why doesn't he just quit?"

Because there aren't any other fucking jobs he can get! Flip wanted to scream but didn't, sitting instead with his head slightly downward and Jackson's note not to talk peeking at him from the spiral notebook. *Because it was hard enough for him to get this job, because he doesn't have money to move to a bigger city, and because he has five student loans and a shitty car! It's not his fault no one wants to hire young liberal arts grads when they can hire an empty-headed dude-bro from the suburbs who slept through an economics major but picked up a bunch of internship experience! If I didn't have to spend all those summers working back at home I could have found some amazing opportunities that would have led to better things.* Upon finishing this thought Flip realized he wasn't sure what opportunities he could have found or what kinds of things they'd have led to, but he felt certain they must have been there somewhere.

"The financial angle's good though," Craig said with his leg still rocking up and down. "It works because his lack of money adds tension. Maybe this guy isn't getting ready to move out of his parents' house—maybe he isn't saving money at all because he's charging a bunch of stuff on his credit cards. Maybe he's shelling out money for his internet porn habit or he just bought a speed-boat and now he's got to figure out a way to pay for it. Maybe the repo men are coming to take the boat away, or maybe they already took it and now he can't impress this girl he promised to take on a romantic weekend to his uncle's friend's lake house. Maybe he's so strapped that he's got to rob the office or kidnap his boss's daughter for the ransom money while she's walking home from school. Maybe the book *starts* with the kidnapping, but then it goes bad when he has to deal with his boss's loud-mouthed preteen daughter who wants to post the whole thing on her Instagram story—and there's your book right there!"

Lawrence's eyes brightened at this. "I like that! You could even split the kidnapping scene into a short story to send to journals for some extra publishing cred on your CV."

"It's true, man," Craig said. "Publishing a shit ton of short stories in prestigious journals nobody reads is the best way to establish yourself as a writer."

And Melvin said, "I don't necessarily think this book needs an underage kidnapping, but I do think Craig's on to something with the money angle. You might consider how characters react when they're in desperate financial straits, like in Robert MacKenzie's *Shadows of the Tracks*, where the family's been passed up for jobs in the steel mills and has to work minimum-wage jobs to survive. That's the book that really helped me understand what it's like to be poor."

And Brad said, "Also, where are all your female characters? I only counted about two women in the whole thing. Writing a book with lots of women is key to showing agents you care about diversity, and it'll help you win over the female market."

And Kendall, who always seemed to have something to say, said, "I also found the sentences far too long and overloaded with adjectives, so you really need to trim your paragraphs down. All the text messages and handwritten notes also felt like cheap gimmicks to get my attention."

And Stark nodded at this and said thoughtfully, "It's best to be careful with that kind of experimental stuff, since it can make your book feel disorganized."

And Jackson, the message still peeking out from his notebook and his chin still resting in his palm, sat without having said a word.

Flip looked at his watch. There were fifty-three minutes to go.

2

Jackson Grant holds two MFAs and an MA in creative writing, all from large midwestern universities because that's where most of the funding money is. He's currently pursuing his creative writing PhD at a different large midwestern university and plans to figure out something else to do afterward since it's really hard to snag a higher-ed teaching job that pays a livable wage.

After finishing his undergrad he discovered that his English degree wasn't going to get him a job on its own, so he started working as a bartender because the money was good and he could sleep late. However, that all changed when he started his first MFA program and discovered that no one, including his advisor, gave a fuck about his six hundred-page novel that was a cross between In Search of Lost Time and Infinite Jest, which led to his nervous breakdown.

After a recuperative six months reading library books in his childhood bedroom he went back to grad school and started copying the kinds of short stories the other grad students were writing to give himself an easier time during workshop. When working within the same style got boring he stopped writing anything at all, leaving him more time for reading. His favorite things include Daniel Clowes's Ghost World (the movie or the book), Monte Cristo sandwiches, really deep bean bag chairs, and listening to the New Pornographers' Twin Cinema album on repeat. When he has to convince people he's important he sends out a bio that's more professional-sounding than this one.

THREE THINGS happened after the workshop ended.

The first was that Flip took the marked pages of his novel that Stark had tossed across the table, skimmed through enough of them to realize yet again that he was in trouble, and asked Stark whether—as he'd offered during their first class—he had the time to meet and discuss edits. Stark appeared startled by the question and stuttered that yes, they could meet, but that he was only on campus two days a week and was headed to a conference in another part of the state this coming Thursday, so perhaps next week would be better? The stumbling mode of Stark's date-setting made Flip unconsciously emulate his mannerisms and express his own uncertainty about what time before or after his classes or writing center shifts would be best to meet, so that in the end the exchange took longer and provoked far more embarrassment than it should have.

The second was that Brad, who'd been standing by the whiteboard scrolling through his phone while Flip talked to Stark, came over and wrapped his burly arm around Flip's shoulders, a gesture Flip assumed was meant to indicate camaraderie but that actually felt intrusive. Though Brad stood several inches shorter than Flip he was broader and more muscular in the chest, thus giving him the appearance of an individual who spent a lot of time at the gym. His arm clamped forcefully against Flip's shoulder blade as his face contorted into a grin.

"Nice job, buddy," Brad said, though this sentiment seemed to run contrary to all of his workshop comments. "Charlene and I were having some people from the department over on Saturday to watch the first game of the season, and we thought we'd invite some of the new people too."

The invitation came as a surprise to Flip for several reasons, chiefly because it was the first time anyone from the department had invited him to do anything outside of the welcome mixer. He also wasn't sure which game Brad was referring to—the time of year seemed to indicate football, though it was just as possible he meant baseball or some other sport. He felt a twinge of disappointment at the thought of having to watch most, if not all, of an entire football game, but took consolation in the near-certainty that at a gathering of writers said football game would almost certainly be relegated to the background.

"Sounds like fun," Flip said. "I'll be there."

Brad removed his arm from Flip's shoulder and smacked his hands together with a bang. "Great! Send me your info and I'll get you the address. And feel free to bring your plus-one."

Flip's embarrassment at not having a plus-one to bring was worsened by Brad's presumption that he did, in fact, have one, but he felt it best to clear up any misunderstandings. "Actually, it'll just be me."

"Ha ha, a single guy," Brad said with a great booming laugh as he wrapped his arm around Flip's shoulder again. "Must be pretty freeing to start a brand-new grad program without anything holding you back, am I right?"

Flip pretended to laugh and said that this was true, then changed the subject by pulling out his phone to exchange contact info.

The third thing that happened was that Flip walked into the hallway to find Jackson—who'd gone the entire workshop without saying a word—sitting on the bench beside the classroom door. A better word for Jackson's position would have been *splayed* since he'd extended both legs across the bench and was leaning against the table of books left free for the taking by members of the English Department. He was leafing through a faded textbook entitled *Technology & English Composition*, whose cover featured a pale white computer with a tube monitor and external floppy drive, though when he spotted Flip he tossed the book unceremoniously back onto the free table. "Rough break back there," he said.

Unsure what Jackson meant by this, Flip stood his guard. "Yeah," he said, "I guess it could have gone better."

Jackson leaped to his feet, his tall, lithe frame bending easily as he swung his messenger bag over his shoulder. "That's to be expected when you bring in ninety pages with barely a paragraph break," he said with a near-yawn. "Samuel Beckett himself would have had trouble with your book, so of course a bunch of overworked grad students aren't going to give it more than a glance."

This statement took Flip aback. "What do you mean? Like they didn't read it?"

Jackson stuck both hands in his pockets and began walking down the hallway, which Flip took as an unspoken invitation to follow. At four-thirty on a Tuesday anyone with business on the second floor of the English building had long since concluded it. Because the evening classes hadn't yet begun, a sense of tranquility had fallen over the hallway, which barely ninety minutes before had teemed with orange-shirted undergrads crowded outside the classrooms.

"*Reading*'s a funny word," Jackson said. "You can *read* something to immerse yourself with a sense of engagement, like I did the first time I read *The Hitchhiker's Guide to the Galaxy* and couldn't wait to see what happened next. Or you can *read* something to pick up the gist, like I read over the instructions for the blender I bought last week so I'd know which button to push. How closely you pay attention depends on how much trust you have with the writer, and you haven't earned that trust yet."

This insinuation caught Flip off guard. "How do you know that? People in writing workshops should always be open to new perspectives so they can expand their horizons."

Jackson kept his hands in his pockets as he walked. "You've got a lot to learn if you're going to fit in here. You're a first-year MFA student with no publications and no experience, so of course when the other grad students pick up your novel they're going to assume you're no good instead of trying to understand your goals—which means they'll reject anything you hand them that's different. It also didn't help that your chapters jumped all over the place without a clear plot, since that's one rule you're definitely not allowed to break in workshop unless you've already published a book—and then after you've published a book you can break any rule you want."

"What does publishing a book have anything to do with it?" Flip asked. "That attitude blindly favors people who are more established without considering the work itself."

Jackson shrugged. "Maybe the others would be willing to give you a chance if they didn't all have papers to grade and short story submissions to send to prestigious journals and books to read for their other classes, but it's more efficient to read just enough of your novel so they can say something intelligent-sounding about it during workshop and then move on. That's what I call sport editing—it's more about boosting their status in the workshop than about helping you as a writer."

At this point the anger festering within Flip had subsided and in its place appeared a sense of awe at the truths (or what seemed to be truths) tumbling so effortlessly from Jackson's mouth. "What did you think of my novel?" he asked.

"Hard to say," Jackson answered. "I didn't read it—I just skimmed the first chapter ten minutes before class so I could say something intelligent-sounding about it during workshop. What I did read had a restless urgency and lack of focus, but it was smart and passionate and observational in a meaningful way. It's too bad all that was buried beneath pages of rambling."

Jackson paused in his speech but not his stride to extend a sharp salute to an elderly, distinguished-looking man carrying a satchel. The man aimed his gaze squarely toward the floor but looked up when Jackson said, "Hey there—keeping busy?"

The man's eyes relaxed and his mouth fell into a relieved smile. "Always try."

Jackson turned back to Flip. "You also have to be careful about talking during your own workshop—it goes against the rules those guys at Iowa made up eighty years ago. Going against workshop rules makes you look like an amateur since people tend to confuse good writers with people who know how the system works."

As they reached the west side stairs Jackson extended a second salute of equal vigor to a goateed man with a canvas of tattoos below his shirt sleeves who'd emerged from the men's room with a mop and CAUTION sign. Jackson said, "Heya," to the man, and then, "You guys do a great job—this place always looks clean."

The man said, "Thanks, I appreciate that," as Jackson moved on to the stairs.

"People make assumptions about a story because they can't ask the author questions and instead have to guess," Jackson went on. "And since no one in grad school likes to guess, they make confident assertions about what the author's doing and how it's not working. People always trust the workshop speaker with the most authority, so that person's assertions become the consensus that everyone follows to avoid sounding stupid. Eventually people start writing new stories just to meet the consensus." His footsteps echoed through the stairwell as Flip trampled down in pursuit.

"That's a terrible way to run a workshop!" Flip protested. "How are we supposed to create new and innovative art if everyone follows the same standard?"

"You're assuming that the purpose of the workshop is to create new and innovative art," Jackson said. At the bottom of the stairs he pushed open the English building's doors, driving them into the scorching late-afternoon dryness that within seconds had sucked every ounce of moisture from Flip's body. The rush of heat left him feeling disoriented, and as he raised his head to the empty sky he blinked to adjust his eyes to the glare.

A tall, slender, and startlingly attractive girl with blonde hair reaching past her shoulders was walking across the courtyard toward them, her face brightening in recognition at Jackson, who extended a third welcoming salute. She wore a sharply cut red blazer over a t-shirt with a penciled outline of skyscrapers, an outfit too well-assembled for an undergrad yet too daring for a professor. To Jackson she said, "Hey stranger."

"I hear that," Jackson said. "We should meet up."

The girl laughed at this without stopping and said, "You've got my number," as she pulled open the English building doors and was gone.

Identical, flat-walled brick buildings flanked the courtyard around them, and in its center grew a long-branched deciduous tree ringed by flowering bushes. Behind and above the buildings rose the enormous, slate-gray and brown-pillared university football stadium, whose east-facing wall showed off the blaze-orange flames of the Prairie Fire team logo and the words *National*

Champions 1970, 1971, 1994, 1995, 1997. In addition to being the largest structure on campus, it was the first one visible to anyone driving in from the interstate.

"So how is workshop supposed to make us better writers?" Flip asked.

"Good question," Jackson said. "Something about your novel made people want to tear it down, and if you can somehow find the truth behind their posturing you might be able to find out what."

Flip wasn't sure he understood. "Is that what you do when people talk about your writing?"

"I've been in grad school a long time," Jackson said, "and I know enough to get through a workshop with only minor scathing. I will say, though, that you're on the right track by not trusting everything people say when they're trying to boost their reputations."

He turned on to a path beside a gleaming, relatively new, and expensive-looking building towering high above the campus. A sign bearing the university logo declared it to be the Peterson Business Hall.

"I guess it wouldn't have bothered me so much if they'd been able to empathize with the struggles I was writing about," Flip said. "Plus, Kendall seemed to take pride in telling everyone exactly what I'd done wrong."

"I'd be careful what you say about Kendall. He has a short story collection coming out in the spring, so that gives him credibility that you don't have."

"That doesn't give him license to act like a jerk."

"Maybe not," Jackson said, "but academia, especially out here, plays by its own set of rules. It's not like back East where people are more open and used to dealing with different kinds of opinions—in case you haven't noticed, things here tend toward the monocultural."

"I had noticed. Is it normal for a workshop not to have any women?"

"Don't forget people of different ages and races," Jackson said. "Ours is an extreme case for sure, though I think you'll find a lot of things about our program are extreme compared to others. In any case you can thank both the selection committee and the socio-economic conditions that led to our current workshop group, since it takes a certain mixture of ambition, parental pressure, and stupidity to make someone apply for an MFA."

Flip halted for an instant but kept moving, thinking back to the moment when he'd decided to apply for MFA programs but finding that he couldn't quite remember it. Was it possible that he'd always wanted to go to grad school, just like he'd always wanted to become a writer? The answer was no in bold italics. Or was it the case that he just hadn't been certain how one became a writer, especially when one's starting point was a miasma of poorly paid office work? He thought suddenly of the girl in the red blazer, then again of the novel, which had felt so promising only a few hours before. To distract himself he studied the students clustered around the business building's entrance, most of whom were staring at their phones, walking in silent groups, wearing an orange article of clothing with the Prairie Fire logo, or some combination of these.

"You, though, I wasn't sure about," Jackson said. "I read your bio in the department newsletter and figured you were either in for a rude awakening or just bad at making jokes. I grew up in Philly, but my dad moved us all around the Northeast for work. Our kind tends to seek out their own in strange environments."

"I don't like a lot of structure," Flip said, sticking his hands in his pockets in what he immediately recognized as an unconscious emulation of Jackson. "I came here to get away from work rules and people who thought it was weird that I wanted to be a writer. I want to write the kinds of novels that reveal truths about the world people can't explain for themselves but recognize on the page since that's what really resonates."

Jackson raised his eyes to the endless sky where beyond the football stadium and downtown buildings, there were no mountains to hide the horizon and the sun blazed down on them unhindered. "I used to think like that," he said, "but then I realized how the rest of the world works."

They'd reached the south corner of campus where an open green space stretched between the oversized admissions center and the street. Here, a pedestal-mounted statue resembling flaccid egg noodles formed an ominous divide between the university and the city. An archway over the yard's entrance had been decorated with iron-worked bars in the shape of a cornhusk, a flat-toothed sprocket, a herd of cattle, and a test tube spouting a line of bubbles.

"You seem like you know the grad school game pretty well," Flip said.

Jackson nodded once. "I try to stay informed about what goes on around me."

"Are you going to Brad's party on Saturday?"

Jackson laughed. "I've got better things to do, but you should check it out if you want to. Just be warned that sometime during the night Brad's going to ask you to read fiction submissions for the *Long Grass* literary journal, and I strongly suggest you tell him no unless you want to wave goodbye to what little free time you'll have while you're here. Also, before I forget—stay away from downtown on football game day, unless you're a fan of traffic jams and occasional fistfights."

Flip possessed zero interest in either of these things and recalled the mild unease he'd felt upon seeing the gigantic Prairie Fire stadium bulging out from the city as he'd steered the overloaded Honda off the main highway several weeks before. "Better things to do like working on a novel?" he asked.

Jackson laughed again and strolled into the crosswalk without waiting for the signal. "Yes, but you won't see it during workshop. The only stories I submit for workshop are ones I published during my second MFA since they tend to get the usual platitudes and arbitrary criticism. That's a lot less stressful than trying to make the writing I'm really interested in fit the workshop mold."

Flip found this admission unsettling. "So what's your novel about?"

"It's a secret," Jackson said.

Jackson's Secret Novel

A cynical tale of a twenty-something who's grown disillusioned with the world's shortcomings but knows there's nothing he can do to change them, so he decides to stand back, blend in, and coast along while pretending to care.

(He hasn't started writing it yet, though.)

3

It REALLY did bother him how abominably the workshop had gone, since up until Stark had started speaking Flip had been so confident that the novel would resonate with others the same way it did with him. The chapters he'd shown to the writer's group back home had always gone over well, sparking discussions about oblivious bosses and forced workplace conversations and the difficulties he and his friends had all faced getting out on their own after college. Those conversations—held around secondhand kitchen tables in cheap apartments as preludes to games of Carcassonne and Settlers of Catan—had made him feel like his writing held a real place in the world of grown-up artists who moved people. Those were the times he'd felt most like a *creator*, that bigger, all-encompassing category to which *writer*s belonged, a person who opened up new worlds for others. His entire reason for drawing or writing or composing off-key songs on his old Casio keyboard had always been to stir meaningful feelings in people the way so many other pieces of art and writing had in him, and making this happen, he'd realized, was the thing he most believed in.

The problem was that stirring meaningful feelings in people had gotten harder as his friends had all gotten busier with their jobs, significant others, and the mortgages on their fixer-upper houses. The others in the old writing group hadn't suddenly chosen to stop writing; they'd just dropped writing down a few notches on their priority lists until Flip had become the driving force behind their meetings and the only one still bringing new work. This gradual loss of the old Saturday night writing group, even more than escaping that horrible job, had sparked his quest for a place where writing still held meaning.

Flip thought about this as he walked back to his apartment south of downtown, where the east-west streets were all named after consecutive letters and the north-south streets were all numbered. The labeling system had initially struck him as ingenious since it allowed him to find his way from H Street and 11th to C Street and 23rd without so much as a glance at his phone, but within days the grid of identically nondescript streets had become disorienting since it seemed that any local flavor the city's neighborhoods might have aspired to had been sacrificed for ease of navigation. (Were these the kind of suburbs John Updike had written about?) Before making the three-day drive from the Northeast, he'd rented, sight unseen, a second-floor apartment in a square brick building that had been unceremoniously slipped into a line of single-family houses. The building was three stories high with four apartments on each story surrounding a central staircase, and he imagined each apartment having the same living room, the same bedroom, and the same dull teal-colored carpeting as his own. The building's one architectural frivolity was a metal awning stretching over the front steps that evoked a faint image of 1950s urbanity, and beneath it he'd exchanged a few awkward hellos with his cigarette-smoking neighbors in the evenings, though most of the time they just turned and pretended they hadn't seen him.

The apartment had no real furniture since there hadn't been space in the Honda for anything larger than the wood-paneled microwave from his old apartment, the packing trunk he now used instead of a bureau, and the folding card table and chairs he'd set up to double as an eating area and workspace. There'd also been very little time (and even less money) to procure new furniture after arriving, in addition to the difficulty posed by such a task. Back home if he wanted to scoop up a free Craigslist couch, it would have been easy to borrow someone's pickup; out here his options felt decidedly limited. Did furniture stores still deliver, like in old movies? Goodwill and Salvation Army certainly didn't, and anyplace that did wasn't likely to cater to his price range. If he wanted a real bed he could probably tie a mattress to the Honda's roof (also like in the movies) and drive it back to the apartment, but mattresses were expensive and the trip out had cost him more in gas money than he'd expected. He'd done some calculating before his arrival and found that after rent, utilities, groceries, non-deferred student loan payments, and the occasional haircut or clothing purchase, his monthly stipend for working in the university writing center came out a hundred dollars short—an unpromising start to this new chapter of his life. The alternate solution to the bed problem had come from an old friend's air mattress that only had to be re-inflated every four days and would do for the time being.

He threw his bag down in the living room and turned on the air conditioner since the walk through the blistering streets had caused pools of sweat to soak his t-shirt around the armpits and stomach. Before arriving he thought he'd been lucky to find an apartment with air conditioning since no apartment back home short of a luxury condo would ever offer AC, but he'd soon found that all of the buildings in the neighborhood and probably the entire city also had air conditioners mounted from their windows and he'd immediately understood why: the interminable heat of each identical, rainless day left him exhausted after more than a few minutes in the uncooled air. He stuck his face in front of the AC unit to cool himself down and then lay in the center of the living room with his limbs splayed across the carpet.

The others had made good points in that the novel started slow—the mailroom sabotage didn't even come until chapter four—and that it communicated with the reader through long, reflective paragraphs instead of action, but this hadn't felt like a problem until Kendall had pointed it out. Real life, after all, consisted of long empty stretches where people just thought about things rather than springing into action. That's what the novel's style was meant to show, just as the setting and characters were meant to show the confines of an office job where you couldn't be yourself and the only thing anyone cared about was giving you more work to do. Joseph Heller had captured paranoid office politics so perfectly in *Something Happened*, where the lines about feeling powerless and afraid at work had felt so real the first time he'd read them and every other time since. Work hadn't been a fun or stimulating place, and writing about it required a bleaker, more maddening narration that showed readers an exaggerated version of their own jobs. The writing in all the best novels always complemented their plots—*Lolita* worked solely because of its poetic yet playful narration, since only a fellow pedophile could have stomached a detached third-person version of Humbert Humbert's exploits. Great novels explored the limits of what was possible on the page, and when he'd finally felt ready to write his own it had also been the most natural thing in the world to explore those limits as best he could.

The limits of what was possible on the page. In both art and in real life that phrase embodied an escape from the mundane. Month after month processing those same cable invoices had made him feel like he was destined to stay in that office forever while his friends pursued actual career goals and started romantic relationships with people they cared about. For him, by contrast, things had stubbornly refused to move forward, provoking awkward discussions at family gatherings or when he bumped into old friends at the supermarket. As discouraging as things had gotten, though, he'd never regretted his college choices the way some of his friends had, since the exploration and unbridled creativity of his undergrad years had always felt right when so much of what came after felt wrong. The grad school acceptance—and more importantly, the funding!—had been a beacon of hope signifying that he too might finally be moving forward.

Out of habit he pulled out a pen from his pocket and twirled it around his fingers, enjoying the clicks as it rapped against his knuckles. Had the others not understood what he'd shared in the novel, or had they understood and just not cared? Maybe they'd been right and his sentences really were too long and labyrinthine in their use of parentheticals (though he loved the extended, breathless chaos resulting from a long sentence inserted at random, one that caught you in its twists and carried you disoriented around strange corners that turned out not to go anywhere but were fun anyway until they dropped you out the other end, unsure of what you'd gone through but knowing it had been fun) and needed to be tightened up so readers could take a breath. He'd admired Anthony Powell's use of clear sentences and truncated chapters in *Afternoon Men*, though as much as he loved that novel (and that incredible scene of wandering after the main character lost the girl!) its style seemed best suited for a different story. How could a writer convince readers to make sense of something difficult on the page? Some of his favorite books had felt near-impossible when he'd started them, but after many pages and help from skilled teachers he'd found countless payoffs that had made the effort worthwhile. Even if he'd possessed the credibility to keep people reading, it was a stretch to assume that his own novel stacked up to the more complex ones he admired—maybe his was just a haphazard imitation of Heller's *Something Happened*, or worse, Beckett's *The Unnamable*. (You must go on. I can't go on. I'll go on.)

No—*The Unnamable* had crossed a line where form superseded story and reader experience, leaving something that could be admired for its technical achievements but not enjoyed. He'd much preferred *Murphy* with its bizarrely distorted outsider's view of London, not to mention its self-centered characters obsessed with money and sex. That feeling of being the only one sane enough to see the insanity around you had always resonated with him— hadn't Aldous Huxley written about that? Didn't all of his literary heroes—the Holden Caulfields and the Leopold Blooms and the Ignatius J. Reillys—also stand as outsiders in an insane world where readers could recognize their own struggles with not fitting in?

Flip felt a dull ache along his back and rolled onto his side to face the line of books on the upturned egg box he'd rigged up as a shelf. That really was the problem: no one in the workshop had recognized their own struggles in his novel. Perhaps he hadn't accurately captured the materialism of the office world and the uninspired people who worked there. A more skilled writer could have done this through action and dialogue—hell, Fitzgerald did it in *Gatsby* when Daisy talked about waiting for the longest day of the year since her having nothing better to do than wait for it showed her innate flightiness. Having vapid characters say vapid things was always fun—that's what made *Daria* such a great show: *Daria* captured the distorted world the creators had seen all around them and shared with the MTV Generation.

He threw down the pen and rested his elbow on the carpet. What kind of place had he found himself in? Jackson had said that workshops weren't about producing writing that genuinely moved people—what kind of writing, then, did they actually produce? Kendall, too, had spoken with authority in the workshop, and Craig with a great deal of force—even Stark's momentously timed pauses had elicited something relatively close to esteem. If the workshop was really about putting on a show, how then could he find out what people really thought about his work?

Thinking about this reminded him of Brad's party—a party that could very well be an inroad to the grad student social scene. So far his classes hadn't offered much interaction: his Critical Theory class seemed limited to explanatory lectures without pause for discussion, while the elderly professor of the Great Plains Studies course had haphazardly asked for the class's thoughts on the reading and used each one as a jumping-off point for his own expositions. Neither class had been particularly stimulating, but could this also have been his fault in choosing literature electives? Amidst the program's Kafkaesque labyrinth of course requirements he sensed a formal blandness that seemed more like Kingsley Amis's *Lucky Jim* than anything he'd experienced during his undergrad—a bad sign after only two weeks.

There were also likely to be girls at the party, single girls he'd have the potential to flirt with and maybe even date. That had been the other problem back home—between work and the novel and applying to grad school, there hadn't been much time for meeting people, and there had been frustratingly few available dating partners whose outlook and interests had matched his own. How discouraging had it been to find himself attracted to someone (or, more rarely, to find someone attracted to him) only to be turned off by an all-too-common lack of curiosity and unimaginative worldview? His upcoming move to a different time zone also hadn't made for good dating conversation and had prematurely severed any connection he could have made back home.

It was now past seven o'clock, and Flip was getting hungry. That night he had five chapters of a particularly boring novel to read for the Great Plains Studies class as well as some papers to go over before his next day's writing center shift—a brief glance at their opening paragraphs had suggested that they needed a lot of work. He still wasn't sure what to do about the novel, but he could figure that out after he met with Stark. With great pains he lifted himself from the carpet, waited until his head stopped swimming from the onslaught of air conditioning, then went to boil some macaroni and cheese.

4

THE ADDRESS Brad had given him was located deep inside a suburban development conveniently near a Red Robin, a Chipotle, and a drive-through Starbucks. Reaching the house required following one of the four-lane arteries leading south out of the city and turning onto several curving streets whose names, in contrast to the alpha-numeric grid of his own neighborhood, were all named after trees and flowers. All of the houses, including Brad's, were very large and very new, as were the sparkling cars in their driveways.

Brad's first words after opening the door were, "Buddy, you made it!" as he heartily shook Flip's hand, a gesture that felt oddly formal since they'd just seen each other two days before. He wore a bright orange t-shirt picturing the jagged flames of the Prairie Fire logo engulfing a football, and upon releasing his grip he wrapped his other arm around Flip's shoulder. "We didn't think you were coming."

Flip found Brad's manner both physically intrusive and indicative of a false sense of camaraderie. (Didn't people tend to call others "buddy" when they weren't really your friend but wanted to make it seem that way?) He tried to ignore this as he put on a large smile and asked, "Am I the last one here?"

"The game started an hour ago," Brad said. "But I'm glad to see you because there's some people I'd like you to meet. I was also just telling Melvin about some opportunities we have open at the *Long Grass* journal—which, as you may have heard, I'm the associate fiction editor of this year. Melvin's already on board for reading submissions, and I know you'll be perfect for the job too."

Flip recalled Jackson's warning and halted halfway through the dining room near a table of appetizers, the six-pack of beer bottles in his hand suddenly feeling very heavy. "I heard you needed readers for the journal," he said, "but my semester's off to a busy start, and I was hoping to focus more on my classes and my novel."

Brad laughed his effusive laugh and gave Flip's shoulder a firm squeeze. "Of course, buddy! No pressure at all. But if you ever want to come read with us it's a great way to build your CV for when you go on the market."

Flip gave a wry smile and somehow sensed that he'd made the right call. "Of course."

He'd planned on coming fashionably late, but not actually late; back home everyone had always trickled into house parties whenever they felt like coming, and the thought of being exactly on time and getting stuck with only Brad had felt like a poor choice. Now that the week was over he felt ready to relax and be social, and an adventurous spirit rose within him as he moved away from Brad and deeper into the house.

Each of the living room's two couches and oversized armchairs were filled to capacity with people—among them Kendall, Lawrence, Melvin, two girls he recognized from the departmental welcome meeting, and two guys that he didn't. All of them focused intently on a large wall-mounted television showing an assembly of players in white, orange-numbered uniforms dashing in and around a rush of black-shirted players while an off-screen announcer described their performance in a way that seemed complimentary. Two other grad students he didn't know stood leaning against a wall focused on the television, while in the open kitchen a cute, small-framed girl Flip also recognized from the department meeting scraped a light brown substance from a food processor with great concentration. Everyone else in the room wore some variety of orange shirt bearing the Prairie Fire team name and blazing flame logo, and Flip became uncomfortably aware of the purple and black striped shirt he'd chosen before leaving the apartment.

A loud roar erupted across both the TV screen and the living room as some event of interest occurred in the game; onscreen a triumphant player in a white and orange uniform punched the air with his fists as the rest of the team enveloped him in a bear hug. At the same time everyone in the room leaped to their feet, raising their own arms into the air and taking triumphant gulps from their beer bottles while Brad reached over to pound Kendall with a high five.

"Those guys never even got close to him," Kendall announced as he sat back down. "Pretty sorry excuse for a defensive line."

The small-framed girl from the department meeting had briefly paused at the commotion but had almost immediately resumed her scraping, suggesting her own indifference to the game. She had small hands that fit neatly around the food processor's center cylinder and equally small feet and toes that she wiggled inside her sandals as she worked. She also had one of those faces that was offhanded in its prettiness, as if its main objective was to radiate cheerful warmth and any sexual attraction one felt at seeing it came as an afterthought. Flip moved toward the kitchen, ostensibly to refrigerate the six-pack of beer he was still holding but actually to get closer to the girl; once there he uncapped one of the bottles and asked what she was making.

"Hummus," the girl said amiably, still scraping the rest of the mixture. "If you're new here you should know that I make hummus for all the department parties."

The statement felt somehow more inviting than anything else he'd heard that week. It also filled him with a familiar bravado he reserved for moments of light flirtation, the kind that in earlier days had served him well in subtly conveying his interest. "I heard you speak at the department meeting," he said, moving across the kitchen with more assurance. "You sounded really confident, and you almost made me interested enough to actually join student government."

"Aw, thanks," the girl said. "They put me in charge of the recruitment committee this term, though the committee's really just me right now." She extended her hand suddenly in greeting and Flip took it softly, once again struck by the odd formality of the gesture. "I'm Mary-Beth, and I'm a third-year lit PhD. It's cool that you came tonight."

"It's good to get out," Flip said, edging along the counter and away from the living room. "I'm not too up on this football stuff, though."

The girl laughed at this and pressed the rest of the hummus from the spatula onto the edge of the bowl. "I'm not either," she whispered conspiratorially. She pulled out the lower portion of her t-shirt, forming a shallow triangle between her neck and waist that called attention to the orange Prairie Fire flame. "I just root for the Prairie Fire and try to act excited when they win. Going to actual games is fun because everyone in the stadium dresses all in orange and you get this amazing feeling of solidarity with something bigger, especially when they show the photos from the blimp. My fiancé follows them pretty closely, so he can tell you more than I can." She gestured to a broad-shouldered individual on one of the couches staring purposefully at the television.

Flip felt a twinge of embarrassment not just because the girl was unavailable, but because the act of pointing out her fiancé had so clearly been a move to indicate this. Perhaps, however, it was better that she'd taken the step so soon to avoid any misunderstandings.

"Actually, I've never been much of a sports person," he said without showing his disappointment. "Back in high school I tried convincing the administration to let me take extra art classes instead of PE, which didn't go over that well. I was surprised people from the English department take this football stuff so seriously."

Mary-Beth looked away at this. "Oh, I guess that's pretty funny, isn't it?" she said in a way that suggested it wasn't. "In any case, if you're not a football person, make sure you stay away from downtown on game day since the place turns into a madhouse."

"So I've heard," Flip said. "I guess there's not much else to do around here besides football, eh?"

Mary-Beth laughed hollowly and looked away again, causing Flip to immediately regret the comment. "It might seem that way from outside," she said, "but we do a pretty good job of making lives for ourselves out here."

She finished scraping the last of the hummus from the bowl and moved out of the kitchen toward the appetizer table, where she said something to one of the other girls (or women? It was always hard to know which to use) and began talking excitedly. That left no one else in the kitchen, so Flip took the opportunity to stroll away to a leaning position against the burgundy accent wall adjacent to the living room, focusing his gaze on the screen to maintain the illusion of interest. As he approached he was greeted by several *Hellos* and *Glad you could make it*s from the others in the workshop, though each one felt truncated and routine, as if the speaker was responding to a reflex action. Kendall went so far as to lean up from the couch and shake his hand with a brief, "Nice to see you again, Phil," before looking back at the television—had he not grasped Flip's nickname, or was he choosing for some unknown reason to ignore it? The only ones not present from the workshop were Jackson and Craig, and he wondered whether Craig hadn't been invited, had been invited but chosen not to come, or, like himself, was planning a late arrival.

After what seemed like a long time the arrival of a commercial break facilitated movement among Kendall and some of the others toward the kitchen. Flip made quick eye contact with Kendall and nodded to acknowledge that he'd seen him, though the glance may have come too late because Kendall was already turning his head to talk to Lawrence.

"So here's one for you," Lawrence began. "I finally introduced our first paper topic, and after spending the last *three* classes talking about power dynamics and stifled voices most of the class at least had the gist of what I was looking for, with the exception of one student who wanted to write about a celebrity gossip story where some movie star had agreed to a prenuptial agreement and wasn't entitled to any money after her divorce. The student kept arguing that this was a valid paper topic and couldn't get it through her little head that both the movie star and his wife were both coming from positions of privilege and didn't—"

"Yes, yes," Kendall said as he scooped a salsa-laden tortilla chip into his mouth, a move he was somehow able to perform with an air of sophistication. "A lot of the more rural students try to use their own experiences to show how they've been discriminated against without quite grasping the full extent of the term. It's a product of their lack of diversity, though it also represents a kind of persecution complex, so of course when we try to educate them about their own positions of privilege they lash out at us for attacking them."

"Well, this girl was actually from the suburbs," Lawrence clarified. "Though I think the same principle applies."

Flip had been standing a short distance away in quest of an entry point into the conversation and decided Lawrence's comment was the ideal moment. "The concept of pre-nups is pretty crazy anyway," he said, "since asking for one conveys to this person that you presumably want to spend the rest of your life with that you're really focused on your own stability if things don't work out."

Kendall's eyes behind their rimless glasses wandered momentarily toward Flip's, stopped just above his collarbone, then shot back up to Lawrence's as he chuckled. "But don't you think it's better to be prepared since you never know what's going to happen with a relationship, even one you feel sure about in the moment?"

In contrast to Kendall's more controlled reaction, Lawrence expressed more alarm. "And not only that, in cases where one partner has a tenure-track job and makes more money than the other, pre-nups protect the partner who makes more because otherwise what's to stop the other person from taking half?"

"Human decency for one thing," Flip said as if this should have been obvious. "If I'm in a committed relationship that's falling apart, I like to think I could work out a fair breakup deal with the other person. But my point is that asking someone for a pre-nup sends the clear signal that you have doubts. It's like saying you love someone, but not enough to trust them when it comes to money."

Kendall was shaking his head now with a slight eye roll. "It's funny you say it like that, since that's the kind of thing we all believe before we actually get into serious relationships and find out things aren't so straightforward. The whole agreement's about keeping tabs on your own finances—you want to make sure both parties are protected." His eyes met Flip's for an instant before again darting away. "In any case, I'm sure you'll find out just how little our undergrads are capable of when you start teaching your own classes—or are they letting first-year MFAs teach now, too?"

"Not yet," Flip said. "They've got me working in the writing center."

"Right," Kendall said snidely, nodding in a way that caused him to almost but not quite make eye contact. "You'll have to let me know how your own teaching endeavors go—getting these kids to voice an independent thought is like pulling teeth."

Flip had no immediate reply to this and felt like even more of an idiot than he had during the workshop. Sensing intrinsically that the time had come to change the subject he pointed at the blaze-orange Prairie Fire flames on Kendall's t-shirt. "In any case," he said lightly, "I'm sure you'll be able to bond with your students over tonight's homecoming game."

Both Kendall and Lawrence stared at him blankly. "You know we're playing at Purdue, right?" Lawrence said.

Flip felt his face grow red and attempted a chuckle. "Ah, no—I'm not too up on this football stuff. We don't really have college teams in the Northeast, and I did my undergrad at a small liberal arts school where we barely had intramural soccer."

Kendall looked back toward the living room and then again at the spot above Flip's collarbone. "So I've heard," he said, and moved back to his place on the couch.

Flip felt a vaguely unsettled feeling creeping over him—could he really have committed this many faux pas in his first twenty minutes at the party? How was it that a roomful of writers could be so engrossed in a televised football game, something that back home had belonged purely to the domain of people he had nothing in common with? With the believability of his attempt to enjoy the football game now in doubt he headed for the food table and began slipping appetizers first onto a paper plate, then directly into his mouth. Besides Mary-Beth's hummus, the table contained a grocery-store tray of vegetables, a bowl of tortilla chips formed into star-shaped scoops, a Tupperware container of chocolate-chip cookies, a bowl of salsa, two platters of cheese and crackers, some red mini sausages, and a plate of deviled eggs. The hummus was quite good, and Flip found himself scooping more and more of it on to handfuls of crackers layered with cheese slices. In the past several years he'd become aware of his bad habit of overeating in social situations where the food was free, since it both distracted him from his nervousness and gave him something to do, and he now found himself doing so in a way that must have seemed decidedly unnatural to anyone watching. This awareness now came to him in the midst of wiping deviled egg yolk from his upper lip, and with some embarrassment he dropped his empty plate in the trash and stepped around the hallway corner.

The tiled half-circle by the front door was full of shoes, and on the entryway's walls hung small, framed pictures of Brad and his wife with all sorts of different people, some from the department and others he didn't recognize. An umbrella stand stood empty beside the front door and two chairs sat unused below the pictures. He understood suddenly why Jackson had wanted to avoid the party and sensed now more concretely that Craig had stayed away for the same reason. Perhaps Brad's invitation had solely been a move to get him to join the *Long Grass* journal, or perhaps it had been a pity invite so he wouldn't find out about the party later and feel left out. He stepped into a hallway leading away from the rest of the house as a cacophony of cheers, whoops, and high-five slaps from the living room overshadowed the announcer. There were two doors on opposite sides of the hall, one closed and the other opened a crack; out of curiosity he peered through the crack and first saw a tall set of bookshelves, then a desk in front of a window. Next to the desk was a couch, and sitting on the couch reading a book was the girl who'd worn the red blazer in the English Department courtyard.

She looked up rapidly when he opened the door, her expression of surprise turning into embarrassment as she slammed the book closed like a teenager caught with pornography. There passed a brief, terrorizing second in which both of them stared at each other without speaking until Flip realized that the girl must have been doing something illicit, which then gave him more confidence. The girl seemed to realize this about him as well because she rested the book on her lap as a sly, amused smile stretched across her face. "Hi," she said.

Flip slid through the doorway, leaving it open a crack the way he'd found it. "What are you doing here?"

The girl wore a slim, sleeveless turquoise dress with pink stripes along the hems, and as Flip entered, she slid her knees tightly together. "I had to, ah, use the bathroom, and then I saw that Brad's office was full of books, and whenever I see someone's room full of books I always want to know what's there so I can know more about the person, and then I saw this copy of *The Tenant of Wildfell Hall* and I've never read it, so I ah—" She adopted a more suspicious tone. "What are *you* doing here?"

Flip recalled a similar curiosity he experienced whenever he saw bookshelves in an unfamiliar house. "The party was boring," he said, "so I wandered off."

The girl laughed at this, a nervous yet uninhibited giggle that shook her lithe frame as she rested her elbows on the book still sitting on her lap. "That's a good reason. I feel justified in mine, though, because Anne's the only Brontë sister I haven't read, and it doesn't seem right to talk about the Brontë sisters as a whole unless I've read Anne too." She sat straight up as if shifting to a matter of great importance. "Who's your favorite?"

The question caught Flip off guard. "What?"

"Who's your favorite Brontë sister?" the girl repeated.

Flip wondered if he was being given some kind of personality test. "Emily," he said after a pause, "because of *Wuthering Heights*, where Heathcliff has to go somewhere far away and make this mysterious fortune so he can come back and prove his worth to the people who used to look down on him, but then in the end that drive for success consumes him." This summary felt somehow satisfying, so he asked, "How about yours?"

The girl nodded as she swayed forward and back on the couch. "Mine's Charlotte, mostly because of *Jane Eyre*, which is about going after those same goals, except through marriage. I know that sounds trite unless you think about the quest for marriage really being about Jane needing to make a successful life for herself, and marriage just being her way of achieving that as a woman under the standards of the day. You could say she and Heathcliff are really the same in their own screwed-up *Bildungsroman* way."

Flip sensed a slight but distinct flirtatiousness in the girl's manner of swaying, but more so in her manner of relating the two characters. He also found her use of literary terms distinctly appealing and stepped closer to the couch. "I was with Jackson the other day outside the English building when you said hi, but I didn't get to introduce myself. I'm Phil, but I go by Flip."

"I'm Derzen," the girl said with the stress placed on the *zen*. "What's your focus area?"

The time seemed right for Flip to actually sit down next to her, though he was careful to choose a distance that showed his interest without intruding on her personal space. "I'm an MFA," he said. "I do fiction, and I'm in Stark's workshop."

This introduction (unconsciously modeled, he realized, after the countless other grad student introductions he'd heard over the past two weeks) felt decidedly unnatural since at no point had Flip ever thought of himself as *doing* fiction, or especially as someone who *did* only fiction and was therefore exempt from *doing* other things. Saying *I'm an MFA* was also not only syntactically awkward but seemed to envelop his entire personality in a way he didn't feel quite comfortable with.

"That's good," said the girl. (*Derzen*, Flip thought so he'd remember the name, kind of like Dresden in *Slaughterhouse-Five*.) "I used to write fiction but I haven't in a long time. I do poetry here."

"I used to write poetry too," Flip said, "but now I'm working on a novel. I used to do a bit of everything, actually."

"So you understand both worlds," Derzen said. "I started hating all the fiction I wrote because it never came out the way I imagined it. With poetry, though, there's less on the page to keep track of so you can better fine-tune the images to match the ones in your mind. I found it a more natural way to convey truths that people feel but can't explain for themselves."

This thought—one that Flip himself had often tried to express coherently—felt even more extraordinary because she'd expressed it so immediately into their conversation, and he felt his blood quicken in the first critical stages of arousal. "I'm trying to do the same thing with my novel," he said. "It's about a character trying to earn back his dignity while working in an office without any hope of getting ahead."

"It sounds important," Derzen said. "Why can't he get ahead?"

"Because the field he's in is dying and there aren't any opportunities for young people there," he said matter-of-factly. "So in cases like that it's best to seek out something new."

She smiled knowingly at this. "Change is always a good thing."

Flip now felt solidly in his element in a way that reminded him of being in college, or even high school, when a mix of bravery and foolishness had led him to ask out girls more readily than he'd been able to in subsequent years. If this were a party from the old days with more alcohol and a later start time he felt certain he'd be able to escalate his flirtations to the point of asking whether the girl wanted to take their conversation elsewhere—or at the very least, asking for her phone number. This wasn't the old days, though, and while his intent was the same, the ideal course of action felt less certain.

"Why'd you really come in here anyway?" he asked. "There's a party going on."

Derzen scrunched up her face as if someone had just slipped her a sour piece of candy. "If you can call it that. I don't really get the whole football thing."

"Neither do I," Flip said. "It seems weird that a bunch of writers are meeting up to watch sports."

Derzen turned excitedly toward him at this, her bare knees below her turquoise skirt within an inch of touching his. "I've thought that same thing so many times and I've tried suggesting we do something else, but there's not much to do around here besides going out to eat or going to bars, both of which get equally old. I guess that's why I snuck away, because I don't want to feel obligated to watch something I'm not interested in."

Flip swung his elbow onto the back of the couch very close to Derzen's shoulder and said, "I don't like doing things I'm not interested in, either."

"But it's not that simple," Derzen continued with a look of urgency that somehow made him feel very warm. "It's not like the party's straight-up not fun because I still enjoy going out with people and being social. It's like if you really love banana cream pie and you're pretty sure it's your favorite dessert and that you'd probably be happy eating banana cream pie for the rest of your life, but then maybe you start missing other desserts, like chocolate cream pie or strawberry rhubarb pie, and maybe sometimes you don't want pie at all and want some pistachio mousse or a brownie sundae instead. Then maybe you want to figure out some way to have all the desserts you like in proportion to how much you like them, so you could have banana cream pie the most but maybe have chocolate pie once a week and pistachio mousse twice a month, and you could keep all of them in your fridge to have on hand and even mix in some black raspberry ice cream if you felt like it." She leaned back, very close to but not touching his elbow, apparently satisfied with the metaphor. "That would be just perfect, I think."

Flip sensed the advantage of his position and was about to ask what the other desserts symbolized when Kendall poked his head through the doorway, looked at both of them for a terrifying instant, then focused his gaze squarely on Derzen and said, "Honey, there you are—Patrick's about to leave and he still wants to borrow that book of Steven Walter Hendricks stories I left in the car. Do you have your keys?"

And Derzen jumped up from the couch and said, "Yeah, just a sec," with a slight tremble and began fumbling through her purse.

Then Kendall walked over and said, "Thanks, sweetheart," and without looking at Flip placed his hand solidly on the small of Derzen's back.

5

"WHAT IN THE holy name of fuck does a girl like Derzen see in a jerk like Kendall?" Flip exploded, his face fuming with embarrassment and uncertainty. "He even has two first names!"

In the shaded seat across from him Jackson raised his eyebrows as he dipped a spoon into his single-serving cup of vanilla pudding. "Damned if I know. Somerset Maugham made a career trying to answer that one."

"How long have they been together?" Flip asked.

It was a scalding hot Monday afternoon, and the walk from Flip's apartment to campus had caused his body to secrete an overwhelming amount of perspiration. He'd spotted Jackson eating lunch at an umbrella-shaded table by the student union and come over to say hello.

After swallowing his pudding Jackson said, "Two years, maybe. They started dating a few weeks after they started the program. Kendall had been with this other girl when he was doing his MFA in Wyoming but he didn't want to do long distance. He started seeing Derzen on the sly and then broke things off with the Alabama girl when things got more serious. It was a pretty big event at the time."

Flip had listened aghast at his explanation, thinking how neatly Kendall had slotted one girlfriend into the place of another in a way that clearly benefitted himself. "How do you know all that?" he demanded.

"I told you, I like to stay informed about what goes on around me," Jackson said as he scraped the final lines of pudding from the cup. When he finished he set down both the cup and his spoon next to an airport-sized copy of *The Autobiography of Malcolm X.* "As you should too."

"Our whole interaction was so bizarre," Flip said. "I was trying to move closer to her on the couch to show that I was clearly interested, and she must have known that I was clearly interested because she wasn't moving away or anything, yet she somehow neglected to mention that she had a boyfriend."

"Did you ask her whether she had a boyfriend?" Jackson asked.

"I couldn't ask her that!" Flip yelled because he knew he really should have. "It's too direct, so it's better if the person in a relationship finds a way to casually slip it into the conversation like Mary-Beth did."

"I suppose," Jackson answered. "Unless she couldn't find a convenient way to slip it in, so to an observer it would seem like she really was interested and you'd never know the difference."

Flip's head spun at this but he went on. "So instead Kendall caught me hitting on her and we all had to go back to watching that stupid football game and listening to boring small talk until people started slipping out before the game was over. I couldn't even talk to Derzen again because she was busy talking department stuff with the other girls." He recalled the detached, exaggerated manner of speaking Derzen had adopted through the remainder of the evening and shuddered at the change. "The whole thing was an awkward disaster and I'd rather read an entire Francis Bacon treatise than go to another of those parties. And how can Brad afford such a big house anyway?"

Jackson shrugged and scraped a toothpick between his teeth. "Brad's wife's a nurse, so she pulls in way more than we do on our grad student stipends. And if you don't want to go to another of those parties, then don't."

Flip had begun rapping his knuckles on the table. "What exactly is Kendall's deal anyway? First he makes a big show of shooting down my ideas about pre-nups, then he wouldn't even look me in the eye after he saw me with Derzen."

"He probably knew you were hitting on her," Jackson said, shifting the toothpick to the other side of his mouth. "But like I said, you really should be careful what you say about Kendall—he has a short story collection coming out in the spring. He's a pretty respected guy around here."

"Are you saying I should respect him too?" Flip asked.

"No," Jackson said. "I'm saying you should be careful what you say about him because other people respect him." He flicked the toothpick into a trash can several feet away. "It's funny, because when people in real life feel threatened they tend to tone down their reactions and lash out passive-aggressively. It's not like in *The Outsiders* where the characters get in actual fights with knives and punching since conflicts play out in more subtle ways in our world. Maybe that's why writers still throw their characters into direct confrontations: they're more exciting than the power struggles and posturing tactics people use in real life. A bad guy giving the hero the cold shoulder doesn't exactly make for rapid page-turning." He suddenly stood and looped his messenger bag over his shoulder.

"You've got a point," Flip said. "I'm not going to worry about either of them anymore—I came here to finish my novel and that's what I'm going to do. I'm supposed to meet with Stark about it tomorrow, so maybe he can give me some advice."

"I'm sure Stark can help you," Jackson said as he began walking. "He's a pretty respected guy around here too."

6

INSTEAD OF going back up to the apartment after class Flip got into his green Honda with the rust spot on its passenger door and the duct tape stretched across the tear in its driver's seat and drove out of the neighborhood of alphabet streets onto an overpass that rose above the warehouses and brick buildings of the old downtown. Here, beside the scrap yards and factories and grain silos of old industry he felt that he'd embarked on a momentous journey for the first time since his arrival. As the overpass curved around the enormous railroad yard he saw clusters of green, leafy trees with branches hanging toward the road and a distant park with more trees and rolling hills that met the blue sky of the horizon like the old background of Windows XP. When the overpass reached the ground he took a right, then a left, then another right until the trees and houses and driveways fell away into vast, endless fields of corn, taller than he was and green with puffy white threads sticking up from their tops, lined up in rows forever and reminding him of *The Grapes of Wrath*: Got to keep the lines straight, three dollars a day. Between the immense cornfields were more rows of lower, wide-leaved plants that must have been soybeans; though he didn't know for sure because there weren't any soybeans back home to compare them to just like there weren't any cornfields this immense, well-ordered, or perfectly spaced back home, and just like there weren't towering silos beside railroad tracks back home where grain was dumped into freight cars under covered sheds. All of these things were components of an immense agricultural system he'd known about but couldn't have imagined the scope of, like so many other things he'd encountered in his unfamiliar surroundings. Back home you'd be hard-pressed to find a farm larger than a mini-mall parking lot because back home the ground was full of rocks that made farming difficult and had long ago stirred residents on to other endeavors. Of course, back home there were also mountains, lakes, rivers, and forests filling out the landscape for people to enjoy, though now in admiring the vast, unending terrain he felt impressed that people here had built so much farmland where before there'd been only plains.

He drove down the two-lane highway with its single dashed line, watching the square signs for county roads and unincorporated townships and the corn, always the corn and soybeans everywhere. At some point he remembered why he'd come all the way out to this place that was so far from everything he'd ever known because here there were opportunities where back home there'd been so few. As he drove past a roadside restaurant called The Homesteader with an oversized covered wagon on its roof he felt a surge of the same hopeful optimism the pioneers must have felt at entering this wide-open world where successes were made and great things could happen as long as one worked to create them.

The Scandal of Adams County

A Novel

William Stark

Downwinds Press
Torn River, Arkansas

William Stark is the author of two previous novels, *House of Fallen Entropy* and *The Astoundingly Uninhibited Transmogrification of Helen Bixby*, along with a collection of short stories, *Hear Me Out, Say My Name*. He holds an MFA in creative writing from the University of Northern South Dakota and is the recipient of the Arthur L. Wilkes Distinguished Assistant Professorship in fiction.

For my loving wife, Bethany.

CHAPTER 1

The news spun the town into an orchestral hum of voices overpowering one another in sorrowful harmony as they resonated through every barroom, workshop, and breakfast nook in the county: Oscar Sanders had taken up residence with Arnold Bertram's wife.

Arnold was gone, fuming in Room 12 of the Shady Plains Motel on Route 47 without any need to pay the bill because he and Morris Frothingham, who owned the place, had played poker together every Thursday for the past eight years. In that time Morris had won enough pots off poor Arnold to cover six months lodging in the aging single-story motel. "It's the least I can do," Morris told him as he waved away Arnold's well-worn Visa card, "considering the circumstances. A man's gotta look after another man since there are few things in this world besides taxes and companionship that folks can depend on."

Arnold Bertram sat in that motel room for five weeks without seeing his wife or anyone else, driving his dented pickup down Main Street in the evenings to pick up sandwiches and whiskey from the Center Market. The same clerk was always on shift when Arnold came in, and he always rang up Arnold's purchases with a smile and said, "You have a good day, Mr. Bertram," because the clerk, like everyone else, knew what had happened to Arnold and felt the same pangs of sympathy for him. Each time the clerk said this, Arnold would take the bag with a low grunt and drop his change into his jeans pocket.

Oscar Sanders had committed an act so vile that no man or woman in Adams County would have condoned it, least of all because it was Arnold himself who introduced him to his wife, Carol, over helpings of Esther Higgins's award-winning potato salad at the church social the previous fall. It was really a shame since Arnold was only showing Oscar some local hospitality when he introduced his wife to the new driver they'd hired to help out after the police raided Lester

Belton's computer and found the stash of kiddie porn on his hard drive. No one would have believed old Lester capable of such a thing—the man had been with his wife nearly twenty-two years—so when the news teams and lawyers had all had their say and Lester was behind bars, Arnold found himself without a full-time driver and couldn't manage the deliveries between Jake being so busy in the warehouse and Little Matt only coming in when he damned well felt like it. Oscar's coming seemed like a godsend—the man wanted to work, and work hard—and in the weeks after his unspoken departure the shop sank into a turmoil of missed deliveries and upset phone calls with Arnold and Jake working sixty-five-hour weeks to make up the difference. The vendors all knew the story and knew Arnold was doing his best under the circumstances, so they offered their condolences and didn't press too hard.

Oscar began sneaking out to see Carol a few afternoons a week that same summer when he was supposed to be running his deliveries. Their first visit happened innocently enough when Arnold asked Oscar to pick up some order slips he'd left on his kitchen table when Carol was home with nothing to do. School was out for the summer, and her students had traded the drudgery of studying cell membranes for the dubious freedom of part-time jobs and unplanned pregnancies. She welcomed Oscar like she would any other guest— of course she remembered him from the church social since he was the fine man from Taylor County who made the forty-five-minute drive to the warehouse every morning and had been such a help to her husband after the incident with Lester, and would he like to stay a few more minutes for a bite to eat? Such visits became more frequent, more clandestine, and ultimately more intimate until the day Carol asked Arnold to leave and he demanded to know why. That was the end of Oscar's stint as a driver.

Back at the Shady Plains Motel, Morris Frothingham wondered what good, if any, he could do for his brooding acquaintance-but-not-quite-friend in Room 12 whose wife was now openly being seen with another man. Neighbors spotted Carol and Oscar buying fried chicken at the supermarket, riding along the state highway in Oscar's silver Toyota, walking through the town center in broad daylight, and even ordering pulled pork and coleslaw from Lang's Steakhouse, since Carol never ate beef if she could help it for reasons of her own. People took relish in telling Morris these things, as if they expected him to pass them on to Arnold, as if the two men shared that sort of friendship, as if Arnold didn't already know about them. Morris, however, was not one to pour salt on another man's wounds, and when he saw Arnold ambling across the dirt parking lot with his grocery bags of whiskey and beef jerky he always nodded his head exactly once, to which Arnold would—

[At this point Flip tossed the book down and went to stream an episode of *Bob's Burgers*.]

1

"ARE YOU enjoying yourself so far?" Stark asked.

"Oh yes," Flip said. "I've met a lot of people since coming here."

The first of these statements wasn't really a lie (though the way he embellished it seemed to make it one), and the second wasn't a lie at all since technically he really had made the acquaintance of a large number of people since arriving. Stark, with his legs crossed and his chin resting on the crux of his bent wrist, said, "That's good."

They sat in Stark's office, which, through either lack of available options or poor choice, was located near a furniture storage area at the far west end of the English building's windowless third-floor hallway. The chair where Flip sat placed him in full view of anyone walking down the very long and very straight hallway, while Stark sat in a taller, wheeled chair beside the wall safely hidden from passersby.

"So," Stark went on, his small talk apparently concluded, "how do you feel about *Office With a View?*"

"I've been working on it for two years," Flip said quickly. "I wanted to write a novel about being surrounded by people you can't relate to since a lot of my favorite novels are about people who don't fit in with the world around them. I feel like offices are these bizarre places where people spend so much of their time even though everyone really despises them, and they're causing real damage to people's emotional lives, like a modern-day version of *The Jungle* except no one's actually falling into the meat grinder. There's also the problem of more and more young people finishing college with these broader visions of what they can do in the world, but the only places they can get work are these unfulfilling office jobs that don't even offer good benefits. So you've got a generation whose talents are going to waste. I feel like young people are still having a difficult time because companies only want to hire fully trained workers, but young people can't get training without spending time in the working world first. That's the conflict I want to write about, and I want to capture the stresses of office life the way Joseph Heller did in *Something Happened* and show middle-class adults whose lives are as meaningless as the ones John Updike wrote about."

Stark crinkled his nose at Flip's final statement. "The only John Updike novel I've read is *The Witches of Eastwick,* and I didn't much care for it." He switched the crossed position of his legs and said, "But yes, I suppose that's one way of looking at it."

Flip regretted revealing this carefully prepared answer in one long burst since he now had little left to say. The shades of the office window had been pulled all the way down so that only a minimum of natural light entered the room, accentuating the grayish-white walls in a way that contrasted with the pastel artwork and maroon-patterned rug. A table on the opposite wall held an old mechanical typewriter that was interesting to look at but clearly not for practical use. "Do you think any of that came across?" he asked.

"I don't know if it's a matter of what you wanted to say *coming across,*" Stark said after another pause, "as much as how you as a writer *convey* those themes to the reader. That's one of the reasons we have workshop, so you can gauge readers' reactions. I think we, as writers, often get lost in our own worlds and need other people's feedback to rein us back into reality. A big problem I had with your book—and the rest of the class seemed to agree—was that there was so much crammed onto the page and so much rushing through your narrator's mind that we couldn't make sense of the story. You need to give us an entry point into what your book is really about. That's why I started the class by talking about plot."

Flip leaned forward in a feeble attempt to pass off his nervousness as engagement. "But don't you think the others were critical of the novel's style because it was different than what they're used to?"

Stark's reaction seemed to combine a mix of embarrassment and placation. "You have to be careful with things that are different," he began. "A lot of great novels have come from experimentation, but a lot of failed novels have too—far more than we hear about since it's only the winners that get remembered. The problem with trying something readers have never seen before is that they don't know how to interpret it. Literary agents are especially attuned to this—they're looking for books that fit recognizable categories they can market to readers based on what they know will sell."

This statement, if true, spelled doom for everything Flip wanted to do. "But doesn't the best writing challenge people by pushing boundaries?" he asked. "What about when a writer forms a novel's style to complement the story and enhance our experience? When Faulkner wrote *Light in August* he used different prose styles in each section so we'd experience the story from different perspectives. Or how about all those scenes in *A Farewell to Arms* when Catherine and Lieutenant Henry talk to each other without any dialogue tags to show how close their relationship is?"

Stark shifted uncomfortably and spoke with more hesitation. "Of course," he began, "but you have to remember that those novels came from a time when audiences craved that kind of innovation in the era of Modernism. It's debatable, I think, whether today's readers want to be challenged to the point of exhaustion."

"But Steven Millhauser gave us a new kind of experience in *Edwin Mullhouse* by writing the novel as a fictional biography," Flip argued. "Or how about Nicholson Baker novels that spend entire chapters describing minutia like open-slot paper towel dispensers or that metal spout on the side of the Domino sugar box? Both of those writers are still successful today."

"Nicholson Baker got his start in the '80s," Stark said, "and *Edwin Mullhouse* came out even earlier. A lot's changed in publishing since sales plummeted after the 2008 crash. It's harder to sell books now than ever before, and anyone who wants to be a writer these days faces a pretty harrowing challenge." He paused, resting his chin in his palm again and gazing almost restlessly at Flip in his hard-backed chair. "Tell me," he said in a firmer tone, "did you read much in the way of *contemporary* fiction during your undergrad?"

Flip's mind chose this most unfortunate of moments to turn up a blank. "I, uh, took an innovative fiction class where we read David Sedaris."

"And what exactly was your major?" Stark asked.

"Graphic illustration and English lit," Flip said. "I went to a progressive liberal arts school where everyone designed their own majors, and my final project was a graphic poetry book."

"And you were working in an office before you came here?" Stark asked. "Just like the one in your novel?"

Embarrassment rushed over him. "Not exactly the same, but similar."

"I think I understand," Stark said, raising his other palm. He turned to a painting of flowers on the wall before continuing. "A lot of first-time writers start out with autobiographical novels because it's what they know. It's a natural impulse to want to share our experiences with the world but at the same time, we have to consider the market and what kinds of people are willing to appreciate what we write so we can make careers for ourselves, even if that doesn't exactly match what we want for a given project. The admissions committee liked your application essay about millennials facing discrimination in the workplace and decided you'd be a good candidate to round out this year's fiction group since the program's been suffering from an unfortunate lack of—" he chose his next word very carefully "—diversity."

"You mean like how our class is full of white guys?" Flip asked.

Stark nodded again. "That's one aspect, anyway. You can't always plan these things since we don't have control over who actually decides to come, but given the pool of people who can afford to take three years away from their other responsibilities while also being able to craft a decent story, our diversity options can be limited. That's been a criticism of MFA novels in recent years, that they're too white, too middle-class, too male, and written by people who've never worked outside academia. Put a bunch of people from the same demographic in a writing program and of course their writing is going to feel uniform."

Flip had become steadily aware of a lack of diversity in his own novel as Stark spoke, though it occurred to him that this very much represented the circumstances that had led to its creation. "Do you think the writing in our program is all the same?"

"No," Stark said firmly. "Not in the strictest sense, anyway. There will always be differences between individual writers, but if you're referring to bigger-picture views of how the creative-writing world is structured, of course certain styles and topics and ways of setting up a story are going to be more popular. That's because they've been shown to work, and if you want to succeed under these difficult circumstances, it's always better to stick with what works." He paused as if waiting to see whether Flip would protest, and when he didn't, asked, "But tell me, what does your family think about your career plans?"

"My parents have always been supportive," Flip said, surmising that this wasn't the answer Stark was expecting. "They told me to find whatever it was that made me happy, then figure out how to get paid for it. They don't exactly understand writing or art or wanting to play in a band, but if they did they might have tried pressuring me down a different path."

"In that case," Stark asked with a trace of confusion, "why did you decide to go to graduate school?"

"Because I knew I couldn't finish my novel just by working in the evenings and on weekends anymore," Flip said, "and because my old writing group was breaking up and I needed to get out of my old job and find out more about how the writing world worked. So when I looked into what other aspiring writers were doing, an MFA program seemed to be the best path. I guess I considered myself lucky that I was able to get in here with funding since I got rejected from everywhere else."

"What kind of writer's group were you in back in the Northeast?" Stark asked.

"It was a lot of my old creative friends from high school," Flip said, and then, to regain a bit of the ground he'd lost, added, "They looked at most of my novel chapters and liked them a lot."

Stark emitted a noise like a low hum as he leaned over to check the time on his cell phone. "I'm sure they did, though of course you have to remember that not all feedback holds the same weight since not every writer has the skills to tell when a piece isn't working. I think you'll see what I mean when you workshop your next section in a few weeks, and I hope you'll be able to fix some of what we talked about and make the story more ... relatable." He paused again, focusing on an area of empty wall above Flip's head. "That was another thing I found odd about your novel—I kept thinking to myself how any character who'd gone through four years of college could be so naïve as to be surprised to find the working world banal and unfulfilling."

Flip recalled the disgusted disillusionment he'd felt after leaving college and starting work as he felt his face drain to a disconcerting shade of ash. "I guess that could come across as idealistic," he said.

"Are you excited about teaching next year?" Stark asked.

"Sure," Flip said. "As long as I can write too."

"And how about after the program?" Stark added with more concern. "Do you want to go on to a PhD or try going on the market right away?"

"What do you mean?" Flip asked. "Like, with the novel?"

Stark smiled and rubbed his fist against the stubble of side-burn below his ear. "No—when grad students start applying for academic jobs, we call that *going on the market*."

At hearing this explanation Flip was struck by the feeling that he'd heard the phrase somewhere before. "Oh," he said.

"Our own department's more known for its PhD program as a way of preparing creative writers for academic jobs," Stark explained. "We only upgraded the master's to an MFA because we wanted to stay competitive with other schools, but that was before I came here. You'll find that every program has its own nuances, though ours tends to implement a heavy dose of literature and criticism in keeping with its roots."

Flip thought of the particularly mind-numbing article he'd mean-dered through for the Great Plains Studies class that morning. "There's a lot we can learn from the writers that came before us," he said in a way that felt both optimistic and sycophantic.

Stark looked away before continuing. "I also imagine it must have been a big change moving here from the Northeast. Are you married? Or did you come here with someone special?"

Flip hated being asked this question more than any other and glanced down at the floor as if the answer could somehow be found there. "No," he said. "Still single."

"And for this program," Stark said, "graphic poetry aside, do you want to finish this novel as your MFA thesis?"

Flip nodded sickly. "Yes, I'd thought of doing that, especially so I could get it published after I finish."

"A lot of students, MFA or PhD, have that as their plan," Stark said, "and a few of them go on to do it as they advance their careers. You might consider thinking more seriously about your own goals and how this novel can help you achieve them. Keep in mind that writers everywhere always write for an audience—Faulkner and Hemingway wrote for theirs, Steven Millhauser and Nicholson Baker wrote for theirs, and you have to write for yours here. This program has a lot of talented writers, and they can help you figure out what the market's looking for. If you decide not to pursue a career in academia, then we at least recommend that you try to finish a workable novel as your thesis so you'll have something to pitch to agents. Also, if you have a novel forthcoming or already out, even without a PhD you'll have an exponentially better chance at getting an academic job, especially a tenure-track one. On the other hand, lots of students also use PhD funding as a way to buy themselves more writing time and build up more competitive resumes—if that's the career path you're interested in."

Something about the way Stark said this implied that this was very much the career path Flip should be interested in. It was also one that, at that moment due to his lack of options, sounded very attractive. "I hadn't really thought about it," he said, "but I know I want to do something where I can make writing my main focus."

Stark glanced at the shaded window. "Working in academia does give you more freedom—more than I ever got at other jobs, anyway. It's nice having the summers off to just write."

Flip nodded at this but wasn't sure what to say.

"I think a lot of us are in that same boat," Stark went on, "since we all want to write the novels we want to write." He paused again, uncrossing his legs, and looked Flip squarely in the eye. "But we also need to make sure our writing fits into the bigger picture and that we have a secure plan for how to move our careers forward. Do you get what I'm trying to say?"

Here Flip felt the remnants of his earlier argument fading, and he looked through the doorway and down the long, white hallway where the thirty-something assistant professor of nineteenth century lit conversed with one of the grad students Flip had seen at Brad's party. The two of them stood side by side talking with good-natured smiles like in an admissions photo advertising close student-teacher relationships. Something about this scene stirred him more than anything else he'd seen since coming to the Midwest and in it, he saw the antithesis of quarterly goal-setting meetings and forced break room talk about new cars and brokerage invest-ments, just as he also saw the antithesis of being alone at weddings and going on dates where he couldn't find anything to talk about and suffering sleepless nights wondering whether there was any place in the entire world he could be successful while still doing something meaningful.

Flip turned away from the hallway, looking first at the mechan-ical typewriter, then at Stark. "Yeah," he said. "That sounds really nice."

8

"FIRST, NEVER mention Updike," Jackson said as he fell into the oversized bean bag chair in the corner of his living room. "That old-school *New Yorker* stuff won't win you a lot of friends out here. And second, it's Stark's job to tell you those things because he wants you to get published and build your CV so that after graduation you'll get a high-paying tenure-track job that'll boost the department's placement ratings. That way, everyone wins."

Flip had relayed his meeting with Stark to Jackson on another post-workshop walk back from campus, only this time he'd allowed their conversation to continue until they reached Jackson's apartment.

"But doesn't Stark have a point about writing a book in a way that makes people actually want to read it?" Flip asked.

"Of course," Jackson said, pulling out a copy of *The Little Prince* that had been wedged behind the bean bag. "There's no point in writing a book people won't like unless it's a book people will think is important, in which case it's a great reason."

Flip plopped down on Jackson's couch, the arms and back colored a dark cherry red while the cushions were forest green. Jackson's apartment, with its peeling brown wallpaper and collection of oriental rugs, felt like it had been furnished entirely from thrift store purchases: the room was full of small end tables and mismatched chairs, and bookcases of varying sizes filled completely with books set against each wall. Some books were stacked in front of and on top of other books with yet more books piled on the floor. The apartment was located inside a set of aging stone townhouses with ornate roses and vines carved into their exterior and convex windows looking onto the street, the only structure of its kind Flip had seen during his walks around the city.

"But shouldn't the books people like and the books people think are important be one and the same?" he asked. "Don't we remember great books that were popular in their time, and don't popular books sell enough copies to earn the writers a decent living and a place in history?"

"Sometimes," Jackson said. "But I don't see many lit professors putting *Valley of the Dolls* on their reading lists, and I'm sure Franz Kafka wished he could have made a living off his work while he was alive. It's like Salman Rushdie wrote—being a novelist is like a Faustian bargain in reverse, where instead of selling your soul for knowledge and power in this life, you have to give up all your fun, friendships, financial stability, and chances at romantic fulfillment to create something that'll live on after you're dead— unless no one ever reads anything you write and you become a failure after you're dead too."

"True," Flip said. "If the themes of my novel don't resonate with people in the real world, then no agent will want to sign it and no one will want to publish it even after I'm dead."

"You mean if the themes of your novel don't resonate with people in workshop," Jackson corrected. "A fair number of literary agents have been through writing workshops of their own and know the kind of writing that's valued there."

"So you're saying I should write a novel that'll resonate with people in workshop?" Flip asked.

"I'm not saying anything," Jackson said as he slid deeper into the bean bag. "I can't tell you what kind of novel to write and neither should anyone else."

"So I should ignore the rest of the workshop and write the novel I want to write?" Flip asked.

"You could," Jackson said, "but then the people in workshop won't like it, and Stark and the rest of your committee won't like it either when it comes time for your MFA defense because a book like the one you want to write won't get you an agent or a book deal or a shot at a high-paying tenure-track job, especially if you can't convince people that it's important."

"So I should write the novel that people in the workshop will think is important so it'll get me through my thesis defense and win me a writing career?" Flip asked.

"You could," Jackson said, "but then people outside the workshop might not like it."

"Why should I listen to you anyway?" Flip demanded as he began pacing the room. "You told me you haven't written anything in years."

"Harper Lee didn't write anything for decades after *To Kill a Mockingbird*," Jackson said. "And except for *Go Set a Watchman*, people listened to her."

"Harper Lee's different," Flip said. "Millions of people bought copies of *To Kill a Mockingbird*, and it brought her a lot of money and success."

"Millions of people also bought copies of *Go Set a Watchmen*, and it brought a lot of people money and success," Jackson said. "So by that logic anything that makes money is worth listening to."

"Then it's not really about money," Flip said as he paced. "If you're a young, unknown writer who needs to make your way in the world, how are you supposed to find success without compromising your writing?"

"That's assuming the writing you'd be compromising is actually good to begin with," Jackson said. "But you can only know what's good based on what other people think. Take Stark for example— he's an assistant professor at a major midwestern university, he has three novels to his name that probably sold a few thousand copies combined, and people seem to respect him even if they don't actually read his books for fun. Does that mean they're good? At least one agent and a few editors and a university hiring committee seem to think so, and their opinion must count for something. One good way to get people to respect your work is to convince them that a bunch of other people smarter than them respect it already. Academia's a lot like middle school—you're only as good as other people's opinions of you."

"I can't believe that's all there is," Flip lamented as he wrapped both hands around his head. "If my novel was working the way I wanted it to, then the others would have said so; but since they didn't, I must be doing something wrong."

Jackson shrugged. "Three master's degrees and half a PhD have taught me that finding the right readers for your work is important too. Speaking directly to your intended audience shows that you know the business, but more importantly, that you know your readers."

The cool manner in which Jackson delivered this brought to mind something Flip had been curious about. "How old are you, anyway?" he asked.

"Thirty-seven," Jackson said.

Flip hadn't expected this since Jackson's appearance and general manner had made him seem much younger. *Childish* was the wrong word; *youthful* fit more aptly.

"I expect I'll have to leave the grad school game when I finish this PhD, though," Jackson went on. "And since adjunct jobs don't come with health insurance, I'll have to start making a living doing something else."

Flip ran his hand along the back of his neck. "I don't want to coast through life on a pittance of a grad student stipend without ever doing things that matter—I want to make great art but also be successful enough so that I never have to work an office job again." He resumed pacing while Jackson lay still on the bean bag. "But I've also got to write something people can relate to and want to read. The right novel will speak to people and win me an agent and get me through a bunch of MFA workshops *and* help me earn a living, either by selling enough copies or getting me one of those tenure-track jobs everyone's so crazy about. All those things are tied to being a successful writer, and if I can write a novel that checks all the right boxes I'll solve a lot of problems all at once."

"Sounds like a worthy goal," Jackson said with a nod.

A Brand-New Draft of an Awe-Inspiring, Workshop-Friendly, Career-Sparking, Agent-Attracting, Marketable-to-a-Wide Audience But Still Fun, Daring, and Meaningful MFA Thesis Novel About the Frustrations of Office Life That's More Approachable and Speaks to More People Than the First Draft Did

a novel by Flip Montcalm

[Flip stared at the blinking cursor until his eyes began to sting, then shut down his laptop in defeat.]

9

"I DON'T GET it," the student asked, staring blankly out the writing center window.

"I think your teacher wants to know the overall point of your paper," Flip said, an observation he'd based on what he could decipher of the instructor's crooked scrawl. "I mean, what do you want to say about university football? Does it bring joy to people's lives? Benefit the community? Bring people together? Or is it just a distraction for the masses who have nothing better to do?"

Flip had forgotten the student's name within seconds of meeting him and cursed him for coming on an afternoon when he'd hoped to spend his writing center shift finishing a reading response for his Great Plains Studies class. The student wore a blaze-orange hat with the Prairie Fire flame logo, a black and orange polo with the same flames emblazoned on the breast, and had carried a backpack with a Prairie Fire patch stitched to the front pocket. "Not the last one," he said. "But maybe that other thing."

"Which thing?" Flip asked. "Bringing joy to people's lives or bringing people together?"

The student hunched his body down as low as humanly possible without actually bringing his chin in contact with the table's surface. "The bringing people together."

"That's great!" Flip cried out louder than he meant to. "You can use that as the meat of the paper. Now write that down before you forget it!"

The student regarded Flip with skepticism, then wrote *Prairie Fire football brings people together* at the top of the page.

"The point of this assignment is that your teacher wants you to think critically about something," Flip said. "She wants to know that you have a well-thought-out opinion about a topic you can explain using facts and details to convince the reader that football really brings people together. So tell me," he said, looking the student squarely in the eye and drawing his attention away from the girl in the orange high-cut shorts at the next table, back up from the stack of worn Pictionary and Scrabble games on the low writing center bookshelf, away from the empty, aging desktop tower on the opposite table, and away from the *10 Easy Steps to Paper Writing* chart stuck to the whiteboard, "how exactly does football bring people together?"

The student looked down and said nothing.

10

THE PROBLEM with writing the perfect MFA novel, Flip thought as he shivered from the raw gusts of the library air conditioner vent above him, was that molding his novel to suit the workshop's standards seemed to go completely against a story about alienation. His novel needed the high-strung misanthropic voice to give it shape, and making his novel sound more like Stark's would be like asking Thomas Hardy to rewrite *Naked Lunch*.

The icy gale of the air conditioner had become too frigid to ignore, so Flip picked up his books and his unread copy of Kendall's workshop submission and carried them to one of the other empty tables lining the library stacks. Working so close to the windowless brick walls of the library felt mildly depressing, but it was preferable to sitting in a wobbly folding chair and paying the cost of running the air conditioner back at the apartment. He looked again at Kendall's workshop packet and thought about how much he didn't want to read it before wondering whether the air conditioning in this new spot would be just as annoyingly powerful as in the old one.

The real question was which aspects of the novel he could compromise on to appeal to a wider audience. Was it a mistake to hold off mentioning the narrator's name until page twenty-eight? Or to save the conflict of his getting the window office until page sixty-two? Would the novel be more approachable if written in the third-person? This might also lead to less embarrassment since people tended to associate first-person novels with things that had really happened to the writer. He recalled Kendall's comment about there being too many coworkers and to check whether this was true, he pulled out his character notebook from his bag and counted forty-nine in the novel as it now stood. Perhaps this was too many, and it'd be better to write a novel with only ten or so characters he could introduce within the first fifty pages, with maybe a side character appearing briefly to give the hero sage advice. That could work, couldn't it?

Forty-nine characters was a lot, but *Catch-22* had a lot of characters too and the chaos of having so many had accentuated the chaos of the war in a way that felt deliberate on Heller's part. He'd loved that about the novel even when he'd first read it during that pivotal time in high school when he'd begun to suspect the world wasn't playing honestly with him. Heller had even worked the characters' names into the novel's framework—the wordplay in Lieutenant Scheisskopf's name or the rhythm of referring to the dead man in Yossarian's tent instead of his actual name had made the novel *fun*. Heller, more than even Kingsley Amis, had understood that idea of fun—Christ, he'd filled *Portrait of an Artist, as an Old Man* with literary references and ridiculous novel excerpts that complemented the narrative, and that had made for a great novel.

He put down the badly worn Karl Marx anthology he'd bought off Amazon and rested his chin in both hands. Unfortunately, people hadn't exactly ripped *Portrait of an Artist, as an Old Man* off the shelves when it was published, and if Stark was right then people also wouldn't love *Catch-22* if it came out today because Heller had written it in an earlier time when people wanted different things from the books they read—or maybe when they still wanted books at all. Dickens too had included a lot of characters in his novels, but his work belonged to an even earlier time when fans had mobbed the docks as ships delivered new installments of his novels in serial form, a publishing method that seemed especially antiquated in the age of binge-watching. Now it seemed that nothing short of *Harry Potter* could spark such excitement, though even the *Harry Potter* series had ended and wasn't coming back.

But people still craved stories that excited them—except now they wanted YouTube cat videos and serial Netflix dramas and the next big Marvel movie since that was what genuinely excited people in the twenty-first century. People were always drawn to what Kafka had called an axe for the frozen sea—something real that broke through the stupor of everyday existence. He was certain that books could still stir up that excitement—there were just fewer people reading now and more books than ever before. It also felt like many of the books out there didn't stir up excitement—or didn't stir up excitement in him, anyway. If a book spoke to you like you were a real twenty-first century young person with real twenty-first century sensibilities, then real twenty-first century young people would listen, but doing this required presenting the novel in a way that drew in people rather than pushing them away.

All of us, like Pirsig's Phaedrus, knew what was good and sought to replicate it as best we could. Quentin Tarantino took older cinematic forms he'd loved when he was younger and reworked them for modern audiences; writers did that too, where the books that stirred them as younger readers influenced their own work as adults. However, rather than simply copying what came before them, the best writers transformed these influences into something unique.

Was there some way he could write a spiritual successor to the twentieth century novels he admired? Doing so would require a more elaborate setup that inherently complemented the story, with maybe a few monologues explaining the premise and some hidden signposts for clever readers to catch—a project for another day.

He tore his gaze away from the wall and looked again at the opening chapters of Kendall's novel. Kendall understood what Stark and the others wanted; otherwise he wouldn't have won that book prize and wouldn't be getting his short story collection published. Kendall's collection, though, was only one book among an immeasurable number of books that spoke to an immeasurable number of people. There must be some readers out there who craved stories about the same struggles he'd experienced, so that when they saw those struggles on the page a bond would form that screamed out *Yes—you and I are the same and we look at the world the same way even if other people can't see it!!!*

If the other grad students didn't want to reveal great truths about the world, why had they wanted to become writers in the first place? Had they chosen grad school for other, more material-istic reasons? This seemed like an especially disconcerting thought.

Flip suddenly became aware of an uncomfortable chill in the air around him, now equally if not more intense than what he'd felt at the previous table, and remembered Jackson's comment about Salman Rushdie's Faustian bargain in reverse. Work seemed a good way to get moving again—not novel work, since he still wasn't sure he could face the blank screen, and definitely not more of Marx's reflections on specialization and inequality—but other writing work that would make him feel productive. He opened Kendall's workshop pages and began reading.

The Great Ascension

A Novel by Kendall Warren

Chapter 1

He relished the sight of the sun's timorous sparkle through the limpid sheen of the display case, oblong with its gilded edges, reflecting as it did the sculpture's graceful slope and catching the twisted loop of its claw-like legs. For Graham, the shimmer evoked a feeling almost sensual, akin to taking that first gasp of oxygen after climbing a long spiral staircase or pulling one's body out of the deep end after the afternoon's final lap, for that exacting air of completeness could only be experienced once the sculpture had been placed behind that ineffable pane shielding it from the rest of the world.

The gallery director was taken by the piece but declined to immediately say so, fearing the inevitable haggling and loss of leverage that would result were he to forego the upper hand. Instead he played his negotiations silently, a gambler feeling out his opponent's tells before the dealer turns the final card, and mumbled a number far lower than he would have given an established artist, say, one plucked from a loft in Greenwich Village rather than the flats of Bixby county in a state that most people would have described as "flyover country." He'd gleamed this much in preparing for the meeting and wondered now whether the young man across from him would jump at it, knowing what acceptance from such a distinguished gallery would mean for his budding career.

Rather than responding directly Graham ran his palm along the brown suede of the sofa stretched perpendicular to the director's desk and asked an unrelated question, one necessitating a perfunctory answer and several minutes of small talk—the question of whether so-and-so was acquainted with so-and-so and what they'd shown in which gallery in which year—until he turned wordlessly back to the sculpture still nestled in its ivory packing material and voiced a figure double that of the director's offer.

Such bravado, such debonair, the director surmised, clearly showed the mark of one who knew what he was worth, and so it was that Graham received his first sale as a legitimate sculptor.

[#]

The spectacle surrounding the autumn gallery opening never failed to draw in those both eager for social contact after a summer away from the city and fearful of what would happen should they fail to make an appearance. Graham was careful to note the manner in which they paid more attention to conversational pleasantries than to the art itself, for a farm boy from the rural Midwest didn't simply break into the Chicago art scene on merit alone. With the flute of champagne pinioned against his chest he studied the individuals slowly gathering along the gallery edges.

"These are the people," he whispered to his slender, blonde-haired wife Roxanne, "we have to win over if we want to make it here."

"I really don't see what all the fuss is about," Roxanne murmured back. "You're a much better artist than the rest of them, so you shouldn't have to worry about all this schmoozing."

Graham chuckled and gripped her free hand in his. "Some things just come with the territory." Roxanne, being naturally naïve about the severities necessary to achieve what one might consider success, never ceased to make him chuckle with her child-like belief that the world functioned in a straightforward manner.

He and Roxanne had been married six months earlier in a well-attended ceremony in the city, during which her family had given Graham their blessing despite her father's misgivings about his career path. At the time he'd felt he had something to prove—in many ways, he still did—to that world that looked down on him just because he hadn't been born into it, but in many ways the thirst to attain what they already had had granted him a greater awareness of their surroundings than even they themselves were aware.

Now he studied the participants in their so-called "ballet," each one acting through the motions of his or her part, and it was with a barely perceptible gulp of his champagne that he edged his right foot in front of his left and—

[Here Flip shuddered, raised his eyes from the page, and stared hopelessly at the wall in front of him.]

11

Melvin Glangworth is a member of the National Honor Society,
a recipient of the John H. Compton Scholarship for Academic
Excellence, and was ranked salutatorian of his high school class
with a cumulative 4.43 GPA out of a maximum 4.5. As an under-
graduate he served as the assistant fiction editor of Mylar Bones, a
nationally-recognized undergraduate creative writing journal, and
graduated Phi Beta Kappa with a 3.96 GPA out of a possible 4.0.
He is eager and excited to be embarking on his MFA degree.

THE OFFICE Flip shared with Melvin and the literature grad student
whose name he didn't know was a barren, chalk-colored room on
the third floor of the English building. It was located at the far
east end of the interminably empty hallway, adjacent to the offices
of the professor of medieval literature and the younger of the two
nineteenth century lit professors, both of whom kept their heads
down whenever they walked past his open door. Clever division
of available space had situated the offices of full faculty members
along the floor's perimeter where they had access to windows,
while the larger, windowless shared offices occupied by the grad
students filled in the center area. This lack of connection with
the outside world combined with the office's bare walls and faint
musty odor evoked the feeling of working in a building scheduled
for demolition.

The office contained two three-drawer filing cabinets (both
empty), a seven-foot metal bookshelf (also empty), a microwave
whose discolored interior had been used to overheat at least one
uncovered bowl of spaghetti, a coffeemaker with crevices caked

in rusty brown sludge, and three metal desks dating from an era where the size and weight of one's desk stood in proportion to one's status in a company. Each of the desks was large enough to fit at least twenty-four pieces of paper side by side without touching its edges, and Flip knew this because he'd measured it using the unstapled pages of some Kant reading he'd struggled through during his second week of the Critical Theory class.

At present he'd fanned out several photocopied articles for the Great Plains Studies class on the desk beside his laptop to convey the impression that he was a busy grad student with many things to do, and though this was technically true (he still had to write his Great Plains Studies response, finish Kendall's workshop pages, read and digest fifty pages of Hegel for the theory class, and finish that week's writing center prep), it seemed necessary to convey this to anyone who might be watching. He'd chosen the desk closest to the doorway so that at least he'd have a view of the hallway outside, though said view consisted of only the blank wall and gray tiled floor by the hallway corner. It was, however, preferable to his old work cube.

Melvin's desk was situated on the opposite wall from Flip's, where he now sat reading literary news on his laptop. The room's other desk was occupied by a literature student who on his first week had marched into the office, surveyed his surroundings with a faint sniff, announced "This is it?" without introducing himself, and dropped a black laptop and stack of library books on to the empty third desk. Neither the books nor the laptop had moved since then, and the laptop's light still blinked slowly on and then back off again, gaining power from the charger cable looped over the desk's front edge. Flip wondered how long before the library books would come due.

"Did you hear that Jacob Palter's last book was nominated for the Erickson Prize?" Melvin asked.

"No," Flip said because he didn't know who Jacob Palter was and didn't want to admit this with Melvin having so clearly taken the familiarity of the name for granted. To change the subject he asked whether Melvin had done the reading for the Great Plains class.

"Most of it," Melvin said. "I really liked Danielson's chapter on seasonal fluctuation where she links pH levels with early settlement patterns. I definitely agree with her about the citizens of the Great Plains relying on plant life for their identity, whether natural or through crop production."

Flip hadn't skimmed enough of the chapter to form a coherent response to this, so instead he nodded and said. "Yeah, that makes a lot of sense."

Melvin stopped to check, then respond to, a text message on his phone before asking, "Have you read Blake Anderson's latest novel? It's supposed to be amazing, and Aaron Talrod mentioned it in this interview I was just reading." He spun his chair to face Flip directly. "Actually, I was thinking about your novel this week, and I think where you're going with this office thing is a kind of gritty, Tom Schulman approach like in *Canon of Five* that creates a sense of drama resulting from a desperate situation. The only difference is that instead of five guys hiding in an abandoned warehouse it's your one guy working in an office, so you should definitely check it out."

Flip didn't grasp what, if anything, Melvin meant by this suggestion and decided to ignore it. "How's your novel coming, anyway?" he asked.

"Little by little," Melvin said as he shifted in his chair. "It's hard to have a million things going on in grad school and still work on your own stuff, you know?"

This statement struck Flip as the first thing Melvin had ever said that was worth agreeing with. "What's your novel about, anyway?" he asked.

"It's a family drama," Melvin said, "about three generations dealing with the grandfather's Alzheimer's while the parents are having marital difficulties and trying to secure their children's futures just as they've become empty-nesters and their youngest daughter is struggling with anorexia. The story moves back and forth between the present and the grandfather's youth in the years before World War II."

As impressed as Flip was by Melvin's summation, he suspected the actual novel wasn't anything he'd want to read. "How far along are you?" he asked.

"I've made some good progress," Melvin said without saying how much.

"Will we see it in workshop?" Flip asked.

"Not right away," Melvin said. "But it's a good pitch, isn't it? The novel itself is still in the outline stage, but I've got most of the story laid out. I'm submitting some short stories for my first workshop, but I'm hoping to have a chapter or two written by the end of the semester." He shifted his chair again and asked, "Did you get the email about nominations for student government? I was thinking of going out for one of the first-year graduate representative positions since I don't think many people are interested. You should think about it—it'd be a great way to boost your CV."

Flip wondered whether Mary-Beth had spoken to Melvin about running. "I wasn't planning on it," he said. "I'm pretty busy as it is."

"If you're not interested in student government you should at least think about reading for the *Long Grass* journal," Melvin said. "It seems like there's a lot of opportunity for growth there."

Flip sensed that the time for directness had come. "I really don't want to overextend myself," he said. "I came to grad school to finish my novel and that has to come first, so I don't want to get distracted with a lot of extra-curriculars. Besides, it sounds like you've barely started your own novel as it is."

Melvin laughed abruptly at this. "You know how it is, always juggling professional opportunities and actual writing. Of course, in an ideal world we'd have plenty of time for both, and I certainly try to squeeze in time for writing when I can. But my real plan is to establish myself in these first two years, build a solid CV while I get my novel mapped out, and do the actual writing before my thesis review. Plus, having roles like student government or associate *Long Grass* fiction editor under my belt after Brad leaves will show the tenure-track search committees that I have leadership qualities."

"Sure," Flip said noncommittally, "but are leadership qualities on a CV more important than your actual novel?"

"Both are important," Melvin said. "The difference is that leadership opportunities are available now, and I can always finish my novel later."

Flip sensed a shortcoming in Melvin's plan. "By that logic you'll just keep putting your novel off forever," he said with visible annoyance. "You're still going to be busy next year, so why not start writing now?"

"Because I've got to start reading for *Long Grass* and go out for student government now," Melvin said with annoyance of his own. "Weren't you listening?"

For the first time Flip sensed the crux of Melvin's argument and wondered whether he was doing himself a disservice by not taking on more activities. In any case, this didn't seem like the time for further discussion. He said, "I'll think about it," an answer that seemed to satisfy Melvin, who turned back to his own work.

In the silence that followed Flip put away the Great Plains reading and looked back at Kendall's novel pages. He couldn't read them—each time he tried he began to space out so that though his eyes technically passed over the words, the real part of reading (organizing the sentences into thoughts) failed to trigger. Part of this was due to Kendall's densely overwritten prose, but another, bigger reason was how intensely he hated his protagonist, an egotistical know-it-all who always had a witty reply to anything anyone said to him. Said protagonist (presumably modeled after Kendall himself) now needed to impress his greatness on a world full of pretentious art dealers while calming the skepticism of his wife, who was constantly described in terms of her attractiveness to everyone around her. There was also a lot of thematic harping on the protagonist's quest to prove himself to his wife's over-bearing old-money parents, whose high-ceilinged suburban home was described in envious, unironic terms—more insight, perhaps, into the kind of life Kendall strived for. Still, it annoyed Flip that the novel had an unarguable plot: The protagonist had come to Chicago to establish himself as an artist and win the grant that would finance his work and impress his wife's family while legitimizing himself in the eyes of the art world. As simple as these motivations were, at least Kendall had clearly defined them.

Flip was still staring at the shadowy stretch of hallway thinking about plot when he heard footsteps that he assumed belonged to the professor of nineteenth century literature but that actually belonged to Derzen.

She walked quickly, with a mirthless, business-like gait and her eyes focused straight ahead. In her left hand a clothbound notebook and several paperbacks dangled gloomily toward the ground. Without thinking Flip called, "Hey!"

The greeting seemed to produce a delayed reaction: Derzen first turned her head in Flip's direction without stopping and pivoted her upper body back with her hair falling into the open air. Only then did she stop and say "Hi!" with surprise and take three backward steps so that her torso swung vertically in line with her head, which seemed not to have moved at all. Flip stood and walked to the doorway.

"You look like you're in a hurry," he said.

"Kind of," Derzen said. "I just came from the worst teaching disaster ever." She held her books against her chest the way Flip imagined girls in the 1950s did when accepting invites to sock hops. "Do you ever feel like everyone around you is just going through a series of motions?"

"Every minute of every day," Flip said.

Derzen laughed at this. She wore a jet-black blouse whose neck opened in an elongated vee, and the slim triangle of skin below her collarbone seemed to accentuate the straightness of her body. "It's my first time teaching Intro to Poetry, and if I'd known non-majors could take it just to fill their Arts Appreciation requirement I would have requested something else."

"I'm sure it beats working in the writing center," Flip said. "You should come down there sometime and I'll show you."

Derzen laughed again. "I remember the writing center pretty well, thanks."

Flip didn't know how to respond to this and became momentarily panicked that their conversation would end and Derzen would walk away. His mind fumbled from the writing center back to gen-ed requirements and then further back to banana cream pie and the Brontë sisters, and for lack of any suitable jumping-off points, asked, "Did you have a good time the other night?"

Derzen's face shifted to a less cheerful expression as her eyes rose up and to the right. (Flip recalled hearing somewhere that people always looked up and to one side when lying, but he couldn't remember which one.) "Oh, it was a party, I guess," she said. "Nights like that are pretty much the same. You can be yourself more than you can in, say, the classroom, but you're still surrounded by the same people you see every day."

Flip tried not to think about Melvin sitting on the other side of the office. "I guess I expected more socializing and less football."

Derzen rolled her eyes. "You'd think so. Most of the time I only go to those things because Kendall wants to."

The mention evoked the distressing placement of Kendall's hand on Derzen's back, an image Flip struggled to wipe away. "Yeah," he said. "I was a bit surprised when I realized you and Kendall were together. He didn't mention having a girlfriend in the department."

Upon hearing this Derzen's face shifted first to a look of surprise, then to a look of disappointment, then to a look of nonchalance indicated by a dismissive raising of her eyebrows. "You know how it is," she said. "After a while you just start assuming everyone knows you're a couple." Once this explanation was behind her she began speaking faster. "Kendall told me you were from the Northeast—why didn't you say so before? Jackson and I need more Eastcoasters to keep us company. I'm from New York—not from the city, but a ways outside."

"Long Island?" Flip asked.

"As if," Derzen said. "Just north of the Bear Mountain Bridge. Suburbia meets the countryside, if you can imagine that."

"Is it worse than the Midwest?" Flip asked.

Derzen wrinkled her nose. "No place is worse than the Midwest."

"I guess that's one thing you and I feel the same about."

"Too bad all the teaching assistantships are out here," Derzen said quickly.

"Sadly," Flip said as he looked down at the books Derzen still clutched to her chest, noticing for the first time a stripe of purple nail polish on her ring finger. It seemed somehow to belong there, as if she'd removed all of her nail polish but left that one sliver to disclose an earlier design she hadn't wanted to keep hidden. As he thought about this he sensed she was thinking about something too, so that the silence that followed wasn't awkward, but comfortable, like the kind Uma Thurman's character mentions in *Pulp Fiction*.

Derzen finally said, "I should go work on that stack of papers I have to grade," and lowered the books back to her side. "My office is just down the hall if you ever want to chat."

"I just might," Flip said. "Sometimes it's better to talk one-on-one, without distractions."

This statement seemed to coax a look of agreement into Derzen's eyes. "Tell me about it," she said, and then was gone.

No sooner had Derzen rounded the corner when Flip stepped into the empty hall and silently raised both arms into the air, first with his fists clenched, then his palms open, hissing noiselessly through his teeth and waving to an invisible crowd of onlookers. He followed this with several deep bows and a victory dance where he swung his arms back and forth and jumped around the hallway while swinging his body at erratic angles. He halted when he heard footsteps echoing through the stairwell and ran back to the office, where Melvin proceeded to read him the nomination process for student government.

12

"I JUST WANT to call attention to one sentence I think really captures the heart of Kendall's novel," Lawrence said in his slow, twanging southern drawl, "since it highlights both the main character's conflict and the beauty of the writing." He buried his head in his packet and read, "*So it was that Graham, without ever having functioned within that particular vein, held strong against the current of unrest that threatened his forward-moving course, and in doing so sought to achieve the very thing so many before him had utterly failed to effectuate, that chimerical goal we so aptly call success.*" He raised his head to the rest of the workshop. "And that I think just says it all."

"I was struck by that sentence too," Brad said with a friendly nod in Kendall's direction, "both because of the writing quality and because it describes the concept of success. And what is success, really?" He paused deliberately and continued when no one answered. "Exactly. It's something we can't explain, but we know it when we see it."

Flip sat wondering what in god's name was wrong with everyone around him—couldn't they see the sentence was a string of nonsense? Or was it possible that someone had filtered mind-altering drugs into the department's drinking water through some *X-Files*-esque conspiracy to convince them Kendall's novel was good?

"That's an excellent point," Stark said. "I think what Kendall's getting at is that feeling of being driven to achieve something and sacrificing everything else to get there, like how Graham has to leave his entire family behind to move to the city. We feel the sadness in his decision, but we also feel he's justified in leaving them because setting up his reputation in this cutthroat world is so impossibly difficult that there's not enough room for both the old and the new."

"I'm glad you picked up on that," Kendall said, twisting his pen around his fingers. "I think all of us know the pain of having to let go of something we care about, and in Graham's case I really wanted to stress the closeness of the family relationships that made the separation so difficult."

Why does Kendall get to talk during workshop? Flip thought with sudden fury.

Jackson cleared his throat in response. "I think Graham's conflict comes across especially clearly because right from the get-go Kendall establishes that Graham's getting that funding check determines whether the rest of the world sees him as a real artist."

Judas! Flip thought.

"Jackson makes an excellent point," Stark said with a barely perceptible glance in Flip's direction. "What Kendall's done here is define Graham's motivations right away so that we understand that this book's really about establishing yourself as a young professional in the field, but because that's such an abstract idea it's easier for us to focus on the more material goal of his getting the funding."

Or what if I'm the one who's wrong? Flip thought, and at that moment a great many things seemed uncertain.

"See, that story's totally marketable," Craig said. "Young guy in a new city sucking up to snobby art types, he's overdrawn all his credit cards, and his wife's parents think he's a joke, so he's got to prove he's good enough for their daughter. Agents are going to eat that shit for breakfast and sign you right away, and I mean *right* away—they can sense those marketable hooks like bears sniffing out steaks at a campground."

Flip looked down at his copy of Kendall's manuscript, the margins of which he'd filled with notes like *Feels wordy, Can you cut this?* and *This doesn't feel relevant, somehow.* It occurred to him that if he didn't speak now that the tide of compliments would only gain momentum until he'd lost all chance of voicing even the slightest bit of criticism.

"There's one thing I was thinking, though," Flip broke in before Craig could continue. "It seems like these characters spend a lot of time going to parties and just talking about things—on page forty-seven there's a two-page conversation about how Wall Street should be more tightly regulated, and while most readers would probably agree with that, the topic never comes up again and doesn't feel relevant to the story. It's okay to have your characters talk a lot, but their conversations should show us how they understand the world around them, or at least serve some thematic purpose in the novel."

Kendall turned in Flip's direction with his eyebrows raised and his mouth half-open in surprise. Melvin and Brad also looked uncomfortable.

"I'd be careful about your prose too," Flip continued with less confidence and a faint stutter. "You use a lot of elaborate phrases to describe pretty simple things, so you might want to think about … tightening things up?"

Flip's voice lowered almost to a whisper at this last word as Kendall looked at him with a blank expression, his pen still spinning through his fingers. The silence filling the room was anything but the *Pulp-Fiction* kind.

"I actually thought the Wall Street conversation was quite profound," Melvin said finally. "The lack of regulation that existed before the 2008 crash was inexcusable, and it's well within our power to rein in all those snooty New York bankers, so I'd like to commend Kendall for revealing some profound thoughts about a relevant topic."

"I wasn't disagreeing with him about regulating Wall Street," Flip said defensively. "I just meant that the conversation was tangential to the story."

"Fair enough," Melvin said in a rush to change the subject, "though I also found the writing to be really poetic and meaningful in that scene, as in all of the conversation scenes. Actually, I wanted to share one of my favorite passages, from the part where

Graham starts doubting whether he's good enough to be a real artist: *Graham wondered, as he often did in his most apprehensive moments, whether through some fault of his own or error of judgment, that he might not have been better off taking a different, more certain path with a more definite future, the kind that offered worry-free security for the upcoming decades. Perhaps he should have gone into finance or a STEM field like his father had wanted, but both paths would have lacked the spirit, the passion, and the joy one received from being integrated with the art world."*

Flip didn't say anything for the rest of the workshop.

13

IN THE EVENING when the air began to cool Flip walked behind the music building to the sculpture garden nestled in the shade cast by the towering wall of the Prairie Fire stadium. There were only three sculptures in the sculpture garden, two of which were large enough for the university to have posted DO NOT CLIMB signs on. Though their globular appearance provided little in the way of stimulation, Flip felt a closeness with the place as one that spoke to a less utilitarian mindset.

Beneath a leafy tree he paused, staring at a gap between the music and art buildings through which he could see cars and semi-trucks rushing down the city's main throughway. He dropped his bag onto a picnic table stained with blotches of tree sap, then sat on the table's surface with his feet perched on the seat. He pulled a hard-backed sketchbook from his bag and began to draw the outline of the music and art buildings, though instead of empty space behind them he sketched in the skyscrapers of a city horizon like the one on Derzen's shirt the day he'd first noticed her outside the English building. Something in the cityscape, however, felt wrong, so he turned the page and began penciling in the sides of a tall castle tower, its roof peaked with a triangular flag and its one ovular window looking out on what became a curved river flowing from snow-capped mountains. The mountains back home weren't as pointed or craggy as the ones in the drawing, and snow definitely never clung to them like that when the rest of the trees were still green. Still, drawing cragged, snow-covered mountains made them look more like mountains, which made the whole drawing more clearly resemble what it was supposed to. He added several rocks poking out of the river, then drew a tangled forest with all different kinds of trees like in the forests back home.

The foreground, though, still looked empty, so he sketched out the sharp, scaly tail of a dragon coiling around the tower. On the other side of the tower he drew the rest of the dragon, with wisps of smoke curling from its nostrils and a forked, slithering tongue winding from between its lips. He liked the way the dragon's tongue looked and added half-closed eyes and a pair of horns to make it even more sinister. Without thinking he moved to the tower's window and began sketching a slender, long-haired maiden gazing longingly at the mountains with a sad, empty expression. He penciled in the lines of her hair and dress for a long time to get them exactly the way he wanted. After looking over the whole scene, he decided it needed a hero and drew a chain mail-clad knight sneaking up behind the dragon, his sword and shield in hand and his head in its visored helmet turning back to check for enemies.

Something about this act of drawing relaxed him so much more than sitting down to write did. When he sat down to write the stakes were so much higher because eventually someone would always be there to talk condescendingly about his work or reject it or say that it wasn't good enough to serve as his MFA thesis or get him an agent so that he'd never be published and become successful. When he sat drawing in the sculpture garden for those few minutes before sunset everything felt right with the world.

14

"How do you know for sure they liked it?" Jackson asked.

"Because all they did was gush about how great it was!" Flip said, dashing in front of Jackson as they walked along the scalding hot sidewalk. "Because they spent a full ninety minutes congratulating him on all the things they loved about it and gave him a fucking round of *applause* when they were finished without offering a single piece of criticism, like the novel was absolutely perfect the way it was. And why does Kendall get to talk during workshop?"

"Because he's earned their respect," Jackson said with his hands buried in his pockets and his messenger bag slung against his hip. They were walking along a downtown street beside concrete parking garages, high-rise apartments, and chain restaurants, one of which was blaring country music from exterior speakers. At the end of the block an Arby's complete with a drive-through and a ten-space parking area occupied a corner lot.

"I just wish he hadn't acted so certain about it," Flip went on, "like he'd written the world's greatest literary novel and anyone who questioned that clearly didn't know what they were talking about."

Jackson pulled a tissue from his pocket, blew a loud discharge of snot into it, and tossed the whole thing into a trash can as they passed. "I think that happened partly because the others saw something in Kendall's novel they could relate to, since they're all MFA and PhD writers who want to make it in the academic world as badly as Kendall's character wants to make it in the art world. Who knows whether they realized this consciously or not—the point is that it struck them because of their similar experience and background. But on another level they all sensed the novel was noteworthy and that the socially acceptable course of action was to praise it as such. I fully acknowledge that *Moby Dick* is one of the most important novels ever written, but I don't want to read a bunch of chapters about whale skeletons and ambergris and images of whales in classical painting because those things slow the novel down and most people don't care about them."

"I don't like *Moby Dick* either," Flip said. "I only read it because I thought I had to, like my literary knowledge wouldn't be complete without it."

"You can't completely ignore that aspect of reading," Jackson said. "There's more to a novel or a piece of art than just its enter- tainment value—it can say something about a particular time or place or way of life that's important even if it's not an enjoyable or stimulating read, so when we go through a book like *Moby Dick* it's possible to look past how much we actually enjoyed it and appre- ciate what it says about nineteenth century whaling or man's rejec- tion of God. The hard part comes when you can't see those other, more abstract values, so you have to guess at whether they're really there. That guessing gets a whole lot easier when you know other people have found those values before you. In the case of *Moby Dick*, enough scholars have found enough important things to say about it that we can be pretty sure it's *actually* important rather than outdated trash. We naturally trust the judgments of smarter people who came before us, but when you don't have the luxury of agreeing with decades of distinguished scholarship you have to guess based on the author's reputation or how many books they've published or what the people around you say until the guessing becomes this unspoken awareness that the book itself is *actually* good because everyone thinks that everyone else thinks so."

"So you're saying everyone's just sucking up to Kendall because they think his novel and his short story collection are important?" Flip asked.

"That's something we can't ever really know," Jackson said, "unless everyone in workshop were to speak completely honestly, which will never happen. But I can tell you that Kendall's established trust with his readers because he's been through a lot of workshops and already has an MFA and a bunch of short story publications and a collection coming out in the spring, and because his novel looked and sounded like an MFA novel that people are used to, so it's not hard for them to make the connection."

Flip stared at the large and vacant window of an empty storefront whose interior floor was covered with construction debris. "So apart from all that, what did you think of Kendall's novel?"

"Oh it was trash," Jackson said. "It was empty and rambling and I skimmed as little as I could to get the gist of it. But I could also tell how the others were going to react to it based on what I knew of their tastes and Kendall's reputation, so I described it in solely positive terms so everyone would see that I knew what I was talking about. That's how academia works—you figure out what other people want to hear, then say it over and over so they'll think you're smart."

A towering parking garage rose in front of them, taller than any building on the street and almost as tall as the banks and office buildings further south, and Flip wondered how much of the surrounding suburbs and farmland he'd be able to see from its roof. "How much of Kendall's novel do you think is autobiographical?" he asked.

"You can't read too much into that," Jackson said. "Most writing comes from some form of the writer's own experience, but most often what ends up on the page becomes a distorted fun-house mirror version of that experience, so that figuring out the inspiration for a story involves undistorting its events and guessing at the real image. It's that distortion that lets writers put that *This is a work of fiction* disclaimer on the title page without lying because whenever you change the truth even a little, your story becomes an alternate reality separate from what really happened."

This sentiment reminded Flip of *Lucky Jim* and how Amis couldn't possibly have written it without having suffered through his own version of stuck-up university hell. "That's not what bothers me about it," he said. "What bothers me is that Kendall's novel makes a clearly autobiographical character out to be this hero who's fulfilling his god-given destiny to make it in the art world, but the character's so full of himself that it's impossible to feel sympathy for him for not immediately achieving his lofty ideals."

Jackson stepped around a low bench with rings looped around its seat to stop homeless people from sleeping there. "You're right that Kendall's character's a stuck-up prick, but his predicament taps into something deeper about how we experience stories. Most of the stories that really resonate make us root for underdog heroes who remind us of our own struggles, because we all view the underdogs as the people we want to sympathize with. Nietzsche wrote about that in *The Genealogy of Morals*—if you go all the way back to early civilization, some people back then had power and some didn't, just like today. Of course the people without power got screwed over on a daily basis, so they started hating the people with power who were doing the screwing. That made them see the people with power as Evil, which meant that logically, they themselves must be Good. If the people at the bottom are the Good people, then the qualities they used to protect themselves from the Evil people must be Good too, and the qualities the Evil people used to screw them over must be Evil. That's why we shun greedy, arrogant, and incompetent people and value people who are humble, obedient, and polite since these were tactics the servants and working-class Joes used to stay alive in a crooked world. Meanwhile, the people on top with the money and power were too busy holding feasts at their palaces and sleeping off their hangovers to create any real culture, so the people on the bottom who were disadvantaged, clever, and a little bit desperate did all the storytelling, so they're the ones whose values got passed on. Now it's deeply rooted in our culture to root for the people in the worst predicaments to win against the people who are stronger and meaner, which is why you see this in books and TV and movies. Charlie Chaplin was the most popular movie star who ever lived because he made movies about down-on-their-luck tramps who outwit bullying policemen and monocle-wearing millionaires— people wanted to see Chaplin succeed back then just like we want to see Charlie Brown finally kick the football and ask out the little red-haired girl. It's debatable, I think, whether Kendall's character garners Charlie Brown-like levels of sympathy, but his struggles definitely speak to the ones people in workshop face."

They'd reached a corner in front of a Starbucks where a crowd of undergraduates, most of them tall, many of them blond, and all of them wearing some form of Prairie Fire orange, stood silently waiting at the crosswalk. On the opposite side of the street a window marked PRAIRIE FIRE OUTFITTERS featured several mannequins clad in orange t-shirts, hats, shorts, and sandals all marked with the flame-shrouded PF logo. Jackson stepped around the undergrads as the signal turned green.

"The Chaplin comparison makes sense," Flip said. "My novel's also about an underdog, but I know people can't really sympathize with the character yet. That's what I've got to fix before my next workshop, and I think I just need to figure out what kind of story people are looking for."

"That's a good idea," Jackson said. "For what it's worth, people tend to be more honest with their opinions one-on-one when they're not worried about sounding stupid in front of their peers."

Flip thought about this as he raised his head to the sky, where a crisscross of smoke trails sped onward against the piercing blue, each one moving in a different direction.

15

Craig Prescott's short fiction has appeared in over eighty publications, including WHAM!, The Paul Denton Review, Clockwork and Tea Biscuits, Nothing Important Happened Today, quiet, aLOOF, Explanatrixx, Windowseed, Fingerbang Happenstance, Conspired: A Collection of Revelatory Tumescence, EXI(S)T, Pizazz, Musings on the Edification of a Mercurial Public, UnDerView, Puddle of Despair, Adjacent Times, Deportation, A Completely Unpretentious and Down-to-Earth Journal of Kick-Ass Fiction, CornHOLE, Liquid Metal, RAW: A Journal of Unrevised Writing, *and* Vanderbilt Dingledyne: Stories From America's Most Erratic Writers. *He's currently pursuing his MFA in fiction and working on a novel.*

"THAT'S THE thing about grad school: everybody wants to go out all the time," Craig said as he tore open a cupboard filled entirely with boxes of single-serving coffee pods. "Waste of money if you ask me. Who can afford to drink or even go out for coffee on the eleven hundred bucks they give us every month? I sure as hell wish I'd known that my first week here when I spent my entire month's pay eating out every meal. I see other grad students leasing nice apartments and driving fancy cars and you know they're charging it all on credit cards and student loans and racking up secret debt they don't tell anyone about. That goes hand-in-hand with all the time they waste drinking in bars when they should be writing. Man, you gotta keep away from distractions, which is why I broke up with my girlfriend and quit drinking after I came here, and why I've been avoiding all the empty grad student social interactions so I can spend literally every second of my free time writing."

Flip looked around Craig's first-floor apartment, which had two bedrooms and a large dining room even though he lived alone. Though it was a bright, glaring Saturday in late September, Craig had covered all of the windows with blankets to block out the sun, engulfing the kitchen and dining room in a dim shadow that made it feel like evening. Flip had texted him about meeting up sometime for a drink and to talk shop only to have Craig reply fifteen seconds later inviting Flip to his place for coffee instead.

"Economic shit out here's crazy," Craig went on as he grabbed two different flavored pods and jammed one into the coffeemaker. "Back home you make more, but you also spend more, so everybody ends up working more. I used to work seven days a week overtime, eighty hours minimum, any job I could get my hands on 'cause I liked having money. That was before I wanted to be a writer, though. You gotta do it that way in California, man, where a cup of coffee costs six bucks and a burrito'll run you back ten and you can't order a beer for less than fourteen. Fuck, before I came here I tried to buy my brother one of those custom birthday cakes where they carve the fondant into whatever you want and you can eat all the designs and shit, and since he's a dentist I asked them to make a replica of his dentist's chair with the x-ray machine and that tube thing that sucks all the water out of your mouth because it's more sanitary than those refilling cups we had when we were kids. I brought in all these pictures and explained exactly how I wanted it done and the cake designer told me it'd cost me fucking fifteen hundred dollars. Fifteen hundred dollars for a simple birthday cake! No way you'll catch me paying those prices again when out here I can order chili and a cinnamon roll all day long for four bucks." He pulled the mug from beneath the coffeemaker before it had finished draining and swapped it for a fresh one.

Flip wasn't sure where to sit while Craig was making the coffee since neither the kitchen nor the dining room contained any chairs, so he leaned against the doorjamb as he spoke. "Finding a way to support ourselves without piling up more debt seems to be why a lot of us chose grad school," he said. "It's definitely one of the reasons I'm here. As writers we need some kind of steady income, and the security of a tenure-track job could give us that income for a long time."

"Fuck tenure-track jobs," Craig spat. "You think I want to spend the rest of my life in some midwestern college town reading crappy undergrad stories? Landing a tenure-track job takes far and away more writing credits than we'll ever have. At first I was all gung-ho about getting a literary agent, but they're even worse—all they do is latch onto that month's trendy topic and sign writers who can churn out what sells, like when the *Twilight* books got big and suddenly every chain bookstore had a paranormal romance section. If you want original shit you've got to hit up small presses, the guys outside the mainstream who put out stuff that's actually good."

The coffeemaker emitted another hum as Craig yanked the second mug from below the spout. He then poured both the first mug and the new mug into an even bigger mug and took an enormous gulp.

Flip stared at him. "Were you going to make some for me?"

Craig looked down at his mug and then back at Flip. "Sorry man, I guess I just went on auto-pilot. I drink twelve cups of coffee a day minimum, including one before bed to help me sleep. Gotta stay productive in grad school! I'll make you one now."

"Thanks," Flip said as Craig opened another cupboard also entirely filled with boxes of coffee pods. "You make a good point about agents wanting what people actually want to read, and they must know something we don't because we're just a bunch of lowly grad students."

Craig's response was to hurl an open coffee pod box to the counter in disgust, scattering its contents onto the floor. "Dude, you can't doubt yourself like that. You've gotta have faith in your beliefs and literally fuck whatever anyone else says. The people in workshop are always sucking up to the bigwigs in academia. You've got to do your own shit on your own terms or you'll never make it as a writer."

"Did you think Kendall's novel was good?" Flip asked.

"Good god no," Craig sputtered, the coffee pods lying forgotten on the floor as he reached for his oversized mug. "I wouldn't read Kendall's novel if you had my tonsils in a set of vise grips. His book represents everything that's wrong with MFA fiction, but some fluffy near-bankrupt academic press will sign his book since it's got a bunch of flowing prose and shit. He'll add it to his CV so he can get that tenure-track job he's jonesin' for, then earn enough royalty money from it to buy a new pair of wool socks. So in that sense the novel's a total success, if by success you mean sucking off the upper-class faux-artistic crowd."

He led Flip into the apartment's living room, where boxes and milk crates stacked to shoulder height and jammed completely with books, notebooks, and papers lined the walls. On the far wall sat a long, wood-paneled folding table of the kind found in town halls, but instead of standing on its legs it rested on two half-sized filing cabinets and two other stacks of milk crates so that the only space remaining was a crevice far too narrow for the ergonomic desk chair resting in front of it. Above the table hung a large whiteboard with notes scrawled in no fewer than six different colors of dry erase marker, with smudges of older fragments visible along its edges. Standing out clearly in the board's center was a list written in red:

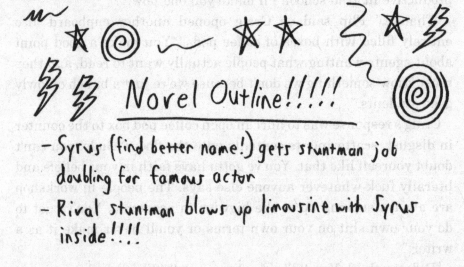

Novel Outline!!!!!

- Syrus (find better name!) gets stuntman job doubling for famous actor
- Rival stuntman blows up limousine with Syrus inside!!!!

- Syrus leaver stuntman job
- Famous actor stalkr Syrus's house, girlfriend
- Syrus escapes to desert, takes peyote and molly and LSD all at once, sees vision of flying dinosaur named Hebert
- Syrus robbed and beaten by hobo thieves
- Syrus meets old psychiatrist outside Walgreens, hooks up with traveling meth lab
- Meth lab explodes outside zoo, killing everyone except Syrus. Elephants escape
- Elephants smash parked cars outside Carl's Jr.
- Syrus finds girlfriend in hospital, apologizes, rescues her from hepatitis experiment

- Helicopter chase!!!!!!

BAM!

—Helicopter crashes outside famous actor's mountaintop mansion by coincidence. <u>Lots</u> of explosions, fistfight in living room. Southeast Asian human trafficking plot revealed. Syrus frees victims, escapes, searches for payphone but finds slots jammed with gum and human feces, bursts into cupcake factory, finally calls police, collapses into giant vat of frosting.

"Don't look at that garbage!" Craig roared, and with a fury of eraser swipes he reduced the list to scattered scribbles. He then uncapped a marker and in the center of the empty space wrote:

Smuggling conspiracy at plastic surgery clinic, breast implants laced with heroin

"That's going to be my new novel," Craig said, tossing the marker aside. "The other one didn't have enough action."

"So they're smuggling drugs in breast implants?" Flip asked. "Wasn't that a plotline on that old show *Nip/Tuck?*"

Craig collapsed into the ergonomic chair and set both feet in their black combat boots on the table. "Maybe—who the fuck knows? Everything sure as fuck's stolen from somewhere else, so any idea you come up with I bet you a million dollars has already been done. You ever read *Fahrenheit 451?* Same book as *Huckleberry Finn* but with no slaves."

"How are those even remotely the same?" Flip demanded.

"I'm telling you, man, same book," Craig said without explaining. "There's only like, four plots that have ever existed. Five, tops."

"Whatever," Flip said, still standing in the center of the room because Craig had taken the only chair. "Regardless of how many plots are out there I want my novel to be unique, and I want it to show how alienating it is to spend day after day in an office with people who don't understand you."

"Dude, your book didn't show that at all," Craig said. "Your book was just the narrator rambling about a bunch of crap I didn't care about. Things have to happen in books, in every scene, on every page, and in literally every sentence. You can't just have one guy talking to other people about what he's going to do later."

"There's more to books than just mindless action," Flip insisted. "Sometimes the action happens through subtle dialogue and character development."

"Real life's boring," Craig said. "And the only way to put action in your book is to show actual action, which is why I stopped reading your book after four pages. If you're going to write a novel about office life it's got to grab me from the very first sentence."

"You can't base an entire novel on its first four pages," Flip said in alarm. "A novel needs time to develop a story."

"That sounds good in theory, but I don't make the rules," Craig said. "Think about TV and how we used to be stuck watching the same sixty-two channels on basic cable—BOR-ing! Now we've got internet streaming where there's literally a billion shows and movies to watch, so when I sit down to unwind I just turn one on that looks cool and if it doesn't one-hundred-percent hook me within the first thirty seconds, BAM, it's on to the next one 'cause there's a billion other potentially better things I could be watching. Books work the same way because people are in a hurry—if somebody's at Barnes and Noble on their lunch break sipping on a seven-dollar latte and wandering through the New Release aisle they're going to see the nine books that James Patterson and Danielle Steel each put out last month, along with a bunch of other books they've never heard of. You're already at a disadvantage because people are more likely to choose a book by an author they know and trust, but let's say for the sake of argument they just happen to pick up yours. First thing they're going to look at is the cover—if your cover looks cool, they're going to open the book, and if they open the book they're going to open to the first page, so your first page sure as fuck better make them want to keep reading. If your first page is just whiny office politics they're going to put your book down and pick up the next one they see with a cool cover. Maybe that one starts with two dudes shoving their dicks in each other's mouths, or a bus full of girl scouts getting eaten by a minotaur, or some ten-year-old whose sister whacks him over the head with a monkey wrench and fucks up his attention span. Shit like that keeps people reading." He took a gulp from the enormous mug. "Who cares if that person actually reads your book, since I guarantee you eighty percent of the books people buy just get thrown beside their nightstands and forgotten about, but it's still a sale, and that's what you need to consider."

Flip shuddered to think Craig might be right. "But that's only one way of getting people's attention," he argued. "Sticking to attention-grabbing openings limits you to telling your story in a certain kind of way."

"Yeah, the best way," Craig said as he tore open a filing cabinet and ran his fingers along a jam-packed set of folders. "I used to write nothing but short stories because I thought if I published in as many places as possible an agent would think I was hot shit and want to sign me, but all those places were crap and no one read them since nobody reads short stories anymore." He pulled a file folder from the cabinet, opened it, and after skimming its contents threw the entire thing in the trash. He then pulled out another folder and handed it to Flip. "How's *that* for an opening?"

Archibald Matthew Carrington pulled his bruised and charred body from the wreckage of his Lamborghini only to discover that he had no legs.

"It definitely grabs my attention." Flip said.

"Of course it grabs your attention!" Craig shouted. "We start with this guy Archibald on the pavement. What happened to his legs? In the next sentence we see his car engulfed in flames after the illegal fireworks truck spun out in front of him and crashed, so now he has to pull himself across the highway to safety before the car explodes, and that's just in the first paragraph. The rest of the story is him crawling through the burning hundred-and-ten-degree desert hoping to hitchhike back to San Marino in time for his youngest daughter's birthday party, but then a Hummer full of escaped convicts almost runs him over and he gets eaten by coyotes."

"That opening makes no sense!" Flip argued. "How did he climb out of the car without legs? Also, how did he get out of the car without *noticing* that he didn't have any legs? And what kind of car accident would tear a person's legs completely off instead of just pinning him in like in *127 Hours?*"

Craig's eyes narrowed to slits as he wrinkled his brow. "Who says a car accident couldn't tear off someone's legs? Are you one of those CSI forensic experts who knows which car accidents can tear off your legs and which can't? I see you've still got both YOUR legs, so how would you know what it's like to lose them? How do you know you wouldn't be in such shock that you wouldn't notice until you'd already crawled out of the car? Maybe you wouldn't notice for hours because the shock was so bad. Maybe you'd go to bed like normal and dream about frolicking through a field of daisies or some shit and only notice the next morning when you woke up dead from blood loss."

"That makes even less sense!" Flip shouted.

Craig put up his hands defensively. "Hey, no need to go crazy on me, cowboy. I'm just saying that not everything a writer puts on paper has to be one hundred percent triple-checked fact." He pulled another folder from the filing cabinet. "How about this one?"

The moment she jammed that eggbeater up my ass, I knew it was love.

"What the hell is this about?" Flip asked as he waved the paper in Craig's direction.

"Exactly!" Craig said in triumph. "I just made you want to know what's going to happen next. The Twitter Generation doesn't have time to slow play—you've literally got to draw them in with one line or else they're going to move right on to the zillion other things they could be reading or watching or playing or listening to, most of which they can get for free."

"You didn't answer my question," Flip asked, wishing again that he had someplace to sit. "What's the story actually about?"

"Who cares what it's about?" Craig said as he threw the folder across the room. "All that matters is that I hooked you from the first sentence. It's a dog-eat-dog world out there, and I for one don't want to get left behind. You know how many query emails literary agents get a week? Hundreds, literally hundreds. With some agents, it's a thousand, and I heard about this one agent who got two thousand query emails a week. Two thousand emails! That's like, five hundred emails a day from people just like us wanting to get their books published. You think agents have time to read them all? Fuck no—they have interns skim them and pick out the ones that don't suck. Last year I sent my short story collection out to fifty book prize contests including the one that chose Kendall's book and I paid a literal king's ransom in entry fees, but it didn't win because the beginnings weren't attention-grabbing enough. So then I wrote a whole new short story collection and sent it to a hundred book prize contests, but none of them took that one either. Want to know why? Because the beginnings still weren't attention-grabbing enough."

"You applied to a hundred and fifty book prize contests?" Flip asked. "That must have cost a fortune."

"It sure as fuck did," Craig said. "Now I'm up to nine grand of credit card debt at twenty-two-and-a-half percent plus my student loans, but that's the price you've got to pay. I was way more impulsive back then, so I thought I knew exactly what I was doing as a writer." He set his feet back on the table and drained the last of his coffee. "I tell you, man, novels are where it's at. If I can get this plastic surgery book or this other idea I have about the psychic zebra-herder off the ground I'll be golden. That's what you should be thinking about. What's your main character's goal?"

Flip lowered his voice in defeat. "He wants to get a new office with a window."

"Man, that's boring," Craig said. "What if he wanted to murder his boss? Maybe the boss made the narrator work too much overtime, so now he wants to sneak through the boss's bedroom window and slit his throat with a rusty hacksaw. Or maybe your guy has a gun and he's planning to shoot everyone in the office who's pissed him off or blow the whole place up with some MacGyver-type bomb he's made from Drano and a car battery. What if he was all set to pull the trigger when he discovers another crazy guy in the same office is planning an even bigger attack, and that snaps him out of it so he can stop the crazier guy in this huge showdown with seven SWAT teams on the roof. *That's* the book I want to read!"

"That sounds like a Robert Ludlum thriller," Flip said. "It's an entirely different story from what I want to tell."

"Maybe the story you should be telling's different than the one you want to tell," Craig said. "What if your main guy wants to fuck one of his coworkers? No, better yet—what if he's already fucking one of his coworkers and he's afraid of getting caught? Or what if they do get caught by the boss and the guy has to give up half his paycheck every week as blackmail so the boss doesn't send a mass email telling everyone? The book could start with the blackmail scene—or even better, it could start with the boss barging into the office supply room where the guy's creaming all over the girl's tits while she's covered in sticky notes because of his weird fetish. That's when the girl freaks out because she's about to marry a guy who owns a chain of frozen yogurt stands, so if the boss sends that email she'll lose everything." Craig's eyes widened as he jumped to the whiteboard and scribbled *Cream on Tits/ Sticky Note Fetish/ Fro-Yo Stands* under the line about the plastic surgery. "Now we know what your book's really about, and any agent who reads that first line about fucked-up sex shit is going to smell money and want to publish the fuck out of it."

He tossed the marker onto the floor and turned to Flip, who stood sullen, confused, and overwhelmed without anywhere to sit. "And you do want someone to publish your book, don't you?"

16

FLIP NO LONGER knew what kind of book he wanted to write, but he did know that he badly wanted a Reuben sandwich with shaved corn beef and extra sauerkraut.

At the grocery store deli counter he found no line, no machine with numbered tickets, and no one working. An orange sign announced a variety of Prairie Fire game-day platters available for order and a Prairie Fire fried chicken special consisting of a breast, a leg, and a biscuit with coleslaw. Instead of sandwich meat, three-quarters of the case was taken up by shelves of potato salads, Amish potato salads, tuna salads, pasta salads, macaroni salads, gelatins, five different kinds of mousse (chocolate, vanilla, cookies and cream, cranberry ambrosia, and chocolate mint), steamed vegetables, dips, a pan of fried chicken, a pan of barbecued chicken, and a pan entirely full of corn dogs. The sandwich meat had been separated into pre-sliced piles in one corner of the case, and there was no seafood section.

Flip called out once, then again, louder, until a young, spindly-armed clerk wandered out of the back room.

"Do you have any corned beef?" Flip asked. "I don't see it in the case."

The clerk mouthed the words silently to himself as he ducked down to look through the pre-sliced meats. He stayed crouched for a long time until he finally rose and shook his head with embarrassment. "Sorry, I guess we don't sell that."

Flip suddenly felt very tired and had zero desire to go to another grocery store. If not a Reuben, he could at least make a Rachel. "How about turkey, then? I'll take a pound of roasted turkey instead."

The clerk bent to grab a handful of thickly sliced turkey from the case, but when Flip saw it he cringed and said, "Not that one—could you cut me some shaved turkey instead?"

"What?"

"Shaved," Flip said. "Could you shave it?"

The clerk bent his head closer. "Could I what?"

"Super thin," Flip said. "Can you slice it super thin, like, as thin as you can get it?"

The clerk smiled and said, "No problem," then bent back behind the counter. After more searching he removed an unopened slab of turkey, struggled valiantly to remove its plastic wrapping, then found a pair of scissors he used to tear it open. He ran the turkey through the cutting machine and held up a slice for Flip's inspection. "How's this?"

The thickness of the new slice was comparable to a volume of CliffsNotes. "Thinner than that," Flip said. "Super thin, as thin as you can possibly get it, like, in little pieces. That's the way we like it back East."

"You got it," the clerk said eagerly before cutting off a second slice the thickness of corrugated cardboard.

"Even thinner," Flip begged. "Turn the machine as low as it'll go."

The clerk turned back with less enthusiasm and gave the dial a very small turn. The resulting slice, though thinner, was still disconcertingly whole. "Any thinner than that, sir, and it'll start to fall apart."

"Falling apart is what I want," Flip pleaded. "The delis back in the Northeast cut it so thin you can clump it all over the sandwich and taste the texture and have the meat fall apart in your mouth. I promise that's exactly how I like it."

The clerk studied Flip with suspicion, then adjusted the dial. He returned from the machine with a slice that was just barely shaved. "So, uh, you want it like this?"

"Yes!" Flip said, excited to find himself so close. "A pound cut exactly like that."

"I can cut it like this for you, sir," the clerk said with uncertainty, "but it'll take a while. The machine's kind of old."

"I don't care how long it takes," Flip said. "I'll wait."

The clerk said, "No problem, sir," and set the slicer in motion; its blade swung automatically back and forth in methodical rhythm as one tiny turkey sliver after another fell through its slot. The clerk watched it for a moment, then picked up a handful to bring into the back room as he shouted, "Hey Don, check out how thin this guy from out East wants his meat cut!" leaving Flip alone at the counter with his blaze orange shopping basket. He turned to look at the adjacent meat case where a man in a white smock unloaded steaks from a multi-shelved cart and a middle-aged customer with a tucked-in shirt studied the label on a two-foot-long tube of ground beef. At the far end of the aisle a toddler tugging on its mother's pant leg howled miserably, a high-pitched, shuddering wail that cracked with each of its gasping breaths and seemed to grow louder the longer Flip paid attention to it. The pile of turkey next to the cutting machine was still very small and the blade still swung evenly back and forth, back and forth, while the toddler wailed and the middle-aged customer weighed the ground beef and a woman in an orange Prairie Fire shirt came to the counter and asked for a half-pound of spicy mustard-flavored potato salad.

17

"HAVE YOU signed up for Ray Javier Martinez's special fiction course yet?" Melvin asked from across their shared office. "The deadline's officially passed, but it sounded like you can still start on Monday and just ask him to sign the registrar's form."

Melvin's mention of the visiting writer's special fiction course felt somewhat familiar from the many emails Flip received on a daily basis from the department listserv. "I wasn't planning on it," he admitted, then turned back to his laptop and the list titled *Attention-Grabbing Openings* he'd been working on for the past hour:

- Show empty, clean office with window—imply longing for freedom?
- Reprimand from boss about detached attitude
- Reprimand from boss about misplaced file
- Reprimand from boss about being sarcastic with new clients
- Awkward confrontation with co-worker at office welcome party, snubbed for differing opinion on prenuptial agreements
- Office scandal [what kind?]
- Cubicle panic attack [provoked by what????]
- Popular guy in office brings in lame project idea, everyone gushes madly over it at meeting

Melvin either ignored or didn't pick up on Flip's reluctance to talk. "Are you sure? It's only a two-week class, and having Martinez come is a big deal since the department only hosts visiting writers in the fall. Martinez will be a great name to network with, and almost all of the fiction writers and even some of the poets are taking his class."

"I would, but I really don't have time for another class," Flip said, thinking again about the stack of papers he had to review for his writing center appointments on Monday and the reading he needed to finish before next week, not to mention the novel pages he still had no idea how to revise before his next workshop submission—though it was easier to avoid the problem of the novel as the least pressing.

Melvin had turned away from his laptop to face him in his chair, a tone of condescending concern entering his voice. "It's just that I also didn't see you at Clayton Rego's Theory Unmasked lecture last week, and you should have come out with Kendall and the rest of us for drinks the other night."

Flip hadn't known about any drinking with Kendall and had possessed exactly zero interest in the lecture Melvin had mentioned. "I'm really trying to focus on my current workload," he said. "That's why I haven't really been socializing or going to events."

Melvin's face returned to its usual blank expression as he began speaking with an air of authority. "I guess that's all well and good, but there are a lot of opportunities here that we really should be taking advantage of, not just in terms of being seen at events, but for networking in general. The people we meet now are going to be our future colleagues one day when we're all working in different realms of academia, and they're the ones we'll be reaching out to when we need book cover blurbs for our novels. You should at least come to Martinez's opening talk with the grad students during lunch on Monday—they're providing sandwiches and pop, and it'll be a solid chance to hear Martinez speak if you're not going to take his class."

Flip's attention had piqued at the mention of a free meal, though it also occurred to him that not only did the talk represent a low-commitment chance at meeting an interesting writer, it might not hurt to try more of the department events people were always talking about. "If it's just one talk," he said, "I'll go."

"That's good," Melvin said. "Also, did you see that email saying the department had increased the travel stipend to two hundred dollars? If you apply and get accepted, you could put the money toward a plane ticket to attend the Creative Writer's Association Conference in the spring."

Flip wondered whether Melvin's mind was capable of focusing on any topic for longer than three minutes and at that moment wanted desperately to escape from that stale, empty office where the sleep indicator on the literature student's laptop was still blinking slowly on and then off again. "I'll be right back," he said.

The third-floor department hallway was deserted on a Thursday afternoon, and as he stepped into it he realized that apart from possibly the men's room he had no clue where he was going or what he might do when he got there. He became aware of a subversive and possibly dangerous thought brewing in the back of his mind: that he could stroll around the corner to Derzen's office to see whether she was there (under, of course, the guise of taking a walk), and if she was there (which she might not be) he could engage her in some distinctly non-flirtatious conversation, and said conversation would have to be non-flirtatious because Derzen was Kendall's girlfriend and engaging in flirtatious conversation with her would not only be wrong but stupid. As casually as he could he strolled around the hallway corner pretending to study the flyers on a bulletin board, meandered past the medieval literature professor's office, and with controlled aimlessness made his way to the end of the corridor to Derzen's office.

The nameplate beside the door listed three names, of which *Derzen Draskovich* was the first, followed by *Mary-Beth Reynolds*, and a third name he didn't recognize. Derzen herself was sitting alone at a computer very close to the open doorway, her eyes moving across the screen with a look of staunch resilience and her front teeth pressing on her lower lip. She continued reading with a vague awareness that someone had approached, her head moving to see who this person was though her eyes remained on the screen until she finally moved them over, at which point she threw back her shoulders with a shrill "Yikes!" that made Flip jump.

"Remind me to knock next time," he said.

Derzen said, "Ha!" very loudly as she relaxed in her chair; the exclamation seemed to echo into the hallway. "I didn't know you were coming."

Flip leaned against the doorjamb trying to create the illusion of nonchalance. "I didn't know I was coming either. What's your appointment schedule look like?"

"Open," Derzen said with heavy emphasis. "If I have to read one more football essay I'm going to quit grad school and join an artist commune."

This seemed like a very strange thing to say since Derzen clearly had no intention of actually joining an artist's commune, hadn't made it clear that she was joking, and the statement itself wasn't actually funny. Her manner also felt distinctly exaggerated, as if a more theatrical part of her had spoken, not to make a joke or communicate information, but to convey a forced feeling of comfort while feeling secretly uncomfortable.

"In any case," he said to steer them both away from the comment, "you've got a nice office. It's decorated a lot better than mine."

Derzen's office contained the same metal furniture and bookshelf as his own, but her books, old and new and of varying sizes, thicknesses, and colors, filled her bookshelf, some with neon sticker flags sticking from their top edges and others incredibly worn with their spines cracked and falling apart from use. Prominently strung from one wall to the other was a line of blue and orange Christmas lights crisscrossed with crepe paper links and a set of Tibetan prayer flags, while posters of animals: a female deer with its fawn, a vaguely familiar print of a panda munching on some bamboo, a line of porcupines walking on a log, and an elaborate dolphin- and coral reef-filled undersea drawing reminiscent of a Trapper Keeper Flip remembered having in elementary school covered the wall above the more cluttered of the other two desks. The desk itself (which must, he sensed, belong to Mary-Beth) had been piled with an array of palm-sized stuffed animals and a basket filled with rolls of Smarties. Photos of several women from earlier eras, though he only vaguely recognized one of them as either Louisa May Alcott or Virginia Woolf hung on the walls above Derzen's desk, in contrast to both. The largest of these wall-pinnings was a letter-sized cover print of Sylvia Path's *The Bell Jar* (one of the many books he'd been meaning to read but hadn't gotten around to) featuring a blood-red dying rose drooping beside the Gothic letters of the title.

"What are you up to today?" Derzen asked.

"I was working on a new outline for my novel and needed a change of scenery," Flip said, his eyes still on the photos.

Derzen's body seemed to turn back to the computer. "And how's it coming?"

Flip maintained his composure. "It's been steady."

"That's good," Derzen said in a way that showed little interest. "I woke up early this morning and wrote two poems, and one of them was the best one I'd written in a long time. Then I came here full of energy and tried to talk about "I Know Why the Caged Bird Sings" with my poetry class and got nothing but crickets, and it was this horribly discouraging experience because they didn't even try to find any meaning in it. Now I'm stuck grading papers for the rest of the afternoon."

Flip interpreted this story as both a general complaint and a plea for sympathy. "I guess that's the risk we run when we try to share things we're passionate about," he said, immediately regretting the pessimism in his voice.

Derzen nodded. "I'd probably be better off if I just bought an Intro to Poetry textbook and ran through it page by page. I guess I thought my role as a teacher would be to open all these young minds to the wonders of poetry when in reality I do things like spend an entire day teaching ag majors how to make a works cited page."

"Don't give up," Flip said. "I think anyone can still be stirred by great writing as long as they come across the right piece."

Derzen lifted her feet onto her chair while clutching her forehead with both hands and letting her fingers fall slowly through her hair. "I wish I had your optimism, but in principle I agree. But then I wonder whether that's just me being naïve and ignoring the reality that most of the world doesn't care about poetry like I do, so I should just stop trying to force it on people."

"I don't think it's a matter of forcing poetry on people who don't care about it," Flip said. "More like finding the people who have some degree of interest and then fostering it."

Derzen pulled her fingers from her hair. "I guess that makes sense."

Flip felt the conversation drawing to a close; at any moment Derzen might turn back to her computer as an unspoken signal that she needed to get back to work, at which point he'd have to abandon whatever course of action he'd set out on and go back to deal with Melvin. The sheer madness of his excursion suddenly became clear since Derzen clearly wasn't in the mood for talk and what unsubstantial talk they were having wasn't going anywhere. Whatever happened to the enticing conversationalist he'd discussed the Brontë sisters with in Brad's study? Maybe he'd remembered wrong, or maybe whatever interest she'd shown that night still hid somewhere waiting to be rekindled. In any case, there was no use pursuing anything other than friendly companionship with this girl because she was in a relationship with Kendall, and girls in relationships didn't just break them off like in *Lucky Jim* or have ruinous affairs like in the John Updike novels just because someone new walked into their offices and talked to them about teaching. Drastic acts like these formed the stuff of fiction, while in real life people stayed for years in relationships that weren't working. Yet it would have been idiotic not to pursue this feeling, this thing he didn't quite have a name for but that had to be investigated.

"Actually," he said. "I could use a change of scenery and was hoping to hear another northeasterner's perspective." He paused to evoke a small but tangible trace of suspense, the way Stark did when talking about even the most mundane topics. "Do you want to go grab a coffee?"

He rarely if ever drank coffee but was running without a plan, and this seemed the most accessible way to get her out of the office.

"Ah," Derzen said, her eyes darting away and her feet in their purple shoes (she wore purple shoes!) pushing against the desk to wheel the chair toward the center of the room—but as soon as she'd done this her eyes moved back to the computer with her front teeth again clenched over her bottom lip. "Not now—I really have to get this grading done."

He felt the rush of disappointment he'd braced for but told himself that at least he'd pulled a McMurphy and tried, goddammit, and had sure as hell done that much—though as he thought this Derzen turned to him, then back to the computer screen, then back to him while drumming her fingers on the desk and burst out, "But how about Saturday?"

18

SOMEONE HAD told him once that if you asked a girl out for a specific day and she told you she was busy it meant that she wasn't interested, but if she told you she was busy and suggested a different day it meant that she really was busy but also possessed some interest. *Interest*, however, could mean many things—interested in getting to know him as a friend (possible), interested in doing something outside the office on a Saturday regardless of whom it was with (also possible), or interested in opening up to his advances because her relationship with Kendall was on the rocks (hard to say how possible).

Still, her eagerness to suggest the alternate day had only added to the list of intimations he'd sensed in those vivid minutes before Kendall had placed that protective hand on her back. What had Derzen's face looked like at that moment? Flip no longer remembered exactly, but it hadn't been the face of someone happy that her boyfriend had rescued her from a stranger's flirtations—no, it had seemed reserved, nervous, and maybe embarrassed that she'd been caught doing something she shouldn't have. He wondered what kind of relationship she and Kendall had, whether Kendall talked to her the same way he talked about other people's writing during workshop, and whether he assailed her with the same know-it-all attitude that came from his always having to be right. What did that do to a couple's sex life? Under certain circumstances it might provide a boost, but something told him that wasn't the case.

Or maybe he was chasing something that wasn't there and Derzen was just a private person who liked meeting people and who really admired Kendall for his knowledge, his successes, his winning of that book prize with the long name, and the prestigious career that awaited him because he'd achieved more than the other grad students had. Thinking about this depressed him since it served as a reminder that all the beautiful, intelligent, and desirable women he'd ever met had always seemed to be taken by someone cooler, smarter, more athletic, or more successful than him, or maybe just by someone who'd gotten there first. He thought of all the times he'd been beaten out for jobs, scholarships, and other opportunities, and how ever since middle school the same people had always seemed to win the class elections and get into National Honor Society because they'd discovered early on how to make people respect them despite their minds being empty of real ideas. It was like being in a tent with Yo-Yo's roomies everywhere you went.

But he'd never really wanted to do all the extra work that came with being class president—all he'd ever wanted to do was write stories and draw in his notebooks and act in school plays and meet other people who wanted these things too, and he'd felt most satisfied in college where there'd been so many others like him, or even in high school where there'd been enough of them to form their own lunch table separate from the popular kids. In grad school, though, the rules seemed rigged so that the popular kids who'd all gotten into National Honor Society and won the class elections were also writing the stories and running the drama club and deciding who could take studio art classes, leaving the misfits who'd built their lives around these things without anywhere to go.

But with Derzen, none of that felt like the case.

"Let's guess how much Prairie Fire merch we can spot in ten minutes!" she said without warning, as if this would be the most amazing game anyone had ever played.

"Does infinity count as a number?" Flip asked.

She laughed. "Tell me your guess and we'll start. I say seventy-two."

"Two hundred and eleven," Flip said. "There's three people in orange t-shirts over there and a bumper sticker on that truck."

It was gameday Saturday, which neither of them had known about when they'd made the plans, though when they'd met Derzen had admitted to forgetting about the game with some embarrassment. He'd had to tell her that it was fine, that they could deal with the crowds of orange-clad football fans crowding not only into the stadium and the city streets but into every bar and restaurant in the city to watch the game on wall-mounted televisions. It was unbelievable how many there were: On the walk to the coffee shop he'd passed scores of sunburned Prairie Fire fans holding orange beer koozies under orange tents, barbecuing, pitching orange bean bags into orange cornhole boards, and clumping around buffet tables heaped with orange potato salad and orange hot dogs. The men wore sleeveless orange t-shirts, the girls wore khaki short shorts with their own orange t-shirts tied off at the midriff, and even one blonde-haired baby slept in an orange one-piece. Flip had walked past them wearing jeans and a green short-sleeved shirt and wondered how he must have looked.

"Twelve shirts waiting at the corner, and four crossing the street," Flip said. "Five more walking and one riding a bike."

Derzen had worn a faded jean jacket rolled up to the elbows with a white-petaled flower pinned to the lapel. "Three hats, a tote bag, and one of those full-body leashes you put on dogs."

They sat on the covered patio of a coffee shop in the old downtown, a three-block neighborhood of brick warehouses with farm and cattle feed advertisements painted on their aging exteriors and where old concrete loading docks lined the narrow streets. Most of the area, however, had been converted into bars, restaurants, coffee shops, and mid- to high-priced apartments to appeal to young professionals with disposable income. The work he and Derzen had brought through unspoken agreement sat untouched on the table between them—for her a stack of ungraded reading responses that she'd pulled from her *Alice in Wonderland* tote bag, and for him a Horkheimer and Adorno textbook with the yellow USED label on its spine.

"Four shirts on the family over there, plus four more and a hat on the guys by the Mexican restaurant," Flip said.

"You missed one. The baby on the father's back has one too."

"Good catch. That makes thirty-seven total."

"How long has it been?"

He couldn't remember.

The game felt perfectly suited to their outing because it emphasized how ridiculous the entire football culture was through its sheer pervasiveness rather than the ridiculousness of any one fan or outfit.

"Where does your name come from?" Flip asked her.

He could tell from her face that she'd been asked this many times. "I think my parents misremembered someone's name they read about or heard when they were traveling. They used to be pretty anti-establishment back when that was still cool, and they wanted to give me the most unique name they could find that people could still pronounce. I guess they didn't want me to have too hard of a time." She rested her elbow on the ungraded stack of papers. "Why do people call you Flip?"

"Everyone's called me that as long as I can remember," Flip said. "When I was little I thought it was my real name because I didn't understand how nicknames worked. Writing *Phillip* on college applications felt like I was taking on this other persona that wasn't mine."

"Filling out college applications is excruciating anyway," Derzen said. "It takes you to this unnatural place where you can't say things the way you'd like to say them."

It was one of those rare times when you connected with someone without ever having to explain yourself.

"What do you miss most about back home?" she asked.

There were so many things. "The mountains."

"Do you like hiking?"

"Sometimes," he said. "But I mostly like knowing that any time I wanted I could drive to a mountain and hike to the top just for fun and see gorgeous views all around. I also realized after I came here that mountains give the landscape variety, which makes everywhere you go feel a little different than just the same flat plains."

"I feel that way about the ocean," Derzen said, "even though I don't go there very often, because at the ocean things stop. Everything has to change when the land ends, and seeing that change creates meaning in this place with waves and rocks and tide pools and clumps of seaweed washed up on shore."

"I think you notice that because there's no ocean here."

She smirked and continued in a serious tone. "But I like knowing I could go anytime I'm home."

"Do you still like it when it's crowded?"

"Sometimes. The beach has a certain energy during peak season when everyone's out having fun and kids are building sand castles and digging those big holes that kids dig in the sand, and I wonder sometimes whether if they dug long enough they could actually make a hole so big that someone could fall in and not get back out. I like watching the couples and trying to guess who's been together a long time and who's on a first date, and seeing the girls who can wear their bikinis without being self-conscious and the old men with those permanent sunburns who stare at them all pervy. But I also hate the sun and the crowds and not being able to get a parking spot, so I usually just drive to the beach in winter when no one's around and the sand's coated with snow and the board-walk shops are all closed except for maybe a convenience store or a townie bar. That's when I like being by myself and just walking and seeing how the beach is still the same, but different when no one's there."

He wondered what kind of life she'd had growing up and how she'd thought to pin a flower on a jean jacket.

"What made you want to become a poet?"

She focused on the brick warehouse across the way. "I used to read a lot of Sylvia Plath and I thought about how her entire life revolved around her writing, which gave it real meaning. I knew I wanted to give my life that same meaning because the people around me were all doing things that weren't meaningful at all. My best friend from high school tracks ad data for a living—she doesn't even make the ads, just looks at how well they're doing. I knew I never wanted a job like that or even one of those jobs where you have to put real energy into something that feels necessary but has no real purpose. Art and poetry are more powerful because they allow us to share something real."

In front of the terrace all the fans dressed in orange plodded steadily toward the stadium, where the game would start soon.

"What made you want to be a writer?" she asked.

"A lot of things," Flip said, "but I always knew I wanted to make something that would move people, and I kept trying all of these ways of doing that, but in the end novels seemed to be the most powerful because they show us how people really think. And then I read *Catch-22* in high school, and a lot of things fell into place."

"I felt that way too when I first read *The Bean Trees*. My mom used to read a lot when she was younger, and though most of her books just sat on the shelves, she kept her copy of *The Bean Trees* under the coffee table—it was that old red paperback edition with the garden on the cover. Finally when I was in ninth grade I just picked it up and read the whole thing one Saturday all by myself. I hadn't discovered Sylvia Plath yet, but that book showed me that it's possible to overcome all the awfulness in the world and really connect with people."

He hadn't read *The Bean Trees* but made a mental note to look it up later. "What's your favorite short story?"

"Definitely 'Days' by Deborah Eisenberg, which is about this young woman in New York who quits smoking and starts running at the Y to deal with her anxiety, and through the course of all these vignettes she realizes she can make her own decisions without relying on other people. And yours?"

"Mine's Hemingway's 'Soldier's Home' where the World War I veteran comes back to his hometown to find everything's changed and he's completely isolated from everyone else."

"What literary character do you most imagine yourself as?"

He thought very hard. "Probably Stephen Dedalus."

She nodded knowingly. "Mine's Lizzy Bennett."

"What food do you miss most from back home?"

"Definitely seafood."

"Good answer. I really miss being able to get a decent sandwich."

There remained, however, the biggest question of all.

"Why did you choose grad school?" he asked.

She wrinkled her nose in concentration. "Because I wasn't sure whether I could write—I mean *really* write—and it felt like I needed to justify my wanting to write poetry by turning it into a career. I also didn't have anything else I wanted to focus on, so teaching seemed just as good a path as any. If I knew another way I could write but also not be poor I'd probably do that, but I'm not sure what it would be."

It made a lot of sense, and he wished he knew what that other way was so he could share it with her.

Then she said, "Plus if I'm in grad school I can at least show my family I'm doing something worthwhile."

That made a lot of sense too.

19

WHEN THE AIR grew cool they walked away from the stadium down the main north-south artery, a five-lane one-way boulevard where only a few cars and pickups drove steadily through sets of green lights now that the football game had begun. They walked evenly in step and because they still had so much to share they kept talking even when a multi-trailered semi-truck roared through the turning lane and the resulting rush of air swept over them like a shock wave. They also kept talking when a deafening roar burst out from the stadium and the people on the orange patio of a sports bar erupted into cacophonous cries of excitement while the cars all honked their horns. None of these things mattered, though, because their conversation was more important.

At a corner beside an immense gray government building Derzen turned left and, when Flip halted instead of following, also stopped so they could finish debating whether Ally Sheedy's makeover at the end of *The Breakfast Club* was a betrayal comparable to Olivia Newton-John's more shameless one in *Grease*. To break the resulting pause he asked what she was doing for the rest of the day.

"I promised Kendall I'd be back before too late so we could have dinner," she said, giving no sign of whether said promise had stemmed from obligation or genuine desire. "I think he's been working in the apartment all day."

"Ah," Flip said, and wasn't sure what to say next. "Is he working on his novel?"

Here Derzen's indifference was more pronounced. "I don't know what he's working on."

Flip felt a strong need to acknowledge the closeness of the last few hours, especially now that she'd mentioned Kendall for the first time. "It was good hanging out with you today," he said. "I needed a break from the Frankfurt School."

Derzen began speaking quickly. "I should have graded more essays, so I'll be stuck with them all day tomorrow."

"Don't let that get you down," Flip said. "Everybody needs a break sometime."

One side of Derzen's mouth bent upward in a smirk. "Things always feel clearer after some time away."

They said goodbye then and she walked off, her *Alice in Wonderland* bag slung over her shoulder and her hair bobbing to either side as she walked. He watched her at the corner for a short time then started in the opposite direction, wondering what, if anything, the afternoon had meant to her. The more he thought about this the less sense the entire thing seemed to make until he could no longer tell the difference between the things Derzen had actually said and the things he'd imagined her saying. He held up his head as he walked and all around him the immense, open horizon blazed orange in a furious sunset that hovered just above the factory smokestacks.

20

Ray Javier Martinez is a second-generation Guatemalan-American whose writing explores the experiences of Hispanic communities in the American Southwest. His novels include Albuquerque Blues, Down and Out at the Seven Star Cantina, Marcus and Me, By the Pueblo's Shadow, *and* Green Chilis, *for which he won the 2015 American CWA Award for Fiction. He is currently an assistant professor at Southwest State University, where he teaches creative writing and Chicana/o literature.*

"IT'S LIKE I was always writing, even when I was a kid and I'd create these fantastic stories for my sisters," Martinez said, "like about dragons and bank robbers and lost treasure. And then when I got older and it came time to go to college, I thought to myself, okay, this is something you have to get more serious about since I knew writing wasn't going to come easy and that my chances of making it were slim." Here, Martinez (again, Flip wondered how best to refer to him) paused, glancing around the conference room with a vague lack of interest. "So I guess the best answer to your question is to just keep writing, and everything else will sort itself out."

Melvin sat steadfastly copying this advice into a notebook while Flip wondered at the banality of this story, which he wished had included more specifics on what Martinez had done after finishing college. Still, he'd spoken with great embellishment that had made the story seem profound, and in the pause that followed Flip reflected on the many, many things he wanted to ask this person who was unquestionably a *real* writer (whatever that meant), who'd successfully published novels while still retaining his youthful demeanor, and who was so well-known that even Stark had expressed his admiration when introducing him. Flip tried again to think up a question Martinez could lend some insight on but came up with nothing; he wondered how much of this uncertainty came from his own lack of focus and how much came from his discomfort at Martinez's detached manner of speaking *at* everyone in the room rather than *to* them, so that he imagined any question he did ask was likely to garner a trite answer wrapped in a lecture.

"At the risk of sounding overeager, I suppose I'll ask another question," Kendall said with a smile and a low raise of his hand. "Unless of course I'm running the risk of using you as my own personal career counselor, ha ha."

Flip had never heard Kendall laugh this way and found the smile on his face equally asinine. Around him, Brad and Lawrence chuckled, as did several of the others, while Martinez slid his mouth slightly upward and back down.

"If you had to choose the single most important quality for building a successful writing career," Kendall asked, "what would it be?"

Flip imagined this was the same tone Kendall would use while kneeling down to kiss the sole of Martinez's shoe.

Martinez seemed to consider the question (or create the appearance of considering it) while resting his arms in their tightly buttoned shirt sleeves on his knees. "Willingness to pick up opportunities, for sure," he finally said. "If you come across a chance to write something, a chance to publish something, meet somebody, help somebody, edit something—take it, because you never know where it'll get you."

"Thanks," Kendall said. "That's really good advice," and Flip felt his heart beat faster in a disconcerting spell of uncertainty.

21

"WHAT DO YOU think I should do?" Flip asked from his place on the stoop railing of Jackson's apartment building.

Jackson's building was even more majestic than he remembered, in a crumbling, dilapidated, used-to-be-elegant-but-now-just-looked-outdated kind of way. The exterior stone curved outward around the first-floor windows and wide, leafy vines hung along the exterior, their leaves just beginning to brown with the coming of autumn. A rusted Maxwell House coffee can half full of sand served dual purposes as an ashtray and doorstop for the paint-chipped front door, though its usefulness as the former appeared questionable since the ground nearby was littered with more ciga-rette butts than were in the can. The stoop's low railings were wide enough for one person to sit comfortably on, and both he and Jackson were now reclining on them with their legs parallel to the angle of the stairs.

Jackson shrugged. "I don't know. Derzen's a hard girl to read. She and I used to talk a lot because we saw grad school problems on similar wavelengths. It was purely platonic, but we stopped hanging out when she and Kendall moved in together, probably because he was jealous. It's funny how even when you're busy you always make time for the things you really want to do."

"Do you think she's interested in me?" Flip asked.

Jackson tilted his head back. "Not for sure. That's something you can't ever really know."

Flip was getting tired of things he couldn't ever really know. "What really gets me is that when she mentioned Kendall her voice had the same fed-up tone she used when she talked about grading her comp essays."

"That could be, but you have to remember that people feel a lot of emotions they don't always act on in the real world. Just because Derzen's fed up with Kendall doesn't mean she's going to break up with him to date you."

"That's true," Flip said. "And I feel the same way since I'd love to make a real move but then I think about how that's a sleazy thing to do and how I really don't want Kendall as my enemy in the department. I'm also still not sure whether Derzen would even consider me that way or if I'm just chasing some crazy fantasy."

Jackson nodded. "That's a lot of reasons not to act."

"But there's more to it," Flip said. "I also can't stop thinking about the novel *Lucky Jim*, where the main character Dixon's unhappy at his academic job and trying to steal his rival's girlfriend, but in the novel it works because the rival's a pretentious asshole who condescends everyone and he's also secretly cheating on the girl, so that puts the reader on Dixon's side when he invites her away from the party in a stolen taxi. It works because Amis sets up all these ways of making us root for the hero and hate the rival with his arrogant way of looking down on everyone, but in real life Kendall's not cheating on Derzen and all he's really done is act condescendingly toward me, so it doesn't really seem like I'm justified in trying to steal Derzen away."

"Hard to say," Jackson said. "A lot's changed since 1950s Britain, but a lot's also stayed the same. Plenty of books have lasted through the generations because they show us things about human nature and society that are still true, even though other aspects of those books become outdated. Think about how a fake priest performing a sham marriage in *The Vicar of Wakefield* feels entirely meaningless and contrived in the age of premarital sex. The trick lies in knowing what's changed and what's still the same."

Flip raised his head to the empty sky.

"Kingsley Amis also gets a lot of flak for his misogyny," Jackson went on, "and I don't think many of his books would pass a literary Bechdel Test today—though I've never been sure how a Bechdel Test would work for books that stick to a close third-person narrator."

"Do you think I'd be a terrible person if I made a move on Derzen?" Flip asked.

"I make it a point not to judge people," Jackson said. "We all need to make our own decisions."

"But not everyone thinks like you. If we lived in a world where no one judged anyone else I'd make a move on Derzen in a second because I believe in taking action to pursue things you believe in. But if I did that, regardless of whether it worked I don't think I could face seeing Kendall again, and I doubt the rest of the department would think highly of me either."

"You've got to be careful about seeing things in terms of taking action versus standing still," Jackson said. "All the best relationships happen through mutual attraction—dating isn't some carnival game where you knock over all the bottles to win the giant stuffed bear. Sure, winning a giant stuffed bear feels good, but knocking over the bottles should be meaningful too. It also helps if the bear actually wants to come home with you instead of just hanging around on the shelf with the other bears."

"You talk a pretty big game for someone who's still single," Flip said.

"If I could find someone worth dating," Jackson said, "I would."

They sat in silence until Flip's back grew sore from slouching on the railing. "You make a good point," he said. "Maybe I'm also not thinking clearly because I still don't know how to fix my novel and I'm just using this as a distraction."

"How long until you have to submit for workshop again?"

Flip felt a cold uncertainty settle over him, the unsparing reality that he'd been wasting time amidst the hopeless tangle of how to proceed. "Two weeks."

"Then take care of your novel first," Jackson said. "Worry about one thing at a time."

There seemed to be nothing more to say, so they sat in the shade of the building while a breeze rustled through the treetops.

Finally Flip asked, "Isn't there anything in the world that pisses you off?"

Jackson tilted his head toward the empty sky. "I always hated it back home when people ran up the steps of the Philadelphia Museum of Art like in the *Rocky* movies."

It was time to go to work.

22

FLIP SPENT the next week working in the writing center and reading for his classes. In the mornings he slept late and in the evenings he binge-watched Netflix shows because he felt too tired for anything else.

23

IT WAS ANOTHER unremittingly hot day, far too hot for October, and hotter still on the black tar of the parking lot that Flip had chosen to cut across after winding around the football stadium. When he finally neared the edge of the green space beside the business office he leaned against the railing to catch his breath, and, feeling the thick pools of sweat coursing down his neck and the sopping mass of hair clinging to his ears (how long had it been since he'd had a haircut?), he trudged across the final stretch of pavement to find the visiting writer Ray Javier Martinez taking a smoke break.

Martinez stood in the mulched shade beneath the thickest branch of a tree still bearing its leaves, his back resting against the business office wall and a half-smoked cigarette between two fingers. While the sleeve of his other arm was still tightly buttoned even in the absurd heat, he'd rolled up the sleeve of the arm holding the cigarette ever so slightly so that Flip could see the colored swirls of a full arm tattoo stretching above his wrist. His eyes followed Flip as he stepped away from the railing.

Flip wiped the sweat from his forehead and extended a barely perceptible nod that Martinez returned, the cigarette still smoldering between his fingers. Martinez's eyes, though strained and exaggeratedly bright during the department meeting, now held a relaxed glimmer of familiarity. It occurred to Flip that he would likely never see the man again.

"So they keeping you busy here or what?" Flip asked.

Martinez raised his eyebrows and flicked some ash from his cigarette. "Comes with the territory. They let me out once in a while, though."

Flip spoke with sudden rapidity. "I didn't get a chance to ask a question at last week's talk. Do you think it's more important to be a great writer whose work people actually enjoy or to have a successful career in academia?"

Martinez wiggled his head as he took a quick drag on his cigarette. "That's not the kind of question I've ever asked myself."

"What do you mean?" Flip asked.

"You've got to pay the bills somehow."

Flip saw Martinez's head turn before he heard Kendall approach. In his arms he carried a cardboard tray with two to-go coffee cups, a stack of napkins, and a handful of sugar packets and cream. His eyes burned with the same coldness they'd shown when he'd caught Flip with Derzen at the party.

"Hello Phil," Kendall said, brushing past him. "I was just escorting Ray to his presentation at the undergrad Creative Nonfiction class."

Kendall's tone and manner suggested that said escort was very much meant to be one-on-one as he held the coffee tray toward Martinez. In response, Martinez stubbed his cigarette into the ashtray and refastened his sleeve button, seemingly at the same time. His gaze fell back to the ground, and when it rose again it carried a familiar glaze of disconnection.

"You're lucky you had the chance to talk with Ray before he leaves," Kendall said, looking squarely at Martinez. "He's been packing a lot of useful craft talk into our workshops, and I must say that we've all been able to learn a lot from him."

Kendall still held the cardboard tray within Martinez's reach, all but gesturing for him to take one of the coffee cups. Instead, Martinez straightened his shoulders and began walking as Kendall dutifully fell in step next to him. With a backward glance in Flip's direction Martinez said, "Nice talking to you."

24

Lawrence Fairweather writes fiction that explores the deeply conflicted past and present of the American South. His stories have appeared or are forthcoming in The New Southern Review, Literary Tales of the South, The Southern Belle Atlantic Review, *and* Panhandles and Grits: Seventeen Stories From the South. *He is currently pursuing his PhD in creative writing.*

WHEN FLIP spotted Lawrence coming out of the student union's copy room his first impulse was to keep walking past the Sbarro line and pretend he didn't see him. This, however, would have been an insulting response to a scenario where Lawrence had almost certainly seen him, so it made sense to at least try making conversation.

"You're really going to like this one," Lawrence announced as he dropped a pile of stapled packets onto a table in the food court. "It's a family drama about the restrictions placed on the daughter's sexuality, told from the perspective of three siblings." He motioned graciously for Flip to choose a side of the plush orange booth.

Flip took the top packet from the stack and weighed it with both hands, considering how attention-grabbing Lawrence's novel pitch had been. "That sounds like a novel I'd like to read," he said. "I talked to Craig a little while ago and he was obsessed by the idea that a first line makes or breaks an entire book."

Lawrence nodded and said, "Oh, definitely!" then looked away and slowly slid his eyes toward the ceiling. He was a tall, gangly individual with an extended neck and sallow complexion whose head swayed languidly from side to side when he appeared to be thinking. "Well, maybe. Hooking the reader with the first sentence is important, but it's also important to write with a powerful, moving voice since that demonstrates your skill as a writer. Demonstrating your skill proves your authority, and proving your authority shows agents you can put together a good story. That's why beautiful language is so important for building trust with the reader."

This made a lot of sense—once again, trust with the reader was crucial. Flip looked at the first page of Lawrence's packet:

A Courage Bound by Fire

A novel by Lawrence Fairweather

Terry

It was just around suppertime when I crept out to the back shed for my nightly drink and caught Mary necking with one of the Forrester boys.

"It definitely grabs me," Flip said. "You start by telling us that the girl's fooling around with somebody the narrator doesn't like and also that this Terry guy's a secret alcoholic."

Lawrence looked at Flip in stupefied alarm. "How did you know Terry's an alcoholic?"

"Because he's out sneaking drinks in the back shed," Flip said. "That's what alcoholics do."

Lawrence's face held its expressionless stare for a moment before it rose into a delighted, eager grin. "Well I'll be darned—alcoholics do drink in secret, don't they? That line really just came to me as I was developing Terry's voice. I've never been one of those writers who *plans* everything since I find that the novel flows more easily if I just let the characters 'take over' in each scene." He accompanied this last phrase with a jerky set of air quotes.

Flip wasn't sure how to respond to this and kept reading:

> It was just around suppertime when I crept out to the back shed for
> my nightly drink and caught Mary necking with one of the Forrester
> boys. It looked to me like he was getting all up in her business, so I
> pounded hard on the glass and shouted, "You!" real loud so he could
> hear. That just about got him, because he pulled his hand out from
> Mary's dress and gave me a look like he'd just got his pecker caught in
> a bear trap, and Mary wasn't too pleased either.
>
> "You get right in here young lady," I said to her, and then to the
> boy. "And you get on home where you belong."
>
> It had been six years since I'd spoken to any of the Forresters, and
> I hated them then as much as I hate them now. We'd had it out for
> each other ever since that time in high school when Clyde Forrester
> took a shit on my letterman jacket while I was in gym class. I could
> have let that one slide, but then Clyde's no-good brother asked May
> out to prom and I gave him the worst beating of his life out behind
> Stetson's bar to prove how we settle disputes.

"Is beating people up behind bars a southern thing?" Flip asked.

"I could tell you stories you wouldn't believe," Lawrence said in
his slow drawl. "I guess that's why I became a writer, huh?"

It struck Flip as odd that Lawrence would say this without actually telling one of the stories he was supposedly so eager to share.
"You've definitely got a strong voice here," he went on. "It's consis-
tent and reveals the character's background at a pace that feels
right."

"Aw," Lawrence said with a swell of pride, "I'm glad you think so.
Terry's voice was the hardest to capture since he's the one who's
stepped up to lead the family after the father dies from alcoholism.
He has to speak in a more powerful tone, especially when talking
dirt about his niece Mary. He spends the whole book trying to
control her sexuality, and it eventually builds up to her running
away with a new boy who comes to the neighborhood."

Flip found several aspects of this description familiar. "He sounds
a little like Jason in *The Sound and the Fury*," he said.

"No no no," Lawrence said dismissively. "That book's much different because in *The Sound and The Fury* Jason's also stealing money from his sister and in the end Miss Quentin breaks into his secret treasury to steal it all back. In my book the relationship between Mary and her uncle is all about power, not money."

"But aren't those the same thing?" Flip asked.

"Not at all," Lawrence said without explaining. "Besides, my story uses less of a William Faulkner voice and more Eli Bridgewater mixed with some Gerald Wright to fit with contemporary southern fiction."

"What do you mean by a William Faulkner voice?" Flip asked. "Faulkner was so versatile that he could harness all kinds of voices when he needed to, so unless you're talking about the later-years, nine-hundred-word-sentence Faulkner, I don't see what you mean."

Lawrence began nodding excitedly. "That's right! It's that long sentence stuff I don't like. My favorite Faulkner novels are the ones with the powerful, moving voices."

Flip didn't feel like discussing this anymore and turned ahead to the next chapter:

Gary

The last customers were just leaving the store when I bolted the door
for the night and saw Paul Forrester strolling down the street.

"Who's Gary and why does his name rhyme with Terry and Mary?" Flip asked.

Lawrence looked at him blankly before bursting into giggling laughter. "Well I'll be a son of a gun—I never noticed that! I guess it comes from working with the characters so much."

"I'd be careful with rhyming names," Flip said. "They're even more distracting than characters whose names begin with the same letter."

Rather than respond to this Lawrence said, "Gary's the more intelligent and sensitive brother who dreams of getting out of Chatanackaseekawa County—that's the fictional county where the novel takes place—but for now he has to work at the local hardware store to save money so he can go away to college."

"So he's kind of like the Quentin of the book, but with Jason's job?" Flip asked.

"No, they're completely different," Lawrence answered immediately. "Gary's the only one who really understands how badly the family's collapsing, and it ends up driving him into a crippling depression so that Terry has to put him on heavy meds. That's much different from *The Sound and the Fury* where Quentin commits suicide in the midst of his depression."

Flip decided to choose his battles. "So if Gary has to save all this money for college I imagine he doesn't want to take out student loans?"

Lawrence's face drooped with disappointment. "Oh yeah, I guess he could just take out loans, couldn't he?"

Flip resumed reading where he'd left off:

> The last customers were just leaving the store when I bolted the door for the night and saw Paul Forrester strolling down the street. It looked to me like he was fuming about something, so I unbolted the door and called, "Need something Paul?" real cheerful so he wouldn't get mad. That just about got him, because he spit a thick wad onto the sidewalk like a mosquito had just flown into his mouth, and he looked like he wasn't too happy to see me either.
>
> "That hothead brother of yours has been threatening my boy," he said to me, and then walked up the steps. "So you're going to tell him to lay off."
>
> It had been a week since Terry had caught Mary out behind the shed with Paul's son Peter, and I felt as indifferent about it then as I do now. I'd had to hear about it all night and the next morning when Terry burst into my room dead-drunk while I was trying to read. I could have let that one slide, but then Terry called Paul Forrester to tell him to keep his no-good son away from his niece and he threw the phone as hard as he could across the room to prove how furious he was about the whole thing.

Flip read the page twice, then turned back to the first section and finally to the Gary page again. "This is the same opening you used before," he stuttered in disbelief. "You've started with an attention-grabbing first sentence, then the character's reaction, then dialogue, then a flashback. You've even used most of the same syntax and phrasing!"

Lawrence looked blankly at him again, then shook his head. "I don't think that's true. See, Terry's chapter starts at the toolshed with Mary and the Forrester boy, and Gary's takes place at the hardware store. Was that not clear?"

"That's not what I mean," Flip said with his hands trembling in frustration. "I mean the style and grammatical structure are the same, and the openings follow the same pattern even though they're about different things."

"I don't think you're seeing the big picture. When you have multiple narrators in a novel, each one has to sound distinct so they can add a new voice to the story."

"So just like Faulkner uses in *As I Lay Dying*?" Flip asked.

"Yeah!" Lawrence spouted excitedly. "That's a great book with a lot of different narrators." He turned ahead several pages and handed the packet back to Flip. "Wait until you get to May, since she's the most unique of all."

May

It's just after one AM when she awakens fitfully at his phone call to hear a voice she hasn't heard in months. It doesn't sound as if it's him at first, so she gathers up her courage and whispers, "Jerry," into the receiver so he'll know she's there. Hearing his own name catches him off guard, because he doesn't answer for some seconds as his silence pulls at her like a cold wind across a cotton field, and she waits breathlessly to hear what he'll say next.

"I want you here, May," he says to her, and then again, slowly. "I want you here in bed with me."

It's been two months since she heard from him, and she yearned for it as desperately then as she does now. They'd been together and apart again ever since those first stolen moments behind the laundromat during the football game when he'd bitten just a little too hard on her eardrum. She could have let that one slide—

Flip grabbed a handful of his own hair to steady himself. "This is the same opening with a different character. The only difference is that you're using third-person present tense for some reason. Also, you can't bite someone's eardrum!"

"May's the only character who speaks in the present tense," Lawrence said proudly, "since she experiences reality more vividly than the other characters and is overall the strongest one in the family. I started writing and her voice just seemed to come out that way."

"So she's like Caddy from *The Sound and the Fury*," Flip said. "And won't it be confusing to have two characters named Mary and May in the same book? That's even worse than the rhyming."

"Oh no," Lawrence said, shaking his head. "Mary's name is different because it has an R." He studied Flip with a look of concern. "You know, you really shouldn't *plan* so much before you write. Just let whatever happens flow naturally."

"But writers have to wield control over their own stories," Flip argued with a vengeance that surprised even him. "You can't just string paragraphs together because they sound poetic, especially if you only know how to write one way."

Lawrence's eyes had taken on a glassy look as he moved to scratch a zit just below his earlobe. "During my MFA I took a visiting writer's workshop with Franklin McConnell, and he taught us that every character you create has to have some inner conflict that stirs us even if we can't see that conflict directly in the scene. These layers make our characters more complex."

"But what about flat characters?" Flip asked, realizing as he said this that Lawrence hadn't responded to his earlier point. "E.M. Forster talks about how not every character can be multilayered and round. Flat characters can resonate around a single recognizable idea, like a character who's comically oblivious and doesn't respond to other people's points."

"Gosh, you just had to bring up more *old* stuff, didn't you?" Lawrence said, scratching at the zit again. "One of the Chatanackaseekawa stories I've written is about a character who was raised in the South but went away to college where he gained some perspective, and he becomes entranced by this old story from the 1930s about a mysterious stranger who comes to the county to build an enormous old-style Southern mansion with a Portuguese architect because he wants to forge a new dynasty, but he only ends up crippling his family through his obsession."

Flip repressed the urge to pound his fists against the table. "That's just *Absalom, Absalom!* expressed in different words— you're taking all your ideas from Faulkner!"

"Don't go jumping to conclusions now," Lawrence corrected. "*Absalom, Absalom!* is way different because the old story in that novel is pre-Civil War, but mine comes from the 1930s. Weren't you listening?"

Flip had no way of responding to this—had no way, it seemed, of responding to anything Lawrence had to say at all. Around them the food court tables had begun filling up as orange-clad students sat together in cheerful groups, their trays loaded with pizza and Chinese food and wax paper-wrapped sandwiches. His gaze wandered to a fountain drink machine beside the Subway that offered no fewer than twelve different kinds of soda (or was it pop?), and the sheer number of choices made him want to drink tap water for free back at the apartment.

"Anyway," Lawrence went on, "you shouldn't force your characters to do things or overthink so much. Go with the flow and see what happens! Speaking of which, I also never see you when we go out—someone should invite you and your special lady friend to come with us for a drink sometime."

Flip felt all the color drain from his face as his heart began pounding at an uncomfortable rate. "What special lady friend?"

"Oh, that girl you introduced me to at Brad's party," Lawrence said. "What was her name again?"

Flip thought of Derzen in her jean jacket with the flower pinned to the lapel and felt as if he might collapse. "You must be remembering wrong—I'm not seeing anyone right now."

Lawrence's face fell into a look of consternation. "Really—a handsome guy like you? Who was I thinking of, then?"

"Anyway," Flip said in defeat, "at least your book has a strong conflict. My next workshop submission date is coming up and I still don't know how I'm going to make my novel connect with readers."

Lawrence tilted his head as if trying to recall something he'd heard long ago. "That's right—your book was the office one, right? If you're stuck, don't forget that you can always ask somebody to switch workshop spots with you to get more time. I'd offer to help, but I'm on my way to the mailroom to pass out my submission right now."

Flip felt a burst of nervousness at the suggestion—switching workshop days, while an excellent way to buy more time, would likely reveal his desperation to everyone else. "I'll think about it," he said.

"I thought your book had a really strong voice," Lawrence went on, "but almost too strong, like the voice superseded the plot. You should try bringing in the other coworkers' voices so they can be heard too." He sat up at once as if emerging from a stupor. "That's it! What if you used multiple narrators in your novel, with each one telling their part of the story in separate chapters with their names at the beginning?"

"That's not what I want to do with this novel," Flip said. "The protagonist has to tell the story himself because it's about him being lonely and not fitting in, and I want the narration to have the wit of a Joseph Heller novel with the observing eye of John Updike and some Kingsley Amis-level craziness."

"John Updike?" Lawrence said. "But *The Witches of Eastwick* was so *bad*. I don't know much about Heller or Amis, but I do remember liking *Money*."

A pained silence spread over the booth, during which Flip turned to stare at a group of men in suit jackets and plaid dress shirts walking across the union in some official capacity. The men were all older and their way of dressing felt oddly outdated; one of them was pointing some feature of the orange booths out to the others, who nodded knowingly.

Finally Lawrence asked, "What are you planning to do after you finish your MFA?"

"I want to get my novel published," Flip said. "Then I want to start a new one and go back to writing short stories and essays and poems and working on my drawing like I used to, and I want to be involved in writing communities that encourage people to make great art, and I want to read all the books I don't have time to read now and devote myself to my work like I also don't have time to do now, and it'd be nice to work with younger writers who are just figuring things out but have a real passion for what they want to do, and I want to mix all these things together in a way that gives my life more meaning."

Lawrence turned away from the men in suit jackets. "No, I mean, are you going to apply for a PhD or try going on the market right away?"

"I don't know," Flip said. "Even Faulkner worked in a power plant when he was writing *As I Lay Dying*, right?"

Lawrence looked away with a nervous, tittering glance. "Sure, you could do that," he said. "It'd be a good way to fill a gap year if you don't get into a PhD program."

After that they sat in silence until it became clear that neither of them had anything left to say.

25

"WHAT ARE you planning to do after you finish your PhD?" Flip asked Jackson as they trampled down the steps to the library basement.

"I think the more pressing question is what you're going to submit for workshop," Jackson said. "I doubt it's going to go well if you use the same pages as before."

"I know," Flip said. "But I feel like I can't even start revising if I don't know what direction to take the novel in."

Jackson led him through the basement landing into an immense fluorescent-lit room filled with narrowly spaced bookshelves. He pulled a slip of paper from his pocket and said, "You don't need a super-detailed blueprint to revise a novel, but you do need a direction to guide your writing if you want to make a change."

"That's my problem," Flip said. "I want to turn the novel into something more approachable, but it still has to feel like the novel I want to write."

Jackson stopped in the middle of an aisle and knelt down to inspect a row of irregularly shaped graphic novels. He hoisted up an oversized hardback of *Little Nemo in Slumberland* and began moving through the stacks again. "Writing without a plan won't get you anywhere, but you also have to make your deadline, so there's that outside pressure to consider."

"So what should I do?" Flip asked. "Turn in something I don't believe in, or turn in something the workshop's just going to tear apart?"

"Either one would solve your deadline problem," Jackson said, "but neither would be helpful in the long run." At the end of the aisle he studied the slip again and turned deftly to the right.

"No it wouldn't," Flip said. "It feels wrong to waste my time on something that doesn't matter so I can get through the workshop and move on, which is why I wanted to ask if you'd trade submission days with me."

Jackson stepped into another set of stacks and halted to pull a jacketless edition of *Fools Crow* from a shelf. "Sure—it's only an extra two weeks, but it'll buy you some time to find the change you're looking for."

Flip felt an all-encompassing sense of relief rush over him. "I appreciate that a lot."

"It's no problem," Jackson said. "Us northeasterners have to stick together. Plus, I'm just going to submit the same well-polished junk from three years ago that'll earn the usual platitudes, so what do I care if it happens sooner or later?" He stopped at a new row of stacks and slid a copy of Balzac's *Lost Illusions* free from the shelf. He held all three books under his arm with his elbow resting against the *Little Nemo* collection.

"What class are you using those for?" Flip asked.

"Just a little weekend reading," Jackson said. "As for your original question, I don't know what I'm going to do when they hand me my PhD and kick me out of here. I certainly don't trust the ultra-competitive atmosphere of academia like Lawrence and Kendall and the rest of them do. Sure, plenty of high-paying tenure-track professor jobs that offer chances at long-term security still come up, but it's not 1965 anymore and those jobs are few and far between, with several hundred PhD and MFA grads vying for each one. Most of the people we'd be up against have CVs far longer than ours with a fat list of publications to make them stand out, and their chances of getting an interview go up exponentially if they know someone on the search committee. We'd have better odds if we had a book or two out and a few stories in high-profile journals, but even Kendall barely has the one short story collection, and there are tons of applicants with credentials even more impressive than his. I guess it could be worse if we were literature students since their job prospects are even bleaker. Don't get me wrong—it'd be great to have tenure because then

I could coast along until I'm eighty with a cushy salary and no chance of losing my job while I taught the same six classes for a few decades and maybe gave some side lectures, but to do that I'd have to claw my way past a slew of desperate job-seekers who wanted that position more than me. Then, assuming I somehow got accepted to one of those professor jobs, to avoid getting booted and actually win tenure I'd have to go to a bunch of boring meetings and make teaching portfolios and do all that extracurricular shit that doesn't have a real purpose but that everyone just kind of goes along with, and that's not even counting the books I'd have to write to prove I was actively contributing to the field. Even if I were passionate about every word I wrote in every single book there'd still be this pressure to write because I'd need those books for tenure, and it wouldn't be the same as just writing for fun or writing to reach people with what I had to say. The world both inside and outside academia pushes people toward the status and material rewards of a comfortable job, but those comfortable jobs are hard to get and young people who want them put themselves through these insane struggles just so they can live easily later on. Meanwhile, the people who've managed to snag those jobs are either exhausted from having to work so hard to get them or lazy from having all that power and money, so either way they stop devoting themselves the way they did when they were young and full of energy. Ideally we'd have a system where everybody could work reasonably hard throughout their entire careers with fair pay, health insurance, and enough opportunities to advance and even the highest-ranked writers would have to answer to their readers so they'd keep producing good work, but you can't fix a system as broken as ours as long as people keep believing it's the only way. It was hard enough getting the funded PhD gig in the first place since programs like ours are shrinking every year and soon there won't be any left at all. After this I think I'll go back to bartending, since the money's a lot better and I get to sleep late." He stopped at another point in the stacks, studied the top shelf, and removed a copy of *The Optimist's Daughter* that he added to the stack under his arm.

This explanation had unsettled Flip deeply. "But the people who have those jobs make good money and get summer and Christmas breaks off, and they can structure their own time so they can write without having to clock in at some regular job, so working in academia must be more conducive to the writing life, right?"

Jackson tossed the slip into a recycling bin as he led Flip back into the center aisle. "Of course—as long as you can hold on to your integrity and pass the tests, it's a dream life for a writer. So if you really want to go for it, you should."

Such an option felt too monumental to consider, and as they passed back on to the landing Flip listened to the soft taps of Jackson's tennis shoes echoing through the stairwell.

from: Flip Montcalm
to: William Stark, M.F.A.
date: Mon, Oct 9, 2017 at 10:47 PM
subject: Switching Submission Dates?

Hi Professor,

Sorry to bother you, but work on my novel has been slow. I've gotten some good rewrites done but haven't gotten as far as I'd like, and I don't want to just bring what I have in to workshop since it won't really be enough for the others to comment on. I also don't want to turn in more pages from the first draft since I still have changes I'd like to make and the originals don't really capture the new tone I'm going for. Fortunately, I talked to Jackson about switching workshop dates and he said he doesn't mind going next week and letting me have his spot, so I really hope it's not too much trouble if we trade. The extra two weeks would really help me get this excerpt ready to go, and I'd be incredibly grateful for the time.

Thanks in advance, and I definitely appreciate it.

All best,
Flip

from: William Stark, M.F.A.
to: Flip Montcalm
date: Tue, Oct 10, 2017 at 6:40 AM
subject: Re: Switching Submission Dates?

Yes that's fine.

26

"IF IT ISN'T the mysterious stranger!" Brad shouted in his great, thundering voice as he clamped an arm around Flip's shoulders. "Kendall and I were just talking about how we never see you anymore, buddy, ha ha."

They were standing outside the east exit of the English building, which opened out next to two benches, a dumpster, an oak tree whose leaves were just beginning to turn sickly brown, and a trash can overflowing with Raising Cane's cups. Still groggy after ninety minutes of lectures on Great Plains ecosystems, Flip jumped when he heard Brad's call. Beside him, Kendall stood with his hands in his jacket pockets, his eyes behind their rimless glasses pivoting away as soon as Flip turned to him.

"Oh, you know how it is," Flip said. "I've been pretty busy lately."

Brad pulled his arm away from Flip's shoulder with a hearty laugh. "Amen to that. But it is what it is, am I right?"

Kendall pulled out his phone and swiped a quick crisscross to unlock its screen. It seemed amiss not to acknowledge him in some way, so Flip looked more obviously in his direction and asked, "How's everything with you?"

Kendall scrolled down the phone screen while he spoke. "Oh, you know, the usual—classes to teach, comps to prepare for, always more books to read."

"I hear that," Brad said vigorously. "But hey, a bunch of us were going out to that new microbrew pub in the old downtown tomorrow after classes, so you should come grab dinner with us."

Flip's immediate impulse was to say no, though then he wondered whether Derzen would be included in said bunch, then whether

Kendall knew about his coffee shop meeting with Derzen, and finally what Kendall thought about their coffee shop meeting if he did know about it. "I think I'll pass," he said. "I was really hoping to do some work on the novel this weekend."

Kendall continued looking at his phone.

"I hear that, buddy," Brad said. "Nose to the grindstone! Staying home to work while the rest of us waste our time drinking. I heard you switched workshop days with Jackson, so I'm sure you've got some secret masterpiece you're waiting to show us, am I right?"

"Oh, it's coming along," Flip lied.

"I'm psyched to finally see it," Brad said, still with his over-arching grin. "I'm sure Jackson already knows about it, though, since I see you guys together all the time in your secret meetings. Guess he must be the one person around here you actually make time for, eh?"

Flip laughed because he didn't know what else to do, then immediately felt sick for doing so and began backing away. "Anyway, I should probably get back to work, but you guys have fun tomorrow."

Kendall said, "You too, Phil," as he looked up and toward an orange construction fence circling the quad.

"We'll drink a flight in your honor," Brad said with a wink as he slapped Flip between his shoulder blades. "And don't forget about reading for *Long Grass*, since we could always use a writer's writer like you on the fiction team!"

"I'll think it over," Flip said, and turned away. He felt more relieved when they were out of sight and he could focus again on figuring out how to fix the novel once the weekend came and he finally had time to do some writing.

27

Flip didn't write at all that weekend.

28

THEN CAME the Thursday when Melvin went to an evening craft talk with a guest lecturer from Idaho and Flip took advantage of the quiet office to decipher (or attempt to decipher) some Foucault reading with his feet up on the desk and his mind focused on something that wasn't the novel, the novel, the novel until Derzen worriedly poked her head through the doorway to ask whether she could borrow two of his office chairs. She had four students coming for a group conference the next morning and Mary-Beth had just texted saying she needed to meet with one of her own students during that time but could do it even during Derzen's conference, so now she was short two chairs and was there any way he could help?

He pulled his feet off the desk and stood—initially out of some base reflex but then because he genuinely wanted to show her his full attention—looking first to the desk occupied by the literature student who still hadn't returned for his books and computer with its sleep indicator still blinking slowly on and then off again, and then to Melvin's desk. Rather than risk giving up either chair he suggested that there might be some extras in the furniture alcove near Stark's office. Derzen made an embarrassed face at not having thought of this first, and since he was already standing it felt natural to walk with her into the empty hallway and down to the furniture alcove where he could see she was tired and stressed from the day or the semester or from something much bigger it didn't seem right to ask about. He made a comment about Mary-Beth hosting an office party that he hoped would make her laugh and when she didn't he began walking faster on purpose so that she also moved faster to keep up until this finally made her laugh and ask why he was in a hurry, to which he jokingly responded that of course he was in a hurry because everyone in grad school was in a hurry always, though it was she who first started running and when he saw that she was running he wanted to run too so that when they reached the halfway point of the hallway they were both pounding their feet against the floor. Derzen was laughing harder and saying she hadn't realized it was a race, to which he replied that of course it wasn't but that they both had many, many things to do and no time to waste, which she said only meant they had to run faster as she shot ahead of him and was first to reach the hallway's end.

Three wheeled chairs had been pushed into the alcove behind one of the oversized desks, though when Flip lifted one of them the metal rod connecting the wheels to the seat slid free and the entire bottom section crashed to the floor, leaving him holding the chair-back while Derzen laughed harder and climbed over the desk next to him to reconnect the wheels so that their faces were very close. He slowly lifted the second chair to gauge whether it was secure and she laughed at this too, and after she'd climbed back over the desk he pushed the chair gently against the backs of her legs so that she slid into its seat with a yelp of surprise and both hands clutching its padded arms. He spun her and the chair into the elongated hallway, and this time Derzen's laughter was so gleefully pronounced that he knew it was okay to push, slowly at first, then faster as the wheels gathered speed. She pulled her legs onto the metal wheel guard still laughing, and when the chair gained enough momentum he found that he could almost pull his arms away and run behind it with Derzen's shrieks echoing down the hallway where there was no one to hear them at seven-thirty on a Thursday. When he was sure he could run without holding the chair he lifted his left hand from its back and felt it begin to slow, and to get it moving again he instead grabbed hold of the armrest and the warm curve of Derzen's wrist. Her skin felt refreshingly smooth, with the edges of her jeweled bracelet stinging his palm, and in the moment she shrieked and clasped her other hand around his wrist as the chair reached maximum speed and they passed the east stairwell where he lunged forward with a push that shot her down the final fifteen feet of hallway squealing in delight and coasting to a halt just inches from the wall. When she leaped up her legs wobbled and she leaned against the corner to steady herself but said she'd race him back for the second chair and so they did, sprinting cautiously at first, then at full speed down the hallway as the air gushing behind them blew back the year-old study abroad posters pinned to the bulletin boards by upper pushpins only and their shoes thudded against the floor wax that shone with a vivid shine as one and then the other of them pulled ahead and Flip's breath came in saliva-filled gasps that grew more desperate as he shot forward with a final burst to meet her so that they finished at the same time and collapsed on the floor.

Their chests heaved up and down, and the collar of Derzen's blouse had become disheveled. She looked at him smiling with her large, sparkling eyes and for that one beautiful, brief moment as he felt the sweat of exhaustion run down his body the one thing he wanted in the entire world was to lie against the wall and rest with her.

29

"WHAT ARE you going to do after you finish your MFA?" he asked her afterward.

They sat in Derzen's office reclining in the borrowed chairs; she tapped the edge of her armrest and shrugged. "I don't know. Everybody's been asking me that."

"Sorry."

"No," Derzen said. "Not like that. When most people ask they do it in this harping, judgmental kind of way, like they're expecting me to list off a bunch of PhD programs I'm applying to or tell them I'm going right on the job market when the truth is I'm not sure whether I really want that."

Flip sat up straighter. "Like you're not sure at all, or you're just hesitating?"

"The second one," Derzen said. "When I came out here for an MFA I swore I'd just stay for three years then get back out into the world through either teaching or doing something else, but the teaching opportunities look pretty bleak right now and I'm not sure what else I'd like to be doing."

"That's always been my problem too," Flip said. "When I was younger I felt sure that all these big things were out there waiting for me, but when I finally felt ready to take them on I realized I didn't know how to go after them or even what they might be. The writing was always there, but the stuff surrounding it's always existed as this nebulous haze."

Derzen had raised her bent knees as she listened. "Yes—the not knowing is the scariest part."

"Lawrence of all people asked me about my plans after I graduated and I didn't know what to tell him," Flip said. "It seemed too early to start planning for that since I don't even know how I'm going to fix my novel, let alone how to make a career. I know Jackson just keeps doing more grad school, but I'm not sure that would help me do the kind of writing I want to be doing."

"Jackson's been in academia a long time, and I think about what he says a lot. I guess I usually take it with a grain of salt, though."

"Me too."

"But then I start worrying about what I'm actually going to do," Derzen said, "and the feeling always gets worse when I'm around other people in the department. That's when I feel most like I have to build up my CV and publish a bunch of poetry books and get into a good PhD program because that's what they tell you leads to success. It sometimes takes a while for me to come to my senses and remember that if I did that I'd be trapped for another four-plus years teaching first-year comp and poetry at some other backwater university when I could be going to readings in New York and riding the subway and meeting lots of cool creative people who are out living their lives, and that's when more grad school doesn't feel like a good choice at all." She paused, then went on. "Plus, Kendall really wants me to stay here for a PhD, at least until he finishes his."

Flip's stomach churned into a disconcerting knot. "I think about what it really means to be living your life too, and I know being here doesn't feel like that, but my old job definitely didn't feel like that either. One of the first times I ever talked to Jackson he mentioned this Salman Rushdie quote about writing a novel being a Faustian bargain in reverse where you have to sacrifice your daily life and happiness to write something that lives on after you're dead, but I definitely don't see people sacrificing their daily lives here, so I think it's possible for writers to have both success and a fulfilling life at the same time. But who knows—maybe if we lived in closet-sized apartments in Brooklyn and worked data entry jobs while writing in the evenings we could get more done than if we stayed here mired in coursework and lesson prep."

Derzen fidgeted in her chair. "Who knows if we could even afford the closet-sized apartments unless we had jobs that paid enough. I think there's always going to be sacrifices involved with writing, but I agree that we can find a balance between work and living a life that matters. I always remember this great Elizabeth Bishop essay where she gets a job working for this crooked mail-order writing course and finds that all the people taking it are desperately lonely and trying to reach out to the rest of the world by becoming famous writers. The thing is, though, that the people taking the class have it all wrong and they should really be embracing their loneliness, since that's what helps writers understand the world around them." Derzen seemed to consider this before continuing. "I think to some extent that's true, but then we also need the companionship that comes from being around like-minded people because those relationships enrich us and help us grow."

"I definitely wasn't finding enriching relationships back home. I couldn't relate to my co-workers, and most of my friends were either too far away or too busy to meet up."

"That's not a good place for anyone to be in."

"No, it isn't."

Derzen's eyes had taken on a melancholy haze. "Sometimes it feels like everyone here is better at academia than me and that they're all off writing and researching these important journal articles while I'm wasting time with friends or binge-watching TV shows, and I think about how everyone else has more publications than me and how Kendall already has a book coming out and then I just start feeling worthless."

"I binge-watch a lot of TV shows too," Flip said. "One time I watched six straight hours of *The Wonder Years* instead of writing."

Derzen didn't say anything but looked past him to the undersea dolphin poster above Mary-Beth's desk. "The reason I bring it up is because I know I'm not strong enough to go on the job market yet, so I started filling out all these PhD applications when the semester started. Not only is it the most boring thing in the entire world, I also feel this weird sense of obligation doing it, like it's just something I have to get out of the way, but I know it'll be my only chance to apply before next year. I've got all these applications with essays and recs and everything all set to go, but I haven't paid the money or clicked send yet. I'll have to make a decision soon, though, and I'm wondering whether I should just apply and see what happens or if I'm better off saving the application fees to put toward moving somewhere exciting after graduation."

Somewhere in the hallway a voice, speaking in a low tone about something indistinguishable, echoed through the doorway and then faded. "Are you also applying here?" Flip asked.

Derzen nodded. "Initially just here, but then I decided to try other places too. At first I told myself the others were just backups in case I didn't get in here, but then I started thinking about seeing someplace new like California or Tennessee or even Hawaii and whether universities there would be any different. I really don't know because the programs all seem the same."

Her eyes had stayed on Mary-Beth's poster but now slowly looked down, hesitating, and it seemed that she wanted to say something she'd been holding back for a long time. "When I came here the choice was easy because this was the only place that gave me funding, but I think the worst thing that could happen would be if both here and another place offered me money so that I'd have to make a choice, and in that case I don't know what I'd choose."

Flip felt his breathing slow as he imagined Kendall, his face dull and expressionless, telling Derzen in a firm and faintly conde-scending voice that he hoped she'd choose to attend the PhD program that would keep her closest to him, and he knew then that something had passed between him and Derzen in the hallway that had caused her to open up.

"When I think about making important decisions," Flip began, "I think about what I really want out of the thing I'm deciding on, and with coming here it was always about making writing the center of my life, so in that sense grad school's just a means to becoming the writer I'd like to be. The only question is whether it's the best means. I don't think anyone necessarily needs grad school to be an artist if they can master the craft some other way— Kerouac couldn't have written *On the Road* if he'd been sitting through a bunch of Iowa workshops instead of driving across the country with his friends."

"I don't know," Derzen said. "Things are different now, and if Sylvia Plath were twenty-six today I'm sure she wouldn't have been able to teach at Smith with her credentials, so she'd be in the same boat as us looking into more grad school. Maybe that would have caused her to stick with teaching instead of moving to Boston because now it would be impossible for her to live in Boston on a secretary's salary and still pay her student loans—but that's the kind of thing you can think about forever and not find an answer to."

"That's true. No two paths are the same."

Derzen began tapping the armrest again. "But a lot of other things haven't changed since then, and women still have a more difficult time finding academic jobs compared to men, and the choices we all face are as real as ever. It's like that line in *The Bell Jar* where Esther talks about sitting in a fig tree and staring up at all the branches loaded with figs where each one represents a different future—one's being a great writer, another's being a brilliant professor, and another's traveling the world, and because she's not sure which one to choose the figs all start turning black and rotting so she can't have any of them. That's what I think about—the world being full of all these figs that I'm afraid are going to pass me by."

Flip wondered what other choices Derzen was thinking about, and it occurred to him that everything she said tied together into something much bigger than academia. "I know that line," he said instead. "Aziz Ansari talked about it on his show, and they did this great montage of him reading the book with all the different fig options forming a mosaic."

The reference felt silly as he said it, and he regretted bringing it up until Derzen said, "A friend of mine back home told me about that since she knows I love Sylvia Plath, and I was glad they used that line because that's how these sentiments get shared with new generations who'd otherwise never read Plath at all."

"Wouldn't it be great if we could share all the things we cared about with everyone all the time?" Flip asked.

Derzen nodded. "I'd like that. And I think about the best way to find the freedom to do the kind of sharing we want to and whether we can really find it by going to academic conferences and workshopping every little thing we write. People aren't reading *The Bell Jar* or *The Bean Trees* anymore because even those books belong to a different generation now. I wish people here could push their writing harder like Sylvia pushed herself with every poem she ever wrote, and I also wish the things we write could naturally reach more people who wanted to read them. I think about all that and wonder whether leaving here would be even worse than staying if I couldn't grab that other fig of being a meaningful poet, so that maybe the only way to become successful is to take the academic path before that fig shrivels up forever. If I miss that chance along with all the others I worry I'll end up destitute and childless on a street corner somewhere wearing a trash bag for a raincoat and rambling to anyone who'll listen how I threw away my only chance because I was afraid of getting too settled."

Or maybe, Flip thought, her uncertainty had only been about academia. It was always hard to tell these things.

30

We were somewhere around Barstow at the edge of the desert when the drugs started to take hold. I remember saying something like, "I feel a bit lightheaded, maybe you should drive..." And suddenly there was a terrible roar all around us, and the sky was filled with what looked like huge figs, all swooping and screeching and diving around the car—

[No, that was bats.]

FLIP'S MIND spun in a mercurial flutter as he walked down the first-floor English hallway the following Monday after the Critical Theory class. He'd made no real progress on the novel over the weekend, though for the first time he'd at least done some writing: a series of openings, not one of them longer than a page, in variations of first-person, third-person, and even a brief, pretentious foray into second-person (*Bright Lights, Big City* it was not), all of which had felt forced and entirely wrong. But trying had felt better than doing nothing, and that feeling of creating something again had driven him to pull out his drawing pad and sketch more pictures of forests and lakes and towering mountains with climbers struggling to reach their peaks as they pulled themselves hand over hand up rugged boulders. Now he had only three days before his rescheduled submission date and still had nothing to show for it—and since Jackson had no more submission dates to offer him, navigating around this problem would require a more cunning plan.

He'd also thought about Derzen. A lot.

He wanted her very badly. He wanted to storm into her office, shove her computer and textbooks and everything else on her desk to the floor, hoist her into his arms like in *Officer and a Gentleman*, and carry her down the English Department stairwell to the Honda (which in the fantasy he'd parked illegally in the east cul-de-sac) and drive until they found mountains and ocean and exciting cities where they could write and live exciting lives and where everything would work out the way they wanted it to. It would be just like in *Lucky Jim* when Dixon pulled Christine Callaghan away from the party in a stolen taxi and in the end she chose Dixon over Bertrand and Dixon finally found the courage to laugh outright at that ridiculous world he'd escaped from in a triumphant victory of the genuine over the false.

When class had ended he'd lingered by his chair slowly putting on his jacket until everyone else had gone; the only people in the hallway now were a pair of women talking wearily by one of the classrooms and an undergrad in a Prairie Fire hoodie listening to earbuds on a bench. In the silence the sound of footsteps coming down the staircase seemed louder than usual, and he sensed that the person on the stairs was Kendall even before he rounded the corner. He ignored the feeling and kept walking toward the west exit until he saw that it really was Kendall coming down the stairwell.

Flip wondered whether to move faster and try to pass the stairs before Kendall completely rounded the corner so he could pretend he didn't see him, or to move more slowly so Kendall would reach the landing well before he did. As long as Kendall turned toward the door without looking to his left Flip would be able to stay behind him out of sight. If Flip maintained his normal pace, however, he would reach the landing at the same time Kendall did, and if this happened then he would have to acknowledge Kendall in some way, maybe with a greeting or maybe just with a nod. No, a nod would be best—the two of them had nothing to say to each other. He wondered what Derzen would think if she knew he was thinking this, and then wondered whether Derzen knew how he felt about Kendall at all, which led to wondering whether Kendall knew how he (Flip) felt about Derzen or how he (Flip) felt about him (Kendall), and finally to whether Kendall knew how Derzen felt about him (Flip), along with whether Derzen had even figured this out herself.

He continued without changing his pace and when Kendall reached the landing Flip nodded slowly in his direction.

Kendall showed no reaction and turned toward the exit.

31

Brad Choude is associate fiction editor of the Long Grass *literary journal, a prestigious publication of poetry, fiction, and creative nonfiction founded in 1934. He originally hails from Appalachia, and his writing tackles the economic and social hardships facing this historically underserved region, with fiction appearing or forthcoming in* The Eastern Mountain Review, The Yinzer Review, *and* Coal: A Critical Study.

"HEY, BUDDY!" Brad exclaimed when Flip poked his head through his office doorway. "Come in and have a seat! What's going on?"

In contrast to the other grad student offices, the one Brad shared with Kendall contained only two desks and was located off a side corridor halfway down the third-floor hallway. Kendall's desk, the barer of the two, contained a stack of thin paperbacks and little else; on his walls hung a three-foot Prairie Fire banner, a poster of two people jogging, and a black and white printout of a solemn middle-aged man bearing the caption *A writer's greatest challenge is to uplift his or her culture's spiritual essence. —Steven Walter Hendricks.* Beside the photo hung a letter that, upon closer inspection, was revealed to be from the Hasenpfeffer-Schweppman Hildridge Book Prize congratulating Kendall on his winning submission. The walls of Brad's side, by contrast, were cluttered with wooden and metal signboards, most of them for diners and roadside ice cream stands with a 1950s flair: *Best Pie in Town! Breakfast Served All Day! Service with a Smile!* High on the wall hung a green street sign that read *Easy Street.*

"You like that?" Brad asked when he saw Flip looking at the Easy Street sign. "That came from some ritzy upper-middle-class neighborhood near where I did my undergrad. The developer had the bright idea to name the place Easy Street, so of course kids started stealing the sign and the town kept having to replace it. They finally got smart and set it on top of this huge pole so tall you'd need an eight-foot ladder and a pickup to get up there. I heard about it from one of the guys in my fraternity."

"You were in a fraternity?" Flip asked. There'd been no fraternities when he was in college, and hearing about them always reminded him of Aarfy from *Catch-22*.

Brad's face shook in a merry chuckle as he waved his hand dismissively. "Hey there, I sense some judgment in your voice. I didn't belong to one of *those* fraternities where everybody just got shitfaced and date-raped sorority pledges. We did a lot of service stuff for the community, but the real reason I joined was to make connections since getting ahead in this world's all about having connections, am I right?"

Brad's manner struck Flip as both defensive and self-involved. "Sure," he said.

"Anyway," Brad said with another chuckle, "one day me and a couple of my buddies from the frat decide we're going to steal the Easy Street sign, so we borrowed this guy's truck and ladder and drove out to this rich neighborhood late at night. And this was a pretty nice neighborhood, I mean, some of these houses probably go for three, four hundred grand, so if any of those old-money types see us college kids hanging around they're liable to call the cops. We eventually found the sign and set up the ladder in the back of the truck so one guy could stand up top taking the bolts out while me and another guy steadied the ladder from the bed and the fourth guy stayed in the driver's seat ready to make a getaway. So when my buddy up top finally gets the last bolt loose it turns out this sign is fucking heavy—I mean way heavier than you'd think a street sign would be—so of course he drops it right on the side of the road and the other guy holding the ladder jumps out to grab it. So he's fumbling with this fucking huge sign while the other guy's climbing down the ladder and meanwhile I reach over the side of the truck so the guy down below can hand it to me."

Brad shook his head and began chuckling with his mischievous, merry grin. "So I'm trying to get the sign from him and he's fumbling with it and all of a sudden I see these headlights coming right at us, so I tell him, 'Hand me the sign!' real loud, but he still can't get a good grip on it, and that's when I see the red and blue lights flash and the other guy in the bed's yelling, 'Man, we gotta get out of here!' while my buddy in the driver's seat starts the engine and I'm reaching over to grab this fucking behemoth of a sign from my buddy outside the truck." He stopped to stifle his laughter before going on. "So that's when he finally hands me the sign and as soon as I get it I yell 'Book it!' and we're fucking out of there before the cops can get anywhere near us!" He burst into ecstatic, knee-slapping laughter that shook his entire body in teetering convulsions. "And meanwhile my one buddy was still standing there dumbfounded in this ditch when the cops came, and they totally threw him in the police car with handcuffs and everything! The guy spent the night in jail and got fingerprinted with a theft and vandalism charge on his record while the rest of us got off scot-free!"

Flip smiled and pretended to laugh. "That's a pretty good one."

Brad slapped his leg again. "But you know what the absolute best part is? After the guy's parents bailed him out we hung the Easy Street sign in the living room of the frat house and a bunch of us were like, 'Yeah, after graduation you should really give that sign to the guy who spent a night in jail for it, since that's the only fair thing to do,' and I nodded and was like, 'Oh yeah, that's definitely the only fair thing to do,' and everybody agreed that giving the guy the sign after we moved out was the only fair thing to do—except that the day after graduation I ripped it off the wall and drove away while everyone else was sleeping!" His entire body exploded into side-splitting laughter as he pounded his fist against the desk. "Isn't that the greatest story you ever heard in your life?"

Flip smiled another meek smile. "Yeah, you guys were pretty lucky."

Still shaking, Brad straightened his torso as if he was about to say something very serious but instead said, "But not that one guy!" and burst back into rollicking laughter. When he finally calmed himself he wiped the tears from his eyes and waved his hand in a circular motion. "So what exactly did you want to talk about?"

"Ah," Flip said lamely, his eyes darting between the Easy Street sign and Brad's round, smiling face. "I'm supposed to submit pages for workshop this week but the ones I've got are still pretty rough, and they'd be a lot stronger if I had more time to clean them up. I saw that you're not submitting until the Tuesday before Thanksgiving, so I was wondering if you wouldn't mind switching with me so I can have more time?"

Brad's face shifted to a look of either genuine or simulated concern as he ran his hand along the folds of his neck. "Switch, eh? I'd have to pull a few strings to get a submission ready in two days—I mean, I *could* do it, but I wouldn't be able to finish the chapters I was planning on ironing out before the holiday."

Flip became aware of a dull, sickening feeling that his plan wasn't going to work. "Honestly, it'd be a huge favor and I'd be really grateful for the help."

Brad nodded and leaned back in his chair. "I mean, I *could* have something ready by Thursday, but then I'd have less time to get through my reading quota for *Long Grass*, and we've been running pretty far behind as it is." He stood and paced slowly around to Flip's chair, sliding onto the edge of the desk while still running his hand along his unshaven neck. "And actually, speaking of *Long Grass*, I kept meaning to follow up about you coming to read for us since we could still use more readers for the fiction team." He aimed a wry smile at Flip from his position atop the desk. "And it'd be an enormous boost for the journal."

Flip saw what Brad was getting at and knew he was in no position to bargain. "Sure," he said slowly. "I could probably read a few stories if I had more time to get those novel pages in."

Brad clasped his palm squarely on Flip's shoulder. "Buddy, that sounds like a great plan." He jumped down from the desk and paced back to his chair. "I'll get you signed into the system right away."

"What do I have to do, exactly?" Flip asked.

"Oh, you know," Brad said as he jotted something on a notepad, "standard slush pile stuff—you read through as many stories as you can and pass the good ones on to me. From there I take the *really* good ones and pass them on to the head honcho, and then once a month the head honcho video chats me from his visiting professorship in Scotland to tell me all the stories I like are crap so he can publish a bunch of stuff by his friends instead."

Flip wasn't sure he understood. "Then why do we have to read submissions if the boss is just going to publish stuff by his friends?"

Brad looked confused for an instant before he burst out laughing with a gigantic, jovial grin. "You know what I noticed about you, Flip, is that you're too serious! You should come out for a beer with us sometime, have a few laughs and make some connections. That's the part about grad school they don't tell you—sure there's a lot of papers to write and books to read that you don't give a crap about, but getting ahead in grad school's really about who you know because even if your book's the greatest thing ever written it's not worth the paper it's printed on unless you convince somebody to publish it, am I right?" His smile seemed to stretch across his entire face. "And to tell you the truth, everybody's wondering about these big novel edits you've been working on all semester. I'm telling you this as a friend, of course, but you aren't exactly the most popular guy around the department, and there's been a lot of buzz about whether you even like it here."

Flip felt the blood drain from his face. "Why would people think that?"

Brad laughed his jolly laugh again. "Tough to say. You're a hard guy to know—you've got that New England coldness about you! And people around here are always afraid of what they don't understand." He raised his arms in an exaggerated shrug. "But of course that's just what people say, and who am I to judge?"

"How about my novel?" Flip asked. "What are people saying about that?"

Brad tilted his chair back and held both hands behind his head. "I mean, I can't speak for everyone, but if you want my honest opinion I'll give it to you."

"Yes," Flip said. "I want to hear the truth."

Brad looked him directly in the eye. "You really want to know?"

"Of course," Flip said. "I want the kind of straight advice I can't get in workshop."

Brad cleared his throat. "If you want my honest answer, your novel's a pile of pretentious garbage and you should dump it. No one's interested in that office stuff—it's just a bunch of first-world white-people problems."

"What do you mean?" Flip asked. "Not feeling motivated at your job is something millions of people struggle with every day."

"But in the grand scheme of things it doesn't mean shit," Brad said. "Your guy's lucky to have a job at all, especially with the way things are nowadays. You want to see real problems, come on down to my hometown where the coal mines are all automated and the corporations are cutting hours so families can't put food on the table. You've got a meth problem, lack of education, and rural poverty at its worst while the rest of the country talks big about disposable potato chip bags, so don't you sit there with your fancy northeastern liberal arts education and your thirty-dollar haircut and tell me that real families' lives aren't more important than one schmuck who's unsatisfied with his job."

Flip felt suddenly embarrassed by the shape and weight of his hair, which he still hadn't gotten cut. "Of course those families' lives are important," he said, "but whoever said there wasn't room for novels about both? There's an infinite number of readers out there with all kinds of different problems, so we need books that appeal to everyone."

Brad shook his head reproachfully as he swayed back and forth in his chair. "Buddy, I hate to break it to you, but no one in the literary world cares about the stuff you're writing about anymore—publishers want novels that give voice to real people's struggles, especially people from traditionally overlooked backgrounds. All the action now's in minority, queer, and working-class fiction, so you've got to dump that middle-class white-people stuff and start writing what's going to get you noticed."

"But plenty of real people struggle with the things I'm writing about," Flip stuttered. "John Updike proved that back in the '60s and it's still true today."

"You mean with that upper-class *Witches of Eastwick* crap?" Brad said. "It's not that publishers aren't looking for novels about suburbia, it's that there are already a million writers more established than us writing about suburbia already, so why take a chance with a no-name MFA student when they could fill their disconnected white guy quota with the latest Walter Lerner novel they know will sell thirty thousand copies based on his name alone even if it's no good?"

A burst of stomach acid rose in Flip's throat that he struggled to gulp back down.

"The real opportunities for guys like us are in diversity fiction," Brad went on, "and underprivileged groups are the hottest thing since Beat culture. The best way to get ahead is to figure out a schtick that matches what publishers are looking for, since everybody wants to be on the cutting edge of this diversity stuff. Of course, that'd be a whole lot easier if we were gay or Asian or women or something, so we have to get more creative. My schtick's that I'm a working-class Appalachian who writes novels about one of the poorest subsections of the country—it's all over my bio! Any publisher who turned me down could easily be labeled classist since I've got peer pressure and socioeconomic affirmative action on my side."

"That's ridiculous!" Flip argued in astonishment. "You can't arbitrarily write about certain groups to meet publishing demands, because that cheapens the struggles of people who feel a genuine desire to tell those stories."

"*Cheapen's* such a strong word," Brad chastised with another wave. "You've got a lot to learn if you're ever going to make it as a writer! See, all businesses make their money by figuring out what people want, then doing that exact same thing over and over until people don't want it anymore, and by that point somebody else always finds another thing people want so they can switch to giving them that. All I'm saying is that in this dog-eat-dog

world of publishing we have to go where the opportunities are."
He scrunched up his face in thought. "So the trick is how to turn
your blue-blood, panini-eating New England novel into something
about an underprivileged group. You weren't ever molested as a
kid, you were?"

"Good god no!" Flip said with a swell of disgust.

"Rats," Brad said, "that's always an easy one. How about growing
up in the inner city? Was your family ever the victims of a drive-by
shooting?"

"No," Flip said. "I grew up in a small town with only a grocery
store and a gas station."

"No sweat," Brad said. "There's always the sexual angle—I mean,
not that it's any of my business, but some people around here think
it's a bit odd that you don't seem to be dating, so if there's something you're hiding or if your parents ever sent you to one of those
de-gayification camps, it might be worth exploring your struggle to
fit in with repressive heteronorms."

Flip felt his eyes widen. "You don't actually think I'm gay, do
you?"

"Just exploring options," Brad said immediately. "I don't suppose
your grandparents were Holocaust survivors, were they? Some
markets still scoop up that Jewish stuff."

Flip stood up with his teeth pressed together and his fists
clenched. "That's cultural appropriation! Real struggles take all
kinds of forms, and sometimes they don't come with convenient
labels. I'm not going to become someone I'm not just to get noticed
as a writer."

"Whoa there, killer!" Brad said as he rose to place a protective
hand on Flip's shoulder. "Who said anything about becoming
someone you're not? The point is to find that aspect of your background that's already been singled out as disadvantaged so you
can fit it into an identifiable spot on the market and present yourself through that lens, which is totally different."

"Are you insane?" Flip asked, his hands shaking in frustrated
uncertainty as a cloudiness blurred his vision. "You can't write
about hardship you don't actually have something to say about

because that makes the writing artificial and stilted. When you've experienced real hardship it'll come out on the page in real ways that people can empathize with no matter what your background is."

"Sounds like you're overthinking this underprivileged thing way too much," Brad said. I'm just trying to help you find your voice since you so generously agreed to help with *Long Grass*, and I like making life easier for people who help me out so that maybe in the future when you get a book deal of your own you might recommend your old MFA buddy Brad Choude who's pitching a novel about Appalachian coal country." He winked in a way that felt glaringly unambiguous. "If you want to write about white people so bad you might try adding a minority or two to create some quick diversity—that way, if people call your book out for being monocultural you can point to your Black or Hispanic character to prove them wrong. It's the same reason I make friends with people from other races wherever I go."

"Don't be shameless," Flip argued. "You shouldn't go adding random minorities unless their race contributes meaningfully to some aspect of the novel."

Brad chuckled again as he shook his head. "I'm surprised you're still not seeing the bigger picture. In the writing world, the meaningful option is always the one that'll get you published, no matter its effect on the story. If you keep talking like that, people are going to think you're standoffish, and that's not what you want, is it?"

Flip glanced at Kendall's side of the room but said nothing.

"In fact," Brad went on, "it almost sounded like you were silently discriminating against me when you found out I was in a fraternity, but I'll let that one slide. My new novel moves beyond the changing coal industry and tackles a topic that literature hasn't explored in any real depth—the devastating effects of the crystal meth boom!"

"Just like in *Breaking Bad*?" Flip asked.

Brad laughed his vigorous, hearty laugh and slapped Flip hard on the back. "That's a good one! The mainstream media latched on to the meth epidemic a few years ago, but there's still plenty of room to explore it in serious literature. See, I've done a lot of careful research into how the meth world works and how it devastates a region socioeconomically. A lot of the novel comes from my own experiences growing up in a three-room trailer while my father worked in the coal mines and my grandfather lay in bed all day coughing from black lung while the rest of the houses on our street sat abandoned or falling into foreclosure."

Flip felt a sharp sting between his shoulder blades where Brad had slapped him and realized he was too tired to argue anymore. "That does sound pretty bad," he said. "You weren't still living there when you came to grad school, were you?"

"Nah," Brad said. "We got out when I was six and my dad took a trucking job in Columbus, but the memories always stay with you. Besides," he said with a laugh, "a good enough writer can make any story come alive—am I right?"

A Tragedy Burned with Meth

by Bradley Choude

Chapter 1

Ace reporter Max Schelemaker drove rapidly down the dilapidated, decaying Appalachian streets on his way to the town's most recent meth lab explosion. *A terrible shame*, he thought to himself, *first the last coal mine in town closes, thus depriving dozens of hard-working families of their income, and now there's been yet another meth lab disaster. This town and its underappreciated people never had it so rough.*

A lifelong resident of Appalachia, Max was no stranger to the area's socioeconomic hardships, having been deeply and personally affected by them in ways that had made it difficult for him to attend college and find what his alcoholic parents referred to as a "real job." The family hadn't had much money growing up, and there were times when Max worried that the crippling lack of opportunities would—

[Flip put down Brad's novel and buried his head in his hands. Then he put on his jacket and walked out into the gloomy evening where a dry chill gripped the air, getting no response when he greeted his black-shirted neighbor scrolling through his phone under the awning. He began walking at random and soon found himself deep inside the grid of alphabet and numbered streets, thinking about everything and nothing.]

32

ALL OF THE *Long Grass* submissions sucked hard.

What made the process so frustrating was that none of the stories were bad in the sense of having clumsy sentences or fake-sounding dialogue, but all of them were bad in the sense of being boring, dense, confusing, or so superficial that no sensible reader could derive even the slightest bit of meaning from them:

> It was on that first adventurous summer after Cynthia's daughter was born that the fox appeared in the meadow behind the barn.

Flip found himself directing an irrational amount of hatred toward this sentence, then hated himself for hating it so much. He hated it because it grabbed his attention by provoking his desire to know more about the fox and for making him somehow believe that Cynthia's baby was in danger of being eaten by said fox, though in retrospect he saw that the sentence hadn't indicated this at all and had implied only that Cynthia's daughter and the fox were somehow linked. The latter observation, however, turned out to not even be true—the fox's bounding path across the meadow was described in a single melodic paragraph before the writer moved on to an overdramatic fox-free story about a thirty-something couple whose marriage hadn't turned out to be everything they'd dreamed. It was the kind of story that might have worked if the couple hadn't clearly brought the emptiness on themselves and if the writer hadn't been so oblivious to their culpability. Stories about empty marriages had all kinds of potential—that's what

Revolutionary Road was about, for Christ's sake—but if the writer couldn't show what made the marriage empty and thus reveal some more universal observation about relationships then the story had no hope of being anything more than a confused lament.

Flip rejected the piece with a note to this effect and moved on to the next one:

> Noel played the mandolin better than any one-armed man I'd ever seen.

He hated this opening sentence too for drawing him in, even though, unlike the first story, this one really was about Noel the one-armed mandolin player and the narrator's encounters with him in a series of dingy bars. The problem with this story, though, was that it didn't go anywhere: The narrator was so infatuated with Noel's whimsically offbeat worldview that he'd neglected to insert any kind of narrative arc, so that the seventeen-page story consisted entirely of stoical reflections on Noel's adventurous spirit peppered by his tendency to speak in annoying aphorisms. The story ended with Noel telling the narrator that most people can't tighten a mandolin string with their feet, a statement that felt both laughably obvious and frustratingly arcane. He summarized this in his note and rejected this piece also.

All of the stories seemed to be of similar length (sixteen to twenty-seven pages) and to cover similar topics. There were lots of families, lots of middle-aged couples, and lots of long descriptions of places and how the characters related to them. Many of the characters taught English at large universities or didn't seem to have jobs at all. A majority of the sentences were the same length, and many of their authors seemed incapable of using the past perfect.

The easiest pieces to reject were the historical fiction ones. Most of them took place in the 1960s and the worst of them included cringeworthy dialect voiced by minority side characters the white protagonists encountered during their efforts to understand the world around them. One particularly boring story seemed to be the centerpiece of the author's *Winesburg, Ohio*esque collection that spent six of its twenty-one pages describing the town's shops and their owners with eloquent descriptions of store windows and bustling sidewalks from a pre-mini mall era; what little plot the story possessed seemed to involve a lost dog that was quickly found again. He felt sorry for these writers who wanted to tell stories that they clearly found meaningful but wished they'd possessed more skill when it came to writing them. With the historical fiction he added gentler notes before adding the NO tag and moving on.

Other stories were so dense that he immediately lost all hope of understanding them since their language and progression of events were so impenetrable. He finished these stories with near-zero comprehension of what they'd been about and when he tried reading portions of them again he got lost trying to follow their myriad of unnamed characters whose thoughts and actions seemed to merge without reason so that the resulting narrative was more confusing than poetic. These stories left him feeling stupid and inexperienced for not being able to unravel them since their writers wrote with such confidence that there must have been some deeper meaning beneath the obfuscation—or was there? In the end he tagged these stories *Maybe* with the note *Brad, can you give this a second look?*

Because so many of the stories seemed the same he began reading their cover letters with more interest. Most of them were short, and many of them began by thanking the editor for his kind feedback on a previous story where he'd encouraged the writer to submit again. He found it odd that most of the letters listed their stories' word counts as exact numbers rather than rounding them to the nearest hundred or thousand, as if the specificity indicated some greater care on the writer's part. After the introductions the cover letters moved on to one-paragraph bios of the writers, all of which followed the same format he'd seen in the department newsletter and on fliers for literary events. Most of the writers noted some form of graduate degree (usually an MFA but very often a PhD) and all of them listed publications in which their fiction had previously appeared or was forthcoming. If he recognized one of the publications it was always placed at the start of the list, though the vast majority of others were literary reviews or magazines he hadn't heard of. Many of the cover letters listed some sort of teaching position that the writer currently held or had held in the past, and one of these mentions caught his eye because the writer proudly announced that *I'm an Assistant Professor of creative writing at—* and then the name of the university. When he read the sentence he couldn't remember whether *assistant professor* should be capitalized when it didn't come directly before a person's name. It wasn't until later that he realized the assistant professor's bio had stuck out because none of the other writers mentioned being any level of professor and instead couched their jobs through phrases like *I currently teach English composition at...*, *I've taught creative writing at...*, and *I'm an instructor of English at...*, which all felt like smoke-and-mirror ways of saying they were adjuncts. He felt sorry for the writers with less prominent publication lists and wondered how much a *Long Grass* acceptance would help them get the careers they seemed to want so badly.

The fiction queue ran for sixty-three pages reaching all the way back to September; at one point he counted forty submissions sent on a single day. He recalled the scene in *Tristram Shandy* where the narrator realizes he's written hundreds of pages of his life story before even getting to the day of his birth and that it's taken him an entire year to write those hundreds of pages, so that if he kept up that pace he'd continue to fall 364 more days behind for every year he spent writing. He wondered how many other grad students Brad had coerced into reading this endless pool of stories and whether it would ever be enough to reach the end of the submission pile while thousands of other stories were being written by thousands of other writers desperate to be published and build up impressive bios that would help them get well-paying tenure-track jobs like the assistant professor's. In that raw, hopeless moment it seemed that Flip was doomed to pore through the submission pile forever while the rest of the world continued to grow, change, and move forward.

33

"HAVE A SEAT," Stark began without looking up from his laptop. "I got your email and I'll be right with you."

Right with you in this case meant the time it took Stark to finish typing out the email he was writing, skim through several more, and fill out a short but official-looking university form while Flip searched for something of interest around the office to look at. When Stark finished he turned to Flip and asked, "So, what did you want to talk about?"

That Stark could somehow be oblivious to why he was here struck Flip as either forgetfulness or a carefully staged show of ignorance so he could avoid making the first move. "Did you read what I wrote about switching dates with Brad for my second workshop?"

Stark nodded without indicating judgment. "Yes, I did."

Flip now regretted meeting with Stark directly since this would force him to admit his shortcomings face-to-face. "I suppose I just wanted to make sure that was all right and that you knew I was taking until Thanksgiving to finish my submission."

Stark uncrossed his legs. "Of course that's fine. The schedule's meant to be flexible, and since everyone's in different places with different projects I don't want you to feel like you *have* to submit pages at a certain time." He paused to let this more amiable summation settle before continuing. "But then you also know that you've only got so much time and funding to get your MFA thesis done, and novels take a lot of time and energy to finish—especially when you're just starting out."

"Yes," Flip said as guilt overcame him again. "I know."

"I also don't want you to feel pressured into thinking that you have to finish a perfect, publishable novel during your MFA," Stark went on. "My first novel was over four hundred pages, and what little plot it had didn't go anywhere, so it wasn't until my second one that I was actually able to get it picked up. Melvin just talked to me about finishing a short story collection for his thesis instead of a novel, so you might think about that direction too. It'd also give you time to get some more publication credits, which will be a good boost for your CV when you go on the market."

Flip wondered how much of this was Stark's way of telling him that both his novel and his reputation didn't hold water. "I know that," he said, "but this novel means a lot to me and I'd really like to finish it."

Stark rested his chin in his palm and didn't say anything while Flip heard the dull thud of footsteps in the hallway. When Stark finally spoke his words carried less conviction than before. "If that's what you'd like to do, that's fine," he said. "I only suggest you keep editing it more vigorously. It's tempting to get attached to our early drafts because they mean a lot to us, so you shouldn't be afraid to kill your darlings and try something new if you think it'll help your novel. Does that make sense?"

Flip said "Yes" very quickly.

"Good," Stark said and then looked Flip over as if trying to decide whether he was lying. "Is everything else going all right?" he asked with more concern.

Flip wanted to tell Stark that things weren't going all right, that his novel had no direction, his classes were mind-numbing, his officemate was an idiot, his career prospects were hopeless, and that he had no furniture, one friend in the entire department, and a hopeless crush on someone else's girlfriend.

"Everything's going fine," he said.

Stark nodded again. "That's good because grad school isn't easy, and you guys have a lot to keep on top of. Things were hectic when I did my MFA fifteen years ago, but I can't imagine managing everything you do now, especially with the stipends having stayed the same." He looked at the typewriter by the window, then back at Flip. "Of course you've got to focus on your writing, but you can't forget that grad school is also about getting to know your colleagues and learning how to be a contributing member of the academic community. The people you meet in grad school are the ones who'll help you as you move through your writing career, but they're also there for companionship and to go out for drinks with because at the end of the day we all need to get out of our own heads. It's scary to suddenly realize that your station in life is set and that the time for freedom and experimentation is gone, so you start to wonder whether you should have taken more advantage of those earlier times." He gestured at the heap of books and papers on the desk. "I sometimes remember how different my life was before I started working here—even being a grad student felt liberating compared to the responsibilities that come with an academic job." His eyes took on a disconcerted look as they moved toward the window. "But I shouldn't say that because after you get settled all the responsibilities that come with being a career writer start to blend together into this larger conversation that's fulfilling in its own way, until after a while that becomes your life. Then, it just is what it is."

Stark had begun speaking more and more slowly until he finally trailed off to stare at the drawn window blinds and the slivers of light poring through their edges. He sat like this for some seconds, his forehead wrinkling and his lips tightening as his eyes focused on something far, far away. It was the look of someone who existed separately from the rest of the room, separately from the rest of the English building and the campus and the entire Midwest, the look of someone existing solely within the mind and its secret, endlessly rushing thoughts. Stark held this far-off look for what seemed like a long time before turning back to Flip with his eyes wide. "Does that make sense?"

34

Mary-Beth Reynolds is a fourth-year literature PhD whose dissertation, A Nose by Any Other Name: The Olfactory Organ in Nineteenth Century Literature, *focuses on the symbolic uses of the human nose in British and American literature of the period. Her scholarly articles have appeared or are forthcoming in* The Kentucky Journal of Victorian Literature, The Journal of Arcane American Lit, *and* The Wilkins Micawber Journal of Literary Studies.

TIME WAS running out.

There wasn't going to be any MFA thesis novel if Flip couldn't write one, and this revolting realization forced him to sit at the folding table and squeeze out new, painfully labored openings that all felt horribly forced but that he relegated to a hard drive folder optimistically labeled *Alternates* since he feared his final submission day would arrive and find him still laughably empty-handed. He knew the openings were garbage, knew they would continue to be garbage without the confidence of tone and certainty of a story arc that moved readers into a novel, and knew at every moment of the strained, futile process that his novel lacked these things and stood no chance of functioning in even the most mediocre sense without them. When the hopelessness grew too great to ignore he would step away from the laptop and lie on the empty living room's carpet and think about the novel and what it could do and what it wasn't doing and what people like Stark and Craig and Lawrence and Kendall and Brad wanted it to do. Sometimes these spells of lying led him to jot down promising, vitally coherent notes he felt sure held the potential to drive the novel up from mediocrity, yet

the next time he opened his notebook and saw the trite or inco-
herent thoughts he'd scribbled out for the misplaced drivel they
were he gloomily slashed X's through them before moving on.

As the failures grew more frequent and the doubt that he could
ever fix the novel more real, he began reflecting more and more on
the way the novel's characters and events connected so that when
he walked through the grid of alphabet streets or sat pretending
to read a student's paper at the writing center or lay on the air
mattress thinking about what it would be like to sleep with Derzen
his mind returned always to the novel as it had so much more
often in the days when writing it had been new and exciting and
sitting down to work had been a matter of merely squeezing all of
his ideas onto the page. The difference was that in this new, more
difficult writing stage the whole thing felt like an intricate puzzle
needing to be solved while everyone in the department watched
over his shoulder.

In this way the time passed quickly until November was halfway
over and the last of the leaves fell from the city's trees, though
without any snow to cover the university commons the campus
stretched onward in a sickly shade of brown. The Tuesday-before-
Thanksgiving deadline loomed frighteningly close, and when he
had only a week to go and nothing to show for it he slumped in his
office chair with his head on the desk hoping no one would walk
past and see him stewing in his failure. It was this feeling that
stirred him, for the first time in weeks, to go see Derzen.

Derzen wasn't in her office, but Mary-Beth was, and when he
stepped through the doorway her head jerked away from her
computer like a baby bird eager for food. "Hi!" she exclaimed with
her cheeks raised in youthful excitement. "What brings you here?"

Since the night of Brad's party Flip's only contact with Mary-
Beth had been their occasional meetings in the hallway, where-
upon Mary-Beth would smile her energetic smile and call out, "Hi
Flip!" often from very far away. These conversations, however,
had never progressed beyond superficial summaries of his classes
or Mary-Beth's teaching. Now she sat at the desk opposite
Derzen's surrounded by her stuffed animals and the violet-hued

undersea poster tacked to the wall. Flip wondered how long she'd been engaged and whether she was as young as her office décor suggested.

"Just needed a break," he said. "Is Derzen around?"

Mary-Beth shook her head, causing her ponytail to bounce back and forth between her shoulder blades. "No, she's been in and out for most of the month. I know she has to get a draft of her poetry thesis to her advisor before she leaves for break."

"Oh," Flip said. He thought of older novels where guys came calling at girls' dormitories while they were out and had to leave elaborate messages with their roommates, scenes that felt decidedly alien in the age of texting. "I haven't seen her for a while either and just thought I'd say hi."

Mary-Beth folded her legs on the seat of her chair and stretched her arms upward in a flexing of muscles that revealed a thin sliver of skin between her jeans and blouse. With her arms still in the air she bent back the fingers of her left hand with her right to stretch the muscles in her wrist, then switched and did the same thing with the fingers of her right hand. She then extended one of her legs horizontally toward Flip, rotating it clockwise at the ankle, continuing this display for several seconds during which Flip thought about saying goodbye but stood unsure how to respond.

He wondered where Derzen was and what she was thinking about.

He wondered whether she'd made any progress on her PhD applications.

He wondered what she'd thought of him after their last meeting.

Then he wondered whether he should have sought her out sooner because it felt like he hadn't seen her in a very long time.

All of these thoughts ran through his head while Mary-Beth finished her yoga pose and brought her arms back to her sides. On the way down her elbow knocked a stuffed rhinoceros off of her desk, and with a cry of "Oops!" she reached over to return it to its place between the giraffe and the hippopotamus. When she finished she said brightly, "Well, she's definitely coming to the grad student gathering on Friday, so I'm sure you'll see her there."

"What grad student gathering?" Flip asked.

Mary-Beth froze in the act of returning her feet to the floor and formed her mouth into a tiny o. "Ah—a bunch of us from the department always go out the Friday before Thanksgiving before the early people leave for break. Kendall's organizing it this year and I know some of the new people are coming, so I thought someone might have invited you." She paused awkwardly as if contemplating the best course of action, then asked, "Would you like to come?"

In a flash Flip considered that such a gathering probably wouldn't be any fun, had clearly been organized to not include him, and would involve at least a few unavoidable interactions with Kendall. However, Derzen was going to be there.

"Sure," he said. "Sounds like fun."

Mary-Beth said, "Okay!" with more certainty than before, then, "I'll add you to the group chat." When they'd exchanged information Flip asked her what she'd been working on when he came in.

"Just dissertation stuff," she said. "Nothing too important."

"That's cool," Flip said. "What's your dissertation about?"

A disconcerted look came over Mary-Beth's face as her cheeks lost their normal rosiness and several stutters emerged from her trembling mouth. "Well," she stumbled, "it's about the different uses of the nose in nineteenth century literature, which seems really silly when you say it like that, but the nose was actually a common symbol of British class structure at the time in terms of its size and whether people bothered to mention it at all, plus the size and shape were really important, like whether someone had a bulbous nose or a hawk nose or even a snub nose. The American Romantics used the nose too, though not to the same ends, and their fascination with the nose was actually more abstractly tied to the ideals of Protestantism and the afterlife, mostly through the act of blowing one's nose as a way to evoke the soul's escape a la sneezing, but then there's also wiping one's nose or the use of handkerchiefs, even though the Transcendentalists were already using this more naturalistic way of conveying the nose as a pathway to our spiritual essence and denoting our singular nature since we have two eyes but only one nose. Then there's the play on words that comes from *nose* and a person who *knows* something or the act of *know*ing something, which then becomes *knowledge* in general, so you have this link between the nose and intelligence which you see more and more often throughout the later period."

Though Mary-Beth's topic had initially drawn Flip in, he'd lost all hope of following her explanation by the end of her first sentence. "Sounds like a big project," he said to end the conversation, and it seemed that Mary-Beth looked secretly relieved when he asked what time the grad student gathering would start.

35

"ARE YOU going out for pre-Thanksgiving drinks with the others?" Flip asked Jackson even though he already knew the answer.

"Nah," Jackson said. "I used to go to events like that before I had my breakdown, but afterward I didn't see the point, and after a while people stopped inviting me."

Flip wondered what the others must think about Jackson and whether they secretly judged him for not attending social gatherings. "If I went, do you think it'd be a good way to form connections with people?"

Jackson smirked. "With people, or with Derzen?"

Flip sputtered before righting himself again. "Both. I feel like what I'm doing now just isn't working and that becoming a more regular part of department life would help me more than staying in my room all the time."

They walked side-by-side along the campus's northern edge away from the football stadium as a dry, empty chill filled the air. The block ahead of them opposite the fraternity row had been barricaded by an orange fence that bulged awkwardly outward and bore a sign reading CONSTRUCTION AREA—SIDEWALK CLOSED. Beyond the fence's circular holes lay an enormous, fifty-foot pit with sloped ramps to allow access for pickups and yellow construction vehicles Flip didn't know the names of. A towering crane in the pit's center moved rust-colored beams from one pile to another and the sound of terrible screeching, engine clattering, and splitting rock filled the street ahead of them.

"If you think being a part of department life's important, then you should go," Jackson said, "especially if your alternative is another hour sitting in front of a blank computer screen. It's the same with Derzen—if you really want to be with her and think that's more important than causing a stink with Kendall, then you should do something about it. We can't help who we're attracted to, but we can help what we do about it."

Flip looked toward the street in search of a place to cross as they neared the construction fence. "I've been thinking a lot about whether you can succeed as a writer in academia while still being yourself, and I know Derzen thinks about that too. I feel like if I knew the answer to that I could sweep her away from Kendall like in *Lucky Jim* so we could make great art together on our own terms. Am I crazy for thinking that?"

Jackson continued past the SIDEWALK CLOSED sign and along the orange fence without speaking, clacking his fingers against the holes while Flip fell in step behind him. "At the risk of sounding like a Haruki Murakami novel, think of it this way. The reality we live in is made up of two different worlds. One's the world you and I talk about where we value real human thoughts and interactions. In this world people are stirred by art and literature that show them things about the world and the actions they take hold real meaning for themselves and others. That's the genuine world. Then there's another world where people do things for material gain because they have to work jobs and make money, so they live their lives in a way that allows them to sustain themselves and maybe even their families. Think about people who go through mind-numbing motions at jobs that insult their intelligence on a daily basis just so they can earn a paycheck, then compare that life to a grad student who writes an article just to score a publication and a CV boost—that's the materialistic world. If someone's born rich or if they're really clever or lucky, sometimes they can join both worlds together and live life in a meaningful way while also making enough to live, but the vast majority of people have to separate the two. Unfortunately, when that happens they end up spending more time in the materialistic world." Without warning he faced Flip with his fingers looped around the links of the construction fence. "Once you get down to it, though, everyone really wants the genuine world as long as they still believe in it, so if you can show that world to people in a way that feels right you can draw them away from the material and toward something much better. Derzen's no different, and I think both of you are more attuned than anyone else here to what really matters."

The sound of drills and jackhammers roared at them from behind the orange fence. "Do you honestly think everyone really wants to live in the genuine world?" Flip asked.

"Yes," Jackson said as he started walking again. "Because that's the only world that has meaning."

36

THE BAR Kendall had chosen for the pre-Thanksgiving outing was a high-ceilinged carpeted lounge on a downtown side street across from a Buffalo Wild Wings, three-quarters empty on a Friday night and staffed only by a cheerful bartender wearing an anachronistic pair of suspenders. The bar's decor suggested that its owners were eager to lure in a more upscale demographic: oversized works of art spray-painted with curls, whorls, and zig-zags that didn't quite cover the entire canvas hung on the walls, and hand-labeled dispensers of cucumber-, peach-, and lemon-flavored water with varying amounts of rind occupied prominent positions beside the bar. A pair of black leather couches sat unoccupied in one corner, while in another a group of middle-aged men and women with their shirts tucked in sat on stools around a high table talking amicably. All of the men and women emitted a striking aura of what Flip viewed as adulthood in its purest, most undefiled form.

Flip had decided not to show up as late as he had to Brad's party but accidentally took 12th Street instead of 11th and couldn't find the bar in its location between O and P Streets. As a result he'd found the other grad students already there, spread out in groups of three or four along with their significant others. Through chance or preoccupation the first people he'd noticed after walking in had been Derzen and Kendall, who stood in front of a railing near the high tables talking with Lawrence and his girlfriend, a blonde girl wearing something very close to a business suit who stood still and nodded along to what the others were saying. It felt disconcerting to see Derzen and Kendall actually together, and though they stood within several feet of one another, Kendall's legs were planted a little too squarely apart and Derzen's posture appeared unnaturally stiff as she leaned against the railing. Kendall wore a green polo shirt and khakis while Derzen wore a black blazer over a turquoise blouse patterned with diagonal lines, a pairing that seemed more in tune with the bar's desired attire.

Flip took in all of this upon entering before abandoning any chance of joining Derzen and Kendall's conversation. Instead he ordered a beer that he resolved to sip as slowly as possible so he wouldn't have to spend money on a second one, and to avoid looking like he had nowhere to be, he made his way to where Craig and Melvin stood talking in a corner.

"There's one thing they don't tell you in grad school, man, and that's that the small press racket is bullshit," Craig announced in a moderately loud voice. "Did you know these small presses get even more query letters than agents do? I found this one press, man, and the guy told me they got four thousand novel queries a week, and that's not even including short story collections!"

"Who told you that?" Flip asked. Across from him Melvin nodded silently in agreement.

"An old friend of mine reads manuscripts for Sandusky Press," Craig went on, his words tumbling out with unceasing momentum, "and he says that even if you make it through all their crazy filters and actually get a book accepted, all they'll give you is a fifteen percent royalty deal plus a few comp copies, so even if you sell a thousand copies, if you tally up all the time you spent writing the book it comes out to like eleven cents per hour, which is literally slave wages."

Melvin nodded again. "True, true."

"But also," Craig went on, "what's the fucking point if they're just going to list your book on Amazon along with the millions of other small press books whose authors are more famous than you, so after you sell all the copies you can to your high school friends who saw it on social media the only ones left to buy it are random people who'll order it on their e-readers by mistake. The industry's fucking doomed, which is why you need a tenure-track job to keep you afloat if you're going to write."

Flip did a double-take at this. "I thought you said tenure-track jobs weren't worth going for because they forced you to compromise your writing."

"I never said that," Craig declared as he sloshed his beer onto the high table. "But if I did it was because I didn't understand how the business worked back then. Those high-paying tenure-track jobs hook you into a bunch of networking avenues you can use to get your books published. How do you network? Go to an academic conference. Who goes to academic conferences? People with tenure-track jobs, that's who!"

Melvin nodded again. "You're definitely right. I've written three query letters for my novel and had them reviewed by professionals, so I figure I'm almost ready to start writing the rough draft. Of course, if I can secure a tenure-track job before the end of my third year I'll be in even better shape since then I'll have my job prospects squared away and can really focus on my writing."

Flip looked away out of frustration and saw Derzen leaning against the railing, now turned almost entirely toward the other side of the room. It was conceivable that she hadn't seen him come in.

Craig had begun swiping rapidly on his phone while Melvin spoke. "Man, you know what's great is fucking Tinder—I went on three dates yesterday and two of them were good, and I'm meeting another grad student who does crop physiology right after I finish up here. I mean, I've been seeing this one girl I'm pretty into on the reg for a few weeks, but it literally never hurts to see what's out there!"

And Melvin said, "Amen to that. My girlfriend's going to move out here and start looking for jobs as soon as she finishes her Marine Biology degree."

Flip turned away out of fear that he might say something sarcastic. He shifted to get a better look at Derzen and Kendall: Derzen sipped from a curved glass of sparkling red liquid with a slice of orange, and he wondered what the drink was called and whether she'd known it would come with an orange when she'd ordered it. Beside her, Kendall nodded very quickly in response to something Lawrence said and gestured with his closed fist in a manner Flip found unbelievably pretentious. Derzen appeared to be engaged in the conversation, but only half so, her responses delayed a split-second as if parroting the actions of someone genuinely interested.

Flip moved closer to the bar to study the other grad students he knew from his classes or from seeing their faces in the English building—even his third officemate who still hadn't come back for his laptop and books was there drinking a Heineken and talking with one of the Comp-Rhet students, and Flip considered the possibility that if he hadn't come across Mary-Beth in the office he would have been the only grad student besides Jackson not in attendance, thus making them department outcasts together.

He heard someone coming up behind him and turned to see Mary-Beth and the broad-shouldered fiancé he'd met at Brad's party. "Flip, you came!" she said with a welcoming burst of energy. "It's good to see you!"

Flip sensed an ulterior motive to Mary-Beth's greeting but smiled to convey the impression that he was having a good time. "Good to see you too," he said.

"You remember Griff, don't you?" Mary-Beth said with an exaggerated gesture at the fiancé, who gave a low grunt as he gripped Flip's palm in an overly firm handshake. "I was just telling him how you were from New England, and his company just sent him on a business trip to Delaware—isn't that funny?"

Flip knew nothing about Delaware besides its being referenced in *Wayne's World*. "How was it?" he asked.

Mary-Beth's fiancé said, "Kinda boring," in a way that made clear he wasn't interested in talking about Delaware. In an attempt to continue the conversation he added, "Business trips get pretty repetitive because everywhere you go is basically the same."

Flip turned to Craig and Melvin in search of some means of escape but found them absorbed in another conversation about agents. "Yeah," he said to the fiancé, "I hear that."

Mary-Beth announced that she was going to get a drink and left Flip with the fiancé in an awkward silence. The fiancé, however, seemed not to care about this and stood holding his beer, his round eyes focused on a point in the distance, the stiff collar of his shirt poking out from the neck of his sweater and traces of curly white hair sticking out of his ear. He raised his eyes to meet Flip's and abruptly asked, "So, have you been to a Prairie Fire game yet?"

Flip said, "No," then, "Excuse me a minute," and walked off in Derzen's direction.

The railing where Derzen stood was about twenty feet away, but reaching it required navigating around the half-wall separating the bar from the rest of the room and sidestepping around a cluster of grad students sharing anecdotes about the head of the department's drinking habits. Flip had just wound around the cluster when he felt a burly arm around his shoulder.

"You worthless son of a bitch," Brad said menacingly as his fingers pressed on bone. "I know what you're planning and you might as well drop it because it's not going to work, you hear me?"

Flip felt every last ounce of blood drain from his face as his head grew foggy and his legs threatened to collapse. His voice seemed incapable of rising above a dull croak. "What do you mean?" he gasped.

Brad held the menacing expression a second longer before bursting into jubilant, gleeful laughter and slapping his palm against his knee. "Ha ha ha! I'm just fucking with you, buddy. You should have seen the look on your face! You must have a guilty conscience or something because I can't remember the last time I got somebody that bad!"

Flip laughed meekly. "You really had me there," he said, feeling Brad's grip steering him further from Derzen and back toward the laughing crowd of grad students.

"You don't know how to take a joke, do you?" Brad asked. "That's because you're the big-time writer working on your super-secret novel, ha ha!"

Flip laughed meekly again. "Ha ha."

"Actually, I'm glad you came tonight because I was hoping we could have a little chat," Brad said as he steered Flip toward an empty table even further from Derzen and Kendall. "I know you've got a novel submission to turn in before next week, but I was hoping you could squeeze in a few more *Long Grass* submissions over Thanksgiving—you know, to help us catch up. And let me tell you what would *really* be perfect," he went on, placing his hands apart and speaking with mounting excitement, "if you could read an extra ninety stories before we get back from break. Ninety might seem like a lot, but it's only ten stories per day, or less than that if you start tonight, and let me tell you, now that you've been reading for a while you'll get through ninety like nothing!" He finished the pitch with a snap of his fingers.

A deep feeling of helplessness had overcome Flip while Brad spoke, but all he could say was, "I'll see what I can do."

"Great!" Brad said and reached out to shake Flip's hand. (Why was everyone in grad school always shaking hands?) "I'll put you down for ninety then—but if you can't finish them all, no pressure." He took a sip from his beer before continuing. "Now if you'll excuse me, I've got to make the rounds, but of course I wanted to stop and see how you were doing."

When Brad had moved on to another table Flip refocused on the task at hand. The Derzen-Kendall-Lawrence group was still engaged as before, Mary-Beth's forlorn-looking fiancé had found an empty barstool and scrolled through something on his phone, and Craig shouted at Melvin as he waved his hands in all directions. Flip took and exhaled a deep breath; this was what it meant to be alone in a public place, though being here felt different than being in the office because at least in the office he had actual work to distract him, whereas here the only alternative to socializing was to withdraw into your own world and stand out even more as someone who didn't fit in. He wished Jackson were here to talk to so that people wouldn't think he was having a bad time, but Jackson was strong enough to not care what people thought and didn't need public acceptance to boost his self-esteem.

He thought again of what Jackson had said about genuine interactions existing separately from ones made for material gain, then recalled times from college or even earlier when both ends had met and the things he'd said and did had mattered while also yielding tangible benefits. Then he thought again of the party scene in *Lucky Jim* where Dixon steals Christine Callaghan away in a pilfered taxi while Bertrand's off schmoozing with Christine's rich uncle, and how well the scene worked because of that bold, beautiful way Dixon took action to make things happen, and how his doing so united both worlds at once.

No one ever got anything by watching from the sidelines. He walked over to talk to Derzen.

She turned in mid-sip as he approached, her eyebrows raised and a sly smile creeping across her face. The smile did wonders to boost his confidence, and he slid alongside her at the railing opposite where Kendall still talked to Lawrence and Lawrence still stared emptily into his drink. Lawrence's girlfriend looked at Flip inquisitively, though Kendall appeared to take no notice of him.

"Are you having a good time?" he asked Derzen.

The glassy look returned to Derzen's eyes as she shrugged and said, "Of course. How about you?"

Flip said, "Of course," too in a tone designed to match hers, then immediately regretted it since his main intention had been to approach her honestly and now he hadn't even been able to do that.

As he pondered what to say next Kendall seemed to acknowledge that his presence could no longer be ignored and turned to face him, edging a bit closer to Derzen while extending his hand for Flip to shake. "Hello Phil," he said brusquely, his eyes darting to the floor. "Glad you could make it."

Flip sensed he was in a weak position and smiled a wide smile. "It's always good to come out and see people," he said, though in the moment this too felt like a lie or at least an exaggeration. Since Lawrence had taken advantage of the pause to begin talking to his girlfriend, Flip looked at Kendall, then back at Derzen, and asked as casually as he could, "What are you two doing for break?"

"I'm flying home early tomorrow," Derzen said with some hesitation. "I haven't been back for a family Thanksgiving in a while, so I decided to take an extra few days off this year."

"That sounds really nice," Flip said, realizing as he said this that it sounded a little too warm. To prove he wasn't excluding Kendall from the conversation he asked, "Are you going too?"

A slight gurgle rose from Kendall's throat. "No trip East for me this year. I'm staying to finish some work and then driving to my family's place for Thanksgiving. My mother's a big fan of the traditional Thanksgivings where she can be surrounded by all her kids, so you know how that goes." He said this with a twinge of disdain that felt carefully rehearsed.

Flip tried to decide the best response to this when Derzen said, "He's exaggerating. She's really only been like that since your brother and his wife moved to North Dakota for that job and he had to work over Christmas, and after that she got a lot more protective of her holiday time. She barely let you come to New York last Christmas, remember?"

"That was different," Kendall said, looking firmly in Derzen's direction. "That was the obligatory bring-the-significant-other-home-to-meet-the-family holiday, and you remember how that went."

Derzen's voice took on a playful tone. "I thought it went okay."

"It would have been if they'd kept their jokes to themselves," Kendall said. "Certain comments about where people come from can be misconstrued when you're making a first impression."

Flip felt like a small child who'd walked in on its parents fighting and now had to listen to their subdued attempts at disguising it.

"I hear you," Lawrence said, turning away from his still very bored-looking girlfriend. "If I made one mention to my mother about not being home for Christmas she'd tear me a new one, that's for sure."

Derzen's tone, though still gently teasing, now contained a trace of annoyance. "That's what happens to parents when their kids start getting married."

"I don't think that has anything to do with it," Kendall answered in a way clearly meant to end the conversation.

The time was ripe for a change of subject, and Lawrence spoke first, bringing up a recently graduated PhD student whose name felt vaguely familiar from other conversations Flip had overheard. Said student had been lucky enough to procure a book contract with a press whose name also felt vaguely familiar, and said contract had served as a stepping stone to an assistant professor job at a large university in a nearby state. The story's apex concerned some emails Lawrence had recently exchanged with the new assistant professor, and his voice rose in both excitement and pitch as he revealed how their former colleague had admitted to feeling overwhelmed by the multitude of faculty meetings and committee assignments that were making it difficult to finish his book revisions by the deadline. Lawrence revealed this last piece of information with a relish that just barely bordered on gloating.

"That's just as well," Kendall announced with a smirk. "He only got called in for the interview because he'd worked with Kiernan Henderson during his MFA and Kiernan happened to be on the search committee. Frankly, I'm surprised he was able to clean his novel up enough to get it accepted."

Though Derzen's gaze had followed the conversation intently, her face showed a distinct lack of interest as she clutched her sparkling red drink. Lawrence's girlfriend snuck a glance at her watch as Lawrence mentioned a rough portion of the novel he'd recalled workshopping the previous fall.

Flip sensed that the time had come for action and leaned close to Derzen's ear. "Hey," he said in a low voice. "I wanted to say before that I'm beyond jealous of your going back East, so you'll have to get some good pizza while you're there."

Derzen smiled warmly at this. "You have no idea. I've been dying for a real cheesesteak too. And seafood."

Flip imagined a plate heaped with fried haddock and shrimp. "I miss seafood so much."

"When we go down to the city I'm going to order scallops."

"Scallops are the absolute greatest. You won't be working the whole time, will you?"

Derzen raised her eyebrows. "I just might if I can't settle in and focus. I was supposed to have a draft of my poetry collection to my thesis committee by now, and they're not going to be happy if I can't get more poems written."

"I'm in the same boat," Flip said. "I'm toast if I can't get some workshop pages together by Tuesday."

"How many do you have now?"

It felt easier now to admit the truth. "None I feel comfortable sharing."

Derzen's eyes widened in mischievous delight. "That's not many, is it?"

Kendall's interruption prevented Flip from answering, who turned toward them with a cry of, "Don't tell me you're going to spend the weekend before break talking about work." He smiled wryly and his voice carried more exuberance than Flip had ever heard it convey.

Lawrence smiled a grin reminiscent of Bugs Bunny. "I think that's something we can all agree on."

Derzen pulled toward the half-circle around the high table, though her body remained against the railing. "You know how it is," she said. "Work never ends."

Flip's heart began beating faster as he became aware of how close he was to something very real, something that clearly existed between him and Derzen but that kept getting interrupted before it could run its course. More people had entered the bar in the time they'd been talking, older people who now occupied the empty tables and couches so that the room around them had begun to feel very crowded. He watched the people with their tanned cheeks and salt and pepper hair and wrinkled necks and outdated jewelry as if for the first time and contemplated how neatly everything around him seemed to fit together.

"I don't think it's wrong to talk about writing on a night like this," Flip heard himself saying. "I mean, the deadline stuff is a pain, but isn't it important to talk shop with like-minded people as much as possible since it helps us keep improving?"

Derzen appeared interested in this but said nothing.

"Of course talking about writing's a good thing," Kendall said with authority, "but it's always easier to talk about the unpleasant tasks that go along with writing, like deadlines and committee problems, and that's what we're all trying to get a break from."

"Hear, hear," Lawrence said, raising his glass to the ceiling.

"But we could talk about just the writing if we wanted to," Flip said, aware that it was far too late to back down. "I could talk about my novel and you could talk about yours and we could trade ideas and create a closer-knit group that felt more like a real creative community."

Kendall's gaze wandered back to Flip's general direction. "That's what workshop's for, last I checked, and if you're interested in forming some kind of writer's group outside of that I'm sure there are plenty of people in the local community who'd be interested." He said this in a way that implied such activities were beneath him. "That's why I'm glad we don't have any non-degree seekers in our workshop since their approach tends to be more amateurish and you have to do a lot of hand-holding."

"What do you mean, amateurish?" Flip asked in a tone of confrontation.

"Oh, you know," Kendall said, "people who come in because they had some success writing as undergrads or writing for their friends and think they can play with the big kids even though they don't understand point of view or how to use commas with their dialogue. The worst part is when they bring in genre fiction and you have to pretend it's on the same level as all of our work."

"Who says it can't be?" Flip said, aided in part by the effects of the beer he'd begun drinking faster. "Tolkien and Philip K. Dick wrote genre fiction and they've earned their places with the best of them."

Kendall's gaze narrowed. "But that level of genre writing's few and far between, you have to admit."

"Who cares how common it is?" Flip said with more energy. "All that matters is whether people find something rewarding in what they read, even if it's only a few hours of entertainment, and when a writer makes that happen they've done their job."

As Flip finished this sentence Derzen gulped down the last of her sparkling drink leaving only the slice of orange peel, set the glass on the table with a clack, and spoke in a firm tone. "I think that's right—we really should be communicating more about our writing so we can build stronger working relationships."

"Mmmmmm," Kendall murmured. "That sounds like a topic for your personal statement." He held both hands above his head in emulation of a theater marquis. "*Why Most Writers Don't Want to Talk About Writing, But I Do.*"

Derzen's eyes narrowed at this, but Lawrence saved her from having to respond when he broke out of his reverie with a wide gasp. "Oh yeah, how are your applications going, anyway? Did you narrow down your list yet?"

And Kendall said, "Oh, she's working on that. I still say there's value in doing your MFA and your PhD in the same place, but *somebody* isn't sure whether she'll get in." He gave Derzen a falsely playful look.

Derzen nodded and looked slightly away. "We'll see what happens."

Flip decided to steer the conversation away from Derzen's applications before anyone could upset her further. "That's something I've been meaning to ask you guys," he said without thinking. "I can see getting an MFA—you get in, finish a book, learn the tricks of the trade, and get out—but is doing a whole PhD really necessary to become a better writer?"

Lawrence's face seemed to twist halfway around itself in confusion while his girlfriend looked intently at Flip.

Kendall, however, was unfazed. "It's not necessary if you've already got three novels and a hefty stack of journal publications, but in today's competitive climate the extra credentials make you stand out from the MFA crowd."

Flip sensed what Kendall meant by this but wasn't going to give him the pleasure. "Stand out to *whom*?" he said with careful emphasis on the *m*.

Derzen answered with a cool tone. "I go back and forth on the PhD, since on the one hand it gives you more time to publish, but on the other hand you could just as easily write and publish while doing some other kind of work, especially work that got you out in the world doing things and developing your skills."

"That's a really good way to put it," Flip said. "I don't think your career path matters as long as you put the art first and steer the rest of your life toward creating the writing you really want to."

Kendall seemed particularly incensed by this. "That's the old argument," he said. "The days of poets working alone in garrets ended a long time ago. A PhD shows you're serious about your writing and that you know how the academic world works. That's the reality, and unfortunately it's a lot rougher out there for poets than it is for fiction writers, so anyone hoping to make a career in poetry needs all the help they can get."

Derzen's gaze focused coldly on Kendall and her voice cracked as she spoke. "But of course fiction writers could make it on their own if they wanted to, is what you mean?"

"That's not what I mean," Kendall said in exasperation. "It's impossibly hard for any writer to make it on their own, but it's doubly hard for poets since no one's interested in poetry anymore and poets need to be sustained by the few grants and residencies that'll take people outside of academia if you don't want to go the teaching route."

A clear trace of annoyance had entered Derzen's voice. "That's a pretty belittling thing to say."

"I'm not belittling," Kendall spouted. "I'm saying that it's in our best interests to scoop up the opportunities we have inside academia."

"But it's doubly important for poets?" Derzen asked.

Kendall's voice grew firm again. "Don't put words in my mouth."

"That's what you said."

Flip held in his breath, aware that something substantial was about to occur.

"Fine," Kendall erupted as a faint trace of spit shot from his mouth. "Let's just say it outright—poets have a more difficult time than fiction writers, and there's no way you can earn a middle-class living writing poems when fiction writers can barely earn a middle-class living writing novels if they're insanely popular enough." He looked hard at Derzen. "Is that what you wanted to hear?"

"That's not what I'm talking about," Derzen said. "You always make it sound like any capable woman who wants to write poetry needs the crutch of academia to support her while fiction writers can do anything they want."

Kendall spoke coldly. "Stop putting words in my mouth. Poetry's just as vital a literary form as fiction."

"Then why don't you act like it?" Derzen argued with a trembling passion unlike any Flip had ever heard from her. "Why don't you honestly act like they're the same?"

"Because if they were the same they'd be paid the same," Kendall yelled in disgust. "I'm not the one who told everybody fifty years ago to forget about poetry and only sort of forget about novels. I wish poets could make six-figure salaries right out of school by simple virtue of their work being good enough, but we live in a world of people who don't give a fuck about the work we do and aren't willing to pay us for it, so we have to make real, concrete life decisions based on that."

No one spoke for a long time as Derzen ran her tongue around the inside of her mouth and finally, with trembling calmness, said, "I'm going to get another drink," and slid along the railing toward the bar.

When she'd gone Kendall looked at Lawrence and said, "Well, that was unpleasant."

At this point a strange voice spoke: It was Lawrence's girlfriend, whose quiet tone carried an inconceivably pronounced southern drawl even thicker than Lawrence's. "She seemed really upset," she said with a tug on Lawrence's sleeve.

"I know," Lawrence said before his tone turned ill-suitably optimistic. "It sounded like she was just worried about her applications, but I'm sure she'll get in somewhere."

"I'm sure she will too," Kendall said, turning half away from Flip. "The department will let her keep going based on the strength of her collection."

Flip knew there remained no further point in staying. He left his empty glass on the table and backtracked to the bar, where Derzen squeezed through the crowd of people awaiting drinks from the suspendered bartender as he jumped between the beer taps and the billing monitor.

"Hey," he said. "Kendall shouldn't have said that."

Derzen didn't look at him, her chest rising in labored gasps and her fingers shaking as she ran them through the unfolded bills in the rectangular wallet she'd pulled from her purse. "No, he shouldn't have."

"Look," Flip said. "I don't know why I even came here tonight since I see these people every day and no one's having any real fun. Your boyfriend's being an asshole and you shouldn't have to take that from him. I'm going to get out of here, and if you want to get out of here too we can go someplace and have a real conversation."

He looked her squarely in the eye when he spoke and this time he wasn't surprised when she said yes.

37

"I CAN'T stand him when he gets like that," Derzen said, staring down at the sidewalk as she trudged ahead. "Ever since he won that stupid book prize he's been acting like everything's all set for the future and he can do anything he wants."

Flip fell into step beside her with his hands in his jacket pockets. "It's a lot easier to subtly imply that you're better than someone without directly saying so because if you say it aloud you'll be openly labeled as arrogant, which no one wants."

Derzen smirked. "That sounds about right. The sad thing is that I know the money part's true and that poets have a harder time than fiction writers, and facing the reality of how the world sees you makes you feel like your work doesn't matter."

Flip nodded. "Yes."

"It makes me wonder whether I'd still have these problems if I'd kept writing fiction or been born a man or had lots of money so I didn't have to work. But then I wonder whether that's just me being envious of other people and ignoring my own shortcomings, so when I think like that I feel even more worthless because it's not really the rest of the world's fault at all."

Shortly after finishing this thought Derzen reached into her blazer pocket for her phone, read something on its screen that was almost certainly from Kendall, then keyed out a brief reply. The lights of the downtown banks and restaurants surrounded them in a blur that made the night feel very bright against the dullness of the brown, starless sky, while beside them tight lines of cars rushed through a traffic signal only to slam on their brakes when the signal at the next corner turned red.

"I know what you mean," Flip said as he tried not to think about the text. "We all have these things we want to do on our own terms, but the trick is to bring them all together somehow, and I think that looks different for everyone."

Derzen put her hands in her blazer pockets and trembled in the chilly air. "I just wish the path was laid out more clearly, you know? When I was really young I wanted to be a dancer because I loved watching the other girls move in all these flawless ways I'd never seen before, and my parents let me take ballet lessons and even brought me to this high-profile summer program in the city." She stopped and toed her right foot along a sidewalk grate before bounding into a line of angled parking spaces. "And it feels so stupid now, but there were all these older girls there who'd been dancing since they were really young and they used to laugh when I couldn't get the steps right no matter how hard I tried, and that's when I decided I didn't want to be a dancer anymore. Looking back, it was a pretty cowardly thing to do, and I'm not sure whether I let those other girls discourage me from doing something I really wanted to do, or if I wasn't really passionate enough about it to begin with and they just helped me realize it. Who knows—maybe if I still had that drive I could have become the next Martha Graham."

"True, but not many more people go to modern dance performances than read poetry."

Derzen held her mouth open in a strident laugh that reminded Flip of her hands trembling at the bar. "That's a good point."

Somewhere across the city a car horn blared and Flip became aware of his complete lack of a plan for how to proceed. The big move had been asking Derzen to leave the bar, but now that they'd made their escape his goal felt decidedly murkier. For the time being, just walking and listening felt like the right thing to do, and if at any point it no longer felt like the right thing to do, then he'd have to try something different.

"I'm so sick of worrying about money," he said, realizing for the first time how true this was. "I think making art that means something to people is the most important thing, and everything else has to come after that."

Derzen's voice carried a sarcastic tinge. "We all have to eat and pay rent."

"I know. I'd have to make enough to cover necessities, but beyond that I wouldn't need much. I think viewing success as a way of earning money makes you forget the reasons you started doing the thing you loved in the first place, and I don't ever want that to happen."

Ahead of them a crowd of students clad in t-shirts without jackets despite the cold had gathered outside the two largest of the downtown bars, raising their voices in gleeful revelry as they smoked cigarettes, leaned against walls, and circled together in ecstatic conversation. On the corner a hot dog vender Flip had never seen before squirted relish from a green bottle onto a still-steaming bun. From among the crowd there came a sudden shout and a burly, blond-haired student in an orange t-shirt shoved another, lankier blond-haired student with sagging jeans. When the lankier student recovered he shoved the first student back and more shouting erupted among the crowd. Flip motioned silently for them to cross the street.

"You say that now," Derzen said, ignoring the commotion. "But what happens when the people around you start buying houses and starting families and paying off their student loans while we're still toiling away in dingy apartments?"

Flip's words came more easily now, spurred on by his finally being able to explain something he'd never quite been able to put into words. "That's already happening, and of course I care about establishing myself and having enough money to live the life I want to, but I care about the writing more, and that's what I want to prioritize even if it means missing out on other things."

He felt Derzen drift silently closer as they walked past an office building whose clear windows revealed a leather chair-filled meeting room. "I think a lot of people would call that idealistic," she said.

"Maybe," Flip said. "I think a lot of it comes from having the confidence to really do the things you want to do and afterward everything else just falls into place. But that's easy to forget when we're way out here with people in workshops tearing our writing apart. It's also worse because we're short on money and have to deal with the sticky humid weather and being separated from the people we're closest to. I think those stresses wear away at your confidence and make you feel like you're wrong for thinking differently than everyone else. I've been feeling that way since I first came here and it's only been three months, so I can't imagine how it affects you and everyone else who's been here longer. At least at an office job everyone tacitly agrees that the work doesn't matter and that they're just doing it for the money, but since our writing is something we actually care about we have to pretend like those problems don't bother us."

"What worries me most," Derzen said, "is that my poems will never amount to anything even if writing them brings me a lot of joy, and in the end all I'll have to show for it is a couple of publications nobody's read and maybe a chapbook or two. I'll personally feel like a failure if I can't reach people with my work, and the rest of the world will definitely think I'm a failure if I can't find some kind of success. The money's only important because it represents how well you were able to reach people."

They turned on to a three-lane one-way devoid of cars and flanked by a parking garage with an auto mechanic's backlit sign. Beside them an oversized plate-glass window revealed the mechanic's office, where on the walls hung every size of accessory and fan belt imaginable. Flip hadn't imagined so many different kinds could exist.

"In an ideal world those things would match," he said. "But if the money part didn't pan out I think you'd have to realize that your writing was still meaningful even if it didn't bring you the success you wanted."

"True," Derzen said. "But that doesn't change the way people see you."

They cut across an empty parking lot with large FOR EMPLOYEES OF PAUL H. GARRETTY AND SONS ONLY— VIOLATORS WILL BE TOWED signs around its perimeter. The three-foot gap between the parking lot and the sidewalk had been covered with white stones, filling the space between four newly planted trees still held by their support strings to cheap wooden stakes. As they stepped across the rocks Derzen pulled her phone from her blazer pocket, read another message on its screen, then slipped it into her purse. It occurred to Flip just how much of the city had been set aside for parking cars.

"Do you want to stay with Kendall?" he asked.

Derzen didn't answer right away, focusing instead on the ground ahead of her. "I don't know. I think about that a lot and I think about when we first met and we used to have these great talks about writing and how it could influence people, and I'd never been with anyone who understood the power of writing the way he did. We used to show each other our work and talk about what we wanted it to do, but then we kind of stopped because we both got too busy, and now he won't even let me see his new novel."

"It's pretty overwritten," Flip said. "The whole thing's about the main character trying to convince these stuffy art dealers how great he is. The other characters are pretty one-dimensional, especially his wife, who acts as a sounding board for all his great ideas."

Derzen's walk seemed to grow imperceptibly slower. "You mean he's married?"

Flip felt an immediate need to downplay the character's relationship status. "Yeah, in the novel, even though they're both only in their mid-twenties. I figured that was a midwestern thing."

Derzen's mouth rose into a familiar smirk as she resumed her earlier pace. "In some ways. But marriage is still something I think about, like with Sylvia's fig tree and how going after some figs prevents you from going after others, but then some figs you can go after in combination with other figs to build the life you really want. What I think about most is how I could get as many of the figs I really want at the same time. It'd be nice to have a partner I could share my creative work with so we could grow together, and I wonder sometimes about what that's really like and whether I'm too old to move somewhere new and start looking again."

Flip turned to walk backwards ahead of her. "What do you mean too old? Everybody talks like we're settling in for the rest of our lives. I've already left my old life behind once, and if things don't go well here then I'll figure out a new plan and try something different until I get it right."

Derzen blew a stray strand of hair away from her forehead. "That's easy for you to say—you don't have a biological clock."

He considered the implications of this, then said, "I just hate the idea of going through motions your entire life because you feel like you have to." He walked backwards in front of Derzen a moment longer, then slid into step beside her. "You don't feel like you have to stay with Kendall, do you?"

"Of course not. But it feels sometimes like that's the best thing to do since we've been together so long and we live together and have a pretty good life even though we disagree sometimes." Her footsteps clacked slowly against the pavement. "You must think I'm pretty cowardly."

Flip's eyes centered on the gentle aura cast by the streetlamps. "I don't think that at all. But I do think it's easier to break away from a fig that's unsatisfying if you know which fig you're breaking away to."

He expected her to laugh at this but instead she said, "That makes a lot of sense," with her eyes still aimed toward the ground.

The stillness of the night surrounded them in a way that felt emptier than liberating, with the exteriors of the concrete office buildings resembling some unknowable and empty city they'd wandered to after leaving the bar. Now more than ever seemed like the time to take action in pursuit of this elusive thing that felt so meaningful though its specifics remained unclear. With a sudden boldness he asked, "Do you want to go somewhere high where we can see everything?"

She halted and turned, studying him with hesitant curiosity. "Yes," she said finally. "But where?"

Back home it would have been easy because back home they could drive in any direction to a mountain or bridge or river valley where they could admire the night view and feel like they'd transcended everything—but that wasn't the way things worked here.

"How about a parking garage?" he asked.

38

THEY WALKED across the block to the closest parking garage, a bland, shapeless structure with half-height concrete walls circling a half-dozen floors with a faux brick façade running along the bottom and a lit staircase on one corner denoting each level with a different color. Instead of taking the stairs they walked through the main gate as if in a car, passing several soda machines and credit-card-only pay stations beside the empty, glass-enclosed booths where staff sat during the day, then circling the ramps in silence past the late-model sedans and SUVs on each story, their footsteps on the pavement the only sounds. As they climbed higher more lights from the cityscape shone above the concrete half-wall until they rounded the final corner to the open roof and were surrounded by the brilliant, glimmering night with more buildings rising higher than the football stadium, their lights radiating across the city. The cold wind blew harder now, and beyond the central streets the blocks thinned into the smaller buildings of the old downtown near the great overpass curving around the brick warehouses, while farther out the electrical towers trailed along the horizon to the immense railroad yard where beyond that nothing could be seen at all.

They walked to the far wall overlooking the brightly lit night, and as they leaned against its edge the concrete felt rough and cold beneath Flip's fingers. Derzen said nothing but spread her arms wide as if she wanted to either fly away or hurl herself down to the street below, then sunk her head low to her chest. The folds of her blazer muffled her voice so that when she spoke her words seemed to come from far away:

"I just wish I didn't overthink so much."

He leaned close so that their faces were almost touching and said, "You overthink things because you're special. I can't think of anyone I'd rather have come up here with."

She looked at him with hesitant compassion and he wrapped both arms around her shoulders, slowly at first, but more firmly when her face lost its scared rabbit look and she bent her head toward his. The inside of her mouth felt very warm, and he kissed her with more vigor when he felt her fingers clutch his arm. When her mouth no longer moved with his he understood and pulled away.

Neither of them stirred until Derzen said, "That was lovely."

"Yes, it was."

She clutched his arm tighter through his jacket. "It's nice to be with someone who understands. I'm really glad we walked away from there."

"I promise I'll never talk down to you like that."

A shudder shook her neck and shoulders. "I know."

"Are you cold?"

She held him tighter. "Yes."

"Do you want to go someplace warm?"

"Not tonight."

"Do you want to stay here?"

This time she nodded and looked into his eyes as he kissed her again.

39

THEY HELD hands as he walked her home, feeling her palm slightly sweaty as she wiggled her fingers around his in a way that made it impossible to forget that she was there. Sometimes he swung both of their hands up and around in a jump-rope motion that made her laugh, and other times he stepped away from her toward the street while she stayed by the grass and their arms rose horizontally but still together. They talked little, but whenever one of them squeezed the other's palm the other would squeeze back, and whenever one of them made eye contact the other would smile and playfully make eye contact back.

She lived much further from the downtown than he did, and reaching her apartment involved traversing the endless grid of alphabet streets to a neighborhood where the intersections had yield signs instead of stop signs and the houses had low porches with swings. When she stopped beneath the shadow of a thick-trunked tree she raised his hand between them with their fingers intertwined. "Let's say goodnight here. I don't know if Kendall's back yet."

He stopped too and rested his foot against the tree. "Are you sure you don't want to go back to my place?"

She bit her lip as she let herself fall into his arms. "Nice of you to offer, but I shouldn't. I had a really good time tonight, though."

"Then how about tomorrow?"

She laughed and made no move to go. "I'm leaving tomorrow, remember? I've got a lot of thinking to do."

"Deciding which fig you want?"

"Yes."

"Then you should. It's important."

"I'll be back after Thanksgiving. On Saturday."

"So I'll get to see you next Sunday?"

Her hand gently squeezed his. "I'd like that a lot."

"You know I don't even have your phone number?"

"I'll give it to you. You can text me while I'm gone."

They made the exchange behind the tree with their phones held very close, and when they'd finished he kissed her one last time until he again felt her mouth relax and pulled away. Her eyes retained that sly, lingering look as she stepped back once, then again, then turned and walked to one of the porches several houses away, waved a final goodbye, and slipped inside.

40

HE SLEPT until one o'clock the next afternoon, partly because he was exhausted from the week and the semester and the two hours he'd spent lying awake on the sagging air mattress the previous night not quite believing what had happened, but mostly because he needed the silence of the bed to calm himself without people and distractions. When he finally uprooted himself he cooked some oatmeal from the extra-large Quaker Oats carton, heating it too long so that it stuck to the bottom of the pot but didn't burn. As it cooled he sat against the living room wall and ate each layer one at a time. Then he opened the window blinds and watched a bare tree branch blowing back and forth against the vacant sky.

He still held the empty oatmeal bowl, so he put it down and sat on the rug looking at the neighboring rooftops through the window-pane. He sat like this for a long time.

The manuscript of the novel he'd printed weeks ago on the copy center's half-price day sat on the overturned egg box where he'd left it, and without any kind of plan he began running his eyes over it in a rapid, absorbed skim that felt less like reading and more like acknowledging the disconnect between the way he'd imagined the words sounded on the page and the way they actually sounded when he read them. When he'd read six or seven pages in this way he found an instance where the gap between his imagination and the page was too great to ignore and uncapped his pen to cross out the line and replace it with one closer to what he'd imagined. Had that much time really passed since he'd written that scene, that chapter, the entire novel? It felt as if millennia had. He went back to skimming and then scratched out three more lines, an entire paragraph, and then two pages.

In the midst of one of these cross-outs he got an idea for how to change a sentence that felt emptier than it should have and wrote the idea in the right margin (one-and-a-quarter inches—he always set wider margins in his drafts even though it used more paper) to revise later. Then he realized that his description of the new sentence was basically the sentence itself without an ending, so he began writing the actual sentence until he got stuck on a word and sat twisting the end of the pen in his mouth. Not knowing how to end the sentence frustrated him, so he pulled out his thesaurus and consulted several entries until the right word came to him, not from the thesaurus page, but from somewhere else, and he wrote this new and better word in place of the old one. The scene still needed more description, so he wrote another sentence in the margin but now found a disconcerting gap between the new sentence and the rest of the scene, so he crossed out the next two lines and rewrote them too so that the scene felt cleaner and began with more of the energy he'd wanted.

The exchange felt complete but needed another scene to follow it— not immediately, but later, as a payoff for what had just happened, and he turned ahead ten pages and found another scene that was tied to the first but also lacking. This second scene contained only action without proper narration to guide the reader so that anyone unfamiliar with the subtext would miss a large portion of what he wanted to show. That subtext involved a coworker's hidden anger implied by his jostling of the office photocopier; he'd come up with the photocopier line months before, early in the morning when he'd woken up before his alarm and hadn't wanted to go to work, and he'd scribbled it onto the notepad he kept on his old bedside table for just this purpose. After more thought he drew a box around the photocopier line and crossed three slashes across the rest of the page but regretted this immediately and read back through the slashed-out text to rescue two lines that fit the scene and part of a third he could use elsewhere. The photocopier line, though, was powerful because of how much it conveyed through that one bit of action; the rest of the scene just needed to do the same. He reached over to one of the upturned egg boxes and opened one of the spiral notebooks he'd bought for forty cents back home at the local Grocery Barn and opened it to the first page.

The scene as it stood now was without form, and void, and in the empty notebook he wrote a new, clearer opening, then some dialogue, then narration. He then added the photocopier line with only a slight preposition change, then kept writing with his notebook resting on the carpet until he'd finished the two-page scene.

Afterward he leaped up and paced across the apartment with his hands running through his hair, staring out the kitchen window at a neighbor's birdfeeder hanging limply from a chain. Then he grabbed another notebook from the pile and wrote a full character outline on the front and back sides of the first page, then another outline for a second character on the second page, then an outline for a third, fourth, fifth, and sixth character until he'd run out of ideas and returned to another scene that needed fixing, though in the process he got an idea for a seventh character and wrote out a page for that one too.

In this way he wrote until long after the sun had set, working first on the carpeted floor, then, when the pain of bending over became too great, moving to the folding table and setting aside his laptop so he could work with his notebooks and printed pages spread out around him. When his pen ran out of ink he threw it in the trash and uncapped another of the same color and size, and when his wrist grew cramped he paused to massage it before picking up where he'd left off.

It was wrong to say that he wrote without stopping since pauses, reflective moments, and longer sessions of staring listlessly out the window to help him gather his thoughts truncated his work. He recalled a Bill Watterson quote about how cartoonists have to stare at a blank page for most of the day to gather their ideas and how to the layman this must look remarkably like goofing off, but these moments were as much a part of the process as the actual writing because they helped him bring the ideas to fruition and thus didn't feel like breaks at all.

He'd only eaten the bowl of oatmeal since waking up but never thought to stop for food; instead he drank glass after glass of water he refilled from the faucet and set on the floor because the risk of the wobbly card table causing it to spill all over his notebooks was too great. The dryness in the cold midwestern air made his thirst insatiable, and sometimes he reached down to drink without real- izing until the glass reached his lips that he needed to refill it. He also found himself needing suddenly and with painful urgency to urinate and would run to the bathroom to shoot clear, forceful streams into the toilet bowl with the door open, then return to work and again drink more water.

Eventually the hunger became too strong to ignore and he told himself he'd finish first the one scene, then the one chapter, and then the one narrative arc before stopping to eat, but when he'd passed these finishing points he kept going out of fear that if he stopped the next time he sat down to work the blank page would taunt him mercilessly as it had before and he'd never be able to start back up. It seemed better to work as long as he could, as late as he could, for as long as he had the energy, though as he grew fatigued and even hungrier he set the arbitrary stop time of eight o'clock, then eight-thirty, then nine, then stopped looking at the clock at all, and when the pressures of the time melted away he found a new desire to keep going and edited with more vigor until he finished a crucial climax and realized all at once that he didn't know what came next and should stop.

Hovering in the back of his mind had been the desire to text Derzen saying he hoped she'd had a good flight and reiterating that he was glad she'd stepped away from the bar with him, and when he'd texted this simple but meaningful message he lay resting on the carpet with his arms spread wide until her reply came a few minutes later and he dove across the room to his phone to read what she'd said. Hearing from her made him feel even better, and he then cooked a large pot of spaghetti to mix with olive oil and basil because he didn't have any sauce. Since he was hungry and bad at estimating how much spaghetti to cook for one person he threw too much into the pot and had leftovers for the next day. He ate in the corner of the living room away from his notebooks and the folding table, feeling physically exhausted but not sleepy.

Afterword as he rewatched *Annie Hall* on his laptop he laughed especially hard at the line where Diane Keaton's actor boyfriend tells her to touch his heart with her foot.

He slept poorly because he couldn't stop thinking about Derzen and the novel and the fear that he wouldn't be able to write again the next day. When morning came he lay wondering what Derzen was doing and whether it might be better to do something other than write that day to rest his brain even though he knew this was a terrible idea and that if he didn't use the one full day he had left he wouldn't have enough pages to submit for workshop. The malaise felt like a hangover without the headache—only the early morning urge to do nothing was the same.

In this way he wasted a good portion of the day, first in lying in bed too long, then in getting up and showering and eating breakfast more slowly than usual while he wondered whether he could replicate the previous day's feat. As the time passed this feeling grew more and more disconcerting, so he opened his red paperback copy of *Something Happened* and began reading the scenes with Slocum and Virginia and the accident folders, then the scene where the children at the summer camp viciously attack Slocum's son for not trying harder to win the relay race. Reading this filled him with new excitement and seemed to take him somewhere else, though he didn't feel ready to start writing so he also re-read the opening scenes of *Rabbit, Run* until he felt that same driving urge to create something of his own that could in some alternate dimension rival Rabbit's escape from his uninspired life. Some crucial component seemed to be missing, however, so he plugged in his speakers and began playing a St. Vincent album that he could dance and swing his arms and jump around the apartment to without caring whether the people below him were bothered, and the music both excited and separated him from the world outside that he hadn't faced for thirty-six hours: the world of the city and the MFA program and the entire Midwest, the world where the pressure of needing to produce something tangible to please people so you wouldn't be a failure anymore gnawed and scratched and wormed itself into your very being until it blocked out that secret place where the writing really came from. The music brought him back to the world where only the ideas mattered, and when at last his mind began moving entirely within the realm of the novel he turned the speakers off and sat once again with his notebook like Murphy tied to his rocking chair.

41

THE FIG WAS round, plastic, and curved at the tip in a way that was suggestive but not explicitly sexual. Its reddish-brown color closely, but not exactly, resembled the inside of a Fig Newton, and the tip was lighter than the rest, with shallow indents running down its stem to the base. He wondered how heavy or light it would feel when he held the actual one in his hand to give Derzen.

He'd found the fig online, having given up on buying a real one after talking to two confused produce clerks at two different grocery stores. The website belonged to a wholesale plastic food distributor from the West Coast whose products included passion fruit, durian, roasted chicken wings, lobster, okra, and seventeen types of sushi. They promised the most realistic food and beverage replicas sold anywhere, with a ninety-day money-back guarantee and rush delivery available. When Flip called to ask whether the rush delivery would get him the fig by Sunday even with the coming holiday the man who answered sounded like he was driving down a freeway as he assured him with some confusion that yes, it definitely would, but did he really only need just one?

He wasn't exactly sure where the idea of giving Derzen the fig had come from, only that it had appeared while editing a scene completely unrelated to figs or romance or relationships. When the idea came he stopped writing in his excitement and stared transfixed at the wall thinking first that it just might work, then that it very well could work, and finally that it would definitely work because Derzen believed in Sylvia Plath and giving her the fig would show that he understood this and wanted her to choose him. It would be his Dustin Hoffman moment of pounding on the church window in *The Graduate* to rescue Elaine Robinson from the life of upper-middle-class emptiness her parents had laid out for her, and this thought also filled him with rushing excitement as he imagined driving away with Derzen in his scratched-up Honda while Kendall stood shaking his fist.

He was already over budget for the month but the price of the fig and rush delivery didn't matter; the only things that mattered were that he'd found it and that it would arrive by Sunday. When he placed the order he felt the same triumphant thrill he'd felt at the parking garage, the same thrill he'd felt after finishing the first day of writing, and the same thrill he felt the next night when he finished typing out the last of the novel changes and emailed all seventy pages to the workshop members knowing that he'd somehow mustered the skill and dedication to make his deadline.

Then he started in on *Long Grass* submissions, though he read decidedly fewer than the ninety that Brad had asked him to.

42

HE SPENT Thanksgiving with Jackson at an Ethiopian restaurant, where at Jackson's suggestion they split a pizza-sized circle of bread the consistency of a pancake heaped with piles of meat and vegetables. The dinner was partly to celebrate the holiday and partly because neither of them had anywhere else to go.

"I'm glad you got the draft done," Jackson said as he scooped some chicken into a triangle of pancake bread. "I wasn't sure whether you'd be able to finish or if you'd resort to turning in more of the old pages. I will say that the biggest advantage of grad school is having tangible deadlines to guide your writing."

"I guess that's true," Flip admitted. "If I were working on my own I don't think I'd have spent a whole weekend writing like that."

"If you were an absolute master of your craft you could spend a whole weekend writing without even thinking about it. But it takes time to develop that kind of self-discipline."

Flip wiped the sauce off his hands. "In the past, when I've been able to write like that it was because the ideas were coming in too much of a rush to ignore and I didn't have anything else to do, so it was easy to make time to write them down. This time was different because I chose to work even when the ideas weren't coming."

"That's a sign that you're dedicated to the writing process," Jackson said. "I read your submission last night and it was good— there's still some rough spots, but it's ballsy and fun. Writers who fall into that trap of writing just for the sake of finishing lose the connection that comes with creating something fun and exciting, and we as readers can sense that in the finished product. If something's not fun for you as the writer then it's definitely not going to be fun for the reader. That's partly why I don't write anymore, because I realized that nothing I worked on would ever feel as meaningful as the stuff I wrote when I was younger. Your novel had that power from the beginning, but it's cleaner now because you fixed most of the misfires." He paused to swallow the last of his wrap. "Basically, if you're going to break the rules, make sure you do it well."

Flip thought about this as he scooped some beef on to a piece of pancake bread. He and Jackson were the only ones in the brightly colored restaurant apart from the owner, who sat in another booth reading an African newspaper. They ate in silence until Flip said, "Derzen and I left the bar together the other night and kissed on the roof of a parking garage."

Jackson raised his eyebrows but continued eating. "How'd you manage that?"

"She's upset with how Kendall treats her and I think she wants to break away from all that and be with me."

Jackson seemed to consider this as he chewed. "I'm sure Kendall won't be happy when he finds out."

"No he won't," Flip said. "But he'll just have to accept that not everyone wants to settle for a stale academic life with low odds of actually succeeding. Derzen and I talked a lot about this Sylvia Plath quote where different futures are all represented by different figs, and I think she's trying to decide about academia the same way she's trying to decide about me. When she gets back I'm going to give her this plastic fig I bought and tell her how I feel about her and that we can make our writing work together on our own terms, and I think she'll say yes because of what you said about people always wanting what's genuine."

Jackson had begun nodding while Flip spoke. "You make a strong case. Just remember no matter what happens that you went for this thing you wanted even though it seemed crazy. A lot of people never take that step, and being the kind of person who can is worth a lot even if things don't work out."

Any response Flip could have made to this would have felt inadequate, so he scooped up more vegetables with the Ethiopian bread while the restaurant owner turned the pages of his newspaper.

‹ **Derzen Draskovich**

Saturday, Nov 18 · 10:13 PM

Hey...just wanted to say I hope you had a good trip back, and I'm really glad you ditched that party with me ;-) Enjoy the wonders of civilization – we'll miss you out here...

Awww...thanks 😊 😊 It's good to be home, but of course I've been thinking about you a lot 😊

Me too...

I'll see you when you get back...!

Nov 18, 10:26 PM

 Type a Message

Derzen Draskovich

Sunday, Nov 26 ·11:09 AM

Hey there – welcome back. How was Thanksgiving?

Hey! It went really well, actually. We had a quiet dinner and I got to relax and visit my sister in the city for a day.

Very cool. Did you get cheesesteak? Or scallops?

Haha, we got cheesesteak, but no scallops 😞

Jealous.....

Anyway, if you can get away tonight it'd be good to meet up and talk about...everything. We could grab a drink somewhere, unless you'd rather just come to my place...?

Nov 26, 11:34 AM

 Type a Message

< **Derzen Draskovich** ⋮

> Anyway, if you can get away tonight it'd be good to meet up and talk about...everything. We could grab a drink somewhere, unless you'd rather just come to my place...?

I'm really sorry, Flip, but I don't think that'd be a good idea. Kendall and I talked last night and we decided we both want to work things out. I shouldn't have left the bar with you that night or gone to that parking garage, even though I think you're an amazing person, and if things were different I'd definitely want to give it a try. It's just that I have to focus on what I have right now

> I see

> Did Kendall tell you that he didn't want you to see me?

We decided together that it would be best

Nov 26, 12:22 PM

 Type a Message

< **Derzen Draskovich** ⋮

Did he at least apologize for what he said about poets being inferior to other kinds of writers?

He didn't mean it that way. He just misspoke

We talked about that a lot too

That's good, I guess, that you clarified things

Yeah, it was

I also finished a bunch of pages of my novel and they came out really well

That's awesome! I'm really happy for you

Nov 26, 12:53 PM

 Type a Message

< Derzen Draskovich

Yeah, it was

I also finished a bunch of pages of my novel and they came out really well

That's awesome! I'm really happy for you

Thanks

Anyway, I should probably get back to work. I still have a bunch of reading to do and a paper I should be working on

Yeah, me too! Good luck with the rest of your work

Thanks. You too

Nov 26, 1:11 PM

Type a Message

43

IN THE DULL gray haze of the putrid morning he called the writing center to tell them he wasn't feeling well and couldn't come in, then keyed out an email to the professor of Great Plains Studies saying the same thing. He stayed in bed for a long time unable to either sleep or wake up, curled into a ball with his eyes shut and thoughts of frustrated dejection running through his mind while beneath him the air began to slowly hiss out of the inflatable mattress at a more rapid pace until its middle sunk to the floor and left his head and legs sticking diagonally upward. When he finally moved to level out the mattress the air remaining inside shifted bulbously and seemed to run out even faster so that by noon nothing except a thin double layer of rubber remained between him and the hard bedroom floor. He then got up to go to the bathroom and peeked through the blinds, but when he saw only the endless, scathing blue of the midwestern sky above the bare treetops he climbed back under the blankets because it seemed then that nothing in the entire world was ever going to change.

Around three he got up again, ate seven slices of bread spread with peanut butter, then walked out to the Honda and drove south away from the campus and the downtown and the grid of alphabet streets, stopping at traffic lights along the main artery where the setback between the houses and the street grew wider and the houses grew newer and larger until he reached the southern suburban commercial zone with its strip malls and domestic car dealerships and enormous parking lots positioned at odd angles to the street. He turned onto this new road and drove past one shopping plaza after another filled with chain restaurants and specialty big box stores spread between the old grain storage bins rising beside the railroad tracks like the remnants of some ancient Mesopotamian city. He saw signs for Prairie Fire Plumbing and Heating, Prairie Fire Barstools and Billiard Tables, Prairie Fire Windshield Repair, and a towering billboard with a picture of a heavyset, smiling man with blond hair and a cheap blue suit who proudly exclaimed, *Here's to another winning Prairie Fire season from all of us at Andrew Voorhees Realty!*

He passed wave after wave of commercial onslaught until the space between the shopping plazas grew larger and the enormous, sprawling and empty parking lot of a church bigger than even the Home Depot or the Dick's Sporting Goods marked the line where the city ended. Beyond the church there was only empty farmland, with a few turnoffs for housing developments with names like Big Pond Lane and Meadowlark Road even though there were no big ponds or meadowlarks to be found there. When the developments too ended a sign pointed down a straight dirt road labeled 182nd Street and it seemed then that no matter how hard he tried to escape the city he'd still be entrenched within its immense and ordered grid.

He drove along the endlessly straight road past the dismal brown stretches of land lying torn open beneath shells of dead corn stems after the harvest until the land began rising over another road to form a bridge (here, in the middle of nowhere, they needed a bridge!) and he took the exit on to this second two-lane highway that felt older and more established than the one leading out of the city. Here the road ran parallel to a set of rusty railroad tracks and the towering slate-gray grain elevators again rose against the horizon, all of them silent with their bewildering assemblages of machinery, and he had no way of knowing whether they were still in use or had stood abandoned for decades. Some of the factory buildings looked newer, but a closer look at their exteriors revealed the dark bricks and metal roofing of an earlier era, their signs indicating the food products and animal feed and farming machinery and chemical herbicides that were all this strange, monoculturally empty land seemed able to produce.

He hated this new road even more than the first one, so he turned on to a smaller state highway that ran straight through more empty fields and dilapidated towns where only a mechanic's garage or gas station broke up the listless lines of one-story houses that all seemed to be painted white with the occasional Prairie Fire mailbox cover. Each town looked identical to the one before it, and it occurred to him that he couldn't recall the number of the second highway he'd driven down and didn't have his phone or even a midwestern road map to help him find his way home.

With nothing else to look at he began watching the vehicles passing by: almost all of them were white or black pickups driven by men, and all of them were either Fords, Chevys, or the occasional Dodge or GMC. One elderly driver of a white Chevy raised his hand from the wheel in a small but friendly hello, and the gesture felt so foreign in that moment that he had no time to return it before the pickup had passed and there was again only the great, open expanse of farmland and endlessly straight road. For some reason the old man in the Chevy made him think of Derzen in a way he wanted very badly not to think about Derzen. There were no other girls like her anywhere, and certainly not here, and not being able to be with her felt like some bright hopeful chunk of his being had been ripped out of his chest and thrown into a toilet. He wondered how long he would have to drive before he found something new and exciting like a city or mountain range or even a historic marker that would serve as a goal for this ridiculous, aimless trip until it occurred to him that he might not even notice if the landscape began changing gradually in ways the untrained eye couldn't detect, so that even though he'd entered a slightly different place everywhere he went would still look exactly the same. He thought about this as the afternoon sky grew darker (later than he'd expected—he was further west in the time zone than he was back home) and he became aware of a horrendously rancid stench like old dog food he suspected was fermenting inside the Honda's heater but was really coming from the thick clouds of smoke billowing from a factory on the horizon, a factory that grew larger until he could see its flat faceless walls and cramped loading bay where semi-trucks hauling caged trailers pulled in and out. A single warning light mounted on one of its smokestacks flashed on and slowly off again like the sleep light on his officemate's computer, slowly on again and then off. The railroad tracks passed behind the factory where forklifts raced by without end, while in front a chain-link fence topped by barbed wire enclosed a parking lot full of more domestic pickup trucks that were all either black or white. He turned away from the stinking factory but could find nothing else to look at besides the broken cornstalks lined up in battered rows that now appeared even darker and more skeletal in the fading light. He was breathing hard now and driving fast (what was the speed limit in a place like this?) and turned on the radio to find country music, then static, then more country music, then a pop station, then still more country music before he turned the radio off in a fit of rage. In the rearview mirror the factory still belted out gray clouds, with the smokestack light flashing slowly on and then off again and that abominable smell filling the air, and it was then that he looked out the passenger window and saw, far off along the horizon, a wooded grove.

He slammed on the brakes and pulled the Honda into the dust along the side of the road. The grove stretched along the entire horizon—it could have been a real forest, or maybe just a line of trees separating two fields. He watched it transfixed for several minutes until he realized it didn't matter whether the grove was a real forest because the important thing was that it didn't belong there and he had to reach it.

He stumbled out of the Honda into the ditch, losing his balance in the loose roadside dirt and nearly tripped on his way back up to the field where the rock-hard snowless ground had been torn open with cracks that wound their way between the mangled rows of corn. It had grown very cold and he hadn't bothered to zip his jacket; he turned behind him to see the factory smokestacks clearer than ever against the sunset and their stench even ranker and more disgusting now that he was outside. The grove was far away but he knew he could reach it if he kept moving through the lacerated rows of corn husks left behind by the harvester, tripping over some of them as he ran and smacking his shin against others with a sharp, stinging pain that lingered long after he'd resumed moving. Some of the corn husks still had seeds in them, and the yellow bits lining their uneven halves looked like geological remnants thrust from the earth like rocks after the frost thaws back home, though out here there were no rocks, only a brown, flat surface of clay and hollow cornhusks.

He kept moving through the cold but the grove still felt as far as ever while the Honda was now hundreds of yards behind him. He shivered and stopped to catch his breath only to hold it again to keep out the dog food smell, and a fear suddenly overcame him that if a wolf or an insane man with a rifle came at him in the immense empty field that he'd be left without anyplace to take shelter. The confusion of what to do was so overpowering that he fell to his knees. Being low to the ground only made the feeling worse, so he stood back up and spun around like a madman, unsure whether something somewhere was lying in wait for him in this strange and empty place.

One of his shoelaces had come untied. The lights of the factory smokestacks continued flashing slowly on again and then off, slowly on again and then off. The one swatch of color was an orange candy bar wrapper with the Prairie Fire logo caught on a cornstalk. He picked one of the tattered corn husks from the ground and threw it as hard as he could into the emptiness, though it only arched feebly upward before falling a short distance away.

44

IT WAS WITH wrenched, superhuman effort that Flip climbed up the English Department stairs the next morning, his hand tightly gripping the handrail and his head focused intently downward. His stomach felt empty and twisted from not eating, and as he climbed the stairs his vision clouded to a shimmering haze that made him pause until it cleared and he could resume climbing. The drive to the dog-food-smelling field had unsettled him as much as Derzen's text had, and both experiences now blended together in his memory making it difficult to tell where the horrible feelings from one ended and the horrible feelings from the other began. Losing her had hurt, but it had hurt worse knowing how close he'd come and how certain he'd been that she would want to build something real with him. If someone could try that hard under conditions that felt so ideal and still lose, how was it possible that anyone anywhere managed to succeed at anything?

He'd reached the third floor and shuffled past the empty hallway lounge when Kendall stepped out from behind the corner with his eyes narrowed like a demon's.

"Hello Phil," Kendall said, twisting his mouth into what an unknowing bystander would have labeled as a smile. "I thought we might have a little talk before workshop—someplace private, if you don't mind." He glared at Flip from behind his rimless glasses with a wicked, expectant look.

Flip looked back at him without answering, his vision still cloudy and his head spinning until he managed to croak out the words, "All right."

Neither of them spoke while Flip unlocked his office door and gestured for Kendall to step inside, thankful that Melvin never came in before eleven. He shut the door behind him as Kendall strolled to a position near the third officemate's desk and looked around the dull, empty room that now felt more barren than ever. Flip watched him from near the bookcase, crossing his arms in a pose meant to convey intimidation while Kendall took up a position against the filing cabinet, his hip hitting its side with a reverberating thud. "I'm sure you know very well what this is about," he said coldly.

"No idea," Flip said. "Why don't you explain it to me?"

The wrinkles in Kendall's forehead deepened. "You know the most shameless thing about all this is that you honestly don't seem to think you did anything wrong. I think when you pulled Derzen away the other night you were only thinking about your own selfish wants, and she was just vulnerable enough to go along with them."

Flip stood firm. "I asked Derzen if she wanted to leave with me and she said yes. No one forced her to do anything."

Kendall snorted. "I don't know how things work where you come from, but around here making out with someone's girlfriend in a parking garage is a pretty lowdown thing to do. People who do that kind of thing are either desperate or they're jealous, petty individuals who don't care about others. I honestly think you might be both."

This surprisingly accurate condemnation of his motives emboldened Flip with a ferocity he now fought to control. "Maybe if you treated Derzen better instead of belittling her she wouldn't be off exploring other options."

Kendall flared his lips into a sneer as he stepped away from the filing cabinet. "That's enough of that," he said. "I've wanted to tell you off ever since I first caught you hitting on Derzen at Brad's party, but I figured you could take a simple hint to stay away from other people's girlfriends." His expression held firm. "Derzen's been going through a bit of a rough patch, and she's been worrying a lot about what to do after she graduates. MFAs are useful and a solid credential, but she's not quite qualified enough for a decent job and could use more time to boost her CV for the market. There's a lot of paths we could take to develop our respective careers, so we've been talking about the best way to make that work together. Derzen's been naïve about how hard it is to get a decently paying job these days and seems to think everything will be all right if she just meanders along. She doesn't plan for the future like I do—I've had my plan laid out for a long time and I know how much work and sacrifice it takes to get the job and the life I want. Derzen wishes she was more organized when it came to her future, so she's really quite lucky to have me here to help her."

Flip felt himself breathing heavily and was struck by an odd sensation of déjà vu. He wondered whether he and Kendall were heading toward an actual, physical fight, and if so, whether he'd be able to hit him when the time came. "Did you have the same plan when you cheated on your last girlfriend?" he asked.

Kendall's eyes widened. "Who told you that?"

"That's not important," Flip said.

Kendall's mouth moved silently as he looked toward Melvin's desk, then back at Flip. "People here like to gossip," he said. "It's what happens when you're crammed into a small space and secretly competing with everyone around you. What happened a long time ago with Derzen and me was more complicated than what you pulled the other night since Derzen was single then and I was planning to break off my other relationship when the time was right, so you can't really call that cheating at all."

"Do you always spit out horseshit like that early in the morning?" Flip asked.

Kendall's voice betrayed little emotion. "It's different and you know it."

"No," Flip said with sternness rising into his voice. "It's only different because you say it's different and because you're stuck on this idiotic dream of you and Derzen getting six-figure salaried jobs in some other midwestern hell-hole after you magically beat out the other five hundred applicants for the job. You're so obsessed with living happily ever after that you can't accept anything that clashes with your one-track view of how the world works. You have to work yourself stupid and sacrifice your entire life and art to get one of those cushy jobs now that times have changed, and you can't even fathom that people like Derzen and me want something more meaningful. All you care about is impressing people with writing that everyone just pretends to like because they're afraid of looking stupid if they admit the truth."

Kendall had begun moving slowly toward Flip with his fists clenched in unmistakable fury. He stood very close and said, "Of course you'd think that, you arrogant fuck, because you've got your own special little plan all figured out. I know all about where you came from and how you think you're so much better than everybody else. No surprise either that you and Jackson get along so well since he'll still be coasting along on grad student stipends when he's fifty. You think you're too good to go to readings with the rest of us just like you're too good to take workshop with a visiting writer and too good to spend one fucking second listening to opinions that are different from yours. I'm sick of you know-it-all Eastcoasters coming out here with your indulgent experimental novels thinking you're going to turn the literary world upside down without so much as a clue how it all works. You're one to talk about times changing because whatever bygone literary era you're stuck in fucking ended a long time ago. For Christ's sake, when was the last time you read a book from the last twenty years? Maybe if you paid closer attention to contemporary fiction instead of shitting on it you'd realize it's not the Modernist period anymore, but writers like you think you can churn out whatever the fuck you feel like while spending Mommy and Daddy's money in your overpriced New York studio apartments."

He spat these words at Flip with caustic vehemence and charged forward, stumbling into the literature student's office chair and in his rage hurling it against the wall with a crash so that it overturned with its wheels spinning. "Is that what they taught you in your rich hippie liberal arts college while the rest of us had to stay in-state? Where the fuck do you get off writing about anything besides a bunch of rich snobs complaining about other rich snobs? Fucking real life isn't like your fantasy world because in *real life* people have to fucking plan for how they're going to support themselves, so I'm sorry we're all so far beneath you for trying to pursue fucking careers."

Flip tore himself back into the space by the bookshelf. "That's not true," he said, somehow out of breath. "You don't know where I came from or what I want to do. I haven't been to New York since the tenth grade."

Kendall stood without moving. "Oh I know you, and I know how you feel about all of us because I've read your whiny novel draft. I can't believe you had the balls to send that to us, even though it only makes you look like an immature child."

"You're reading too much into it," Flip stuttered as he realized he'd been found out. "The whole point was to write something that showed people the way life really is."

Kendall laughed sarcastically at this, relaxing his upper torso and shifting to lean against the bookcase. "Ha! Maybe that's how life is in your universe. You know what your mistake is, Phil? You honestly believe there are people out there who think the way you do, but in reality *no one* thinks the way you do because they're all too busy living in the real world."

Flip's vision began to cloud and he felt like he might pass out.

"But the real reason I came here was to tell you to stay away from Derzen," Kendall went on. "She and I agreed that you two should keep a strictly professional relationship from now on—small talk and hellos in the hallway and that kind of thing. I'm sure you'll find that's all she wants from you anyway."

Flip felt what little color remained in his face drain out of it as the haze brought on from lack of food and sleep clouded the last of his vision. "You don't control her. She can do what she wants."

"Of course she can," Kendall said. "And she will." He pressed down on the door handle and slipped into the hallway, leaving Flip alone beside the literature student's overturned chair.

An Office with a View

a novel by Flip Montcalm

In the evenings I fall victim to a dull foreboding that immobilizes me in my bed fearful that if I go to sleep I'll have to wake up again and face the void. I feel the same auguries of near-certain doom in the mornings when I lay with my eyes shut not wanting to get up, and in the daytime I feel listless and am prone to pulsating headaches centered around my nasal cavity. People who know me refer to me using words like *detached, morose, oversensitive*, and *tense*, and I scare easily when I see someone I'm not expecting approach from around a corner. When I'm forced to confront people in power I often stutter and feel unsure of what I know to be true, and I worry what few remnants of dignity I have left are being extinguished one after the other. It astounds and disgusts me that my life has turned out this way because I never thought it would when I was younger. After all, I work in an office.

My job would be infinitely more bearable if it wasn't for the work environment, which forces my coworkers to act in a stiffly unnatural manner when they interact with others (especially me). The work I do is itself not so egregiously awful (just repetitive, pointless, and boring), and I might even consider it pleasant if I could do it alone in my room at my parents' house or in one of those cool, progressive West-Coast startups I hear about where the break rooms have foosball tables and employees are entitled to free snacks and massages (sometimes, I imagine, at the same time).

I don't, however, think anyone in my office plays foosball or would ever get a massage during work hours even if one was available—they're under enormous pressure to maintain a strict aura of professionalism and appear much older than they are (even though most of the people I work with are only in their late twenties, they walk, talk, dress, and act much older in a resigned, mirthless sort of way) so their superiors will think highly of them and give them promotions, even though there are very few promotions to be had now since our company is being made obsolete by a changing society no longer as interested in paying for cable television as it once was. My coworkers grip my hand in stiff, formal handshakes the way they must imagine other adults do, and when they talk they seem obsessively reluctant to make mistakes for fear someone will think less of them. (I like to believe that they were once good people who became twisted after years of working here until their personalities began leaking out of their pores and dripping down the parking lot drainage system, leaving only bland work personas that fail to embody the individuals they really are.)

The person with the cube across from mine is named Jake. This is Jake's first job after college; he moved here from a suburb of a larger city far away and is always trying to talk to me about sports, either oblivious to or not bothering with my complete lack of interest. (It amazes me how ubiquitous a place sports holds in our daily discourse when there are trillions of other things we could be talking about, and I'm convinced that a significant percentage of people who seem to really care about sports only pretend to do so because everyone around them seems to really care about sports too.) Often when I'm either daydreaming or actually trying to work I'll hear Jake push his chair away from his desk to announce a baseball victory or news about a football player whose name he expects me to know—I can't conceive how people keep track of so many contemporary athletes when so many are coming and going all the time without any reliable indicator of which will become enshrined in legend and which will have their brief moment and be forgotten. When Jake comes at me I have no choice but to nod along to whatever indecipherable thing he's explaining until he realizes he should be getting back to work and leaves me alone again. Though he possesses the idealistic enthusiasm typical of younger people whose delusions haven't yet been crushed, I've gathered that Jake isn't very good at his job and suspect he won't be getting a promotion anytime soon (or ever) because he appears pathologically unable to start a very large, very important, but very long-term project he's been entrusted with. In spite of this crippling shortcoming I don't think the people in charge will take the more drastic action of letting him go and will instead allow him to drift through a miasma of non-existent advancement until he realizes on his own that he's not cut out for life here.

Another of my coworkers is named Floyd, and while I suspect that Floyd hates this company as much as I do, his hatred has become so intense that rather than allow it to drive him insane he's harnessed it into an exaggerated zeal that favors everything the company does. He has a hyperbolic tendency to fling his hands wildly when he speaks, and when he grows especially excited loose bits of spit will shoot from his overeager, hurried mouth that he appears not to notice. In meetings he outlines his ideas on the pages of legal pads that he scribbles on with leaky ballpoint pens and throws away whenever he gets a new idea regardless of how many pages the pad has left. Once, when we were both waiting for the break room coffee pot to boil, I watched Floyd grab two mugs from the cupboard, yank the pot from the machine when it finished brewing, then fill both mugs with coffee for himself while leaving me to brew my own pot. (The incident left me feeling desolate and confused, partly as to how an individual could be so oblivious to the presence of others, but also because who drinks two separate mugs of coffee like that?) Though Floyd was one of the people I felt most drawn to when I started here, I now find myself annoyed by his inability to move his ideas toward any tangible outcome and avoid him whenever possible.

The person two cubes down is named Timothy (not "Tim" and certainly not "Timmy," but "Timothy" in both official documents and to his face), who goes about his work with a laughably naïve lack of understanding that makes him seem much younger than his actual age. Timothy is the most sincere of all my co-workers and also the most frustrating since he appears to actually believe that the insignificant data entry we work on every day actually serves a vital purpose, and that if he continues working hard enough in a few years he'll rise to a more prominent position in the company that will bring him a higher salary and social status. More than once I've attempted to confide in him my doubts about the company's future, though in response he proceeds to look at me with a detached twinkle in his eyes and dogmatically parrot the company's goal of expanding cable television access to more and more households in addition to its domination of internet. I pity Timothy for believing this and for not understanding the weaknesses in the company's plan, but I suspect he's adopted this unyielding trust as a defense mechanism against his inability to change career paths since the thought of the company he's invested so much time and energy in having no future is so egregiously unbearable that he can't even bring himself to consider it.

Polar opposite of Timothy is Mitch, who I suspect harbors ambitions to take over the company through a heartless series of deceptions made at the expense of others unless he can find another job with a higher salary first. Mitch was friendly to me when I first started here (as he's friendly with everyone who first starts here) but this was only because he needed my help with an enormous project I had no interest in helping with since it technically wasn't my job and didn't come with extra pay. (I regret taking on that enormous project now because at the time I believed it would boost my standing with the company, and for months now I've been trying to bow out without being noticed.) Mitch is most easily characterized by his annoying laugh, disregard for the personal space of others, and plentiful advice on how to succeed within the company that I soon recognized as his attempts to improve his own standing. (Most alarmingly, he's obsessed by the idea that people from other backgrounds are being given unfair advantages due to affirmative action and portrays himself as a victim of systematic oppression so he can steal these supposed opportunities for himself.) If I ever had a good idea—I mean a really good idea for a sales promotion or marketing ploy that would boost our stagnating revenue stream—I'm certain that Mitch would be right there to take credit for it by speaking louder and more convincingly about it than I could, and it's this overbearing quality of his that I'm afraid will lead him to a better job while less outspoken people like me are left in the dust.

All of us in my department (I should say *men* or *guys* in my department, since through some unknown fault of hiring bias or random chance there are no women here) are kept under the supervision of our boss, Stephen Harding, a prematurely balding man in his early forties with two children and a wife who works as a lawyer. I've heard that Harding (I can't bring myself to call him by his first name) attained his position because of his early successes at different companies that made him a much-demanded commodity, thus allowing him to obtain a salary nearly five times what we make. Because of this, everyone in my department grants him a certain amount of respect despite his being timid, weak-willed, and disliking confrontation. Since he inevitably replies to my emails with messages of three words or less, I most often knock on his door to ask him questions (since he, unlike the rest of us, is allowed a real office with a window and more comfortable chairs), though when I come to him he speaks to me in a vague series of surmises that together suggest something very specific he wants me to do without saying it directly. These supposed answers are in all cases an embodiment of the company's way of doing things, which is invariably the same way the company has always done things and will continue to do them in the future despite their no longer really working.

My job would bother me a lot less if it allowed for innovation within the never-ending onslaught of data entry and marketing promotions that all invariably look the same. If I ever had an idea for how to change things I'd have to pitch it to Harding before Mitch could steal it or shoot it down, and assuming Harding approved said idea and that it actually resonated among my coworkers, at that point the gaggle of ancients who control the company would be forced to turn their heads and acknowledge a more effective way of doing things, but I've realized now that this will never happen and that my place lies among the rows of sprawling, identical work cubes stretching across the bare-walled third floor of our building where I'm encouraged every day to put my head down, follow the rules, and talk about sports whenever Jake comes over to say hi. In this way and only this way can I draw my paycheck and hope to somehow scrounge up enough contacts and experience to procure a better opportunity somewhere else.

But the more I consider this the more I'm unsure that another job at a big company is what I really want. I've never really been sure what I want, and maybe my own lack of conviction is why I stay in this faceless, uninspiring place with people who are just as aimless as I am.

The one exception to my string of empty working relationships is with Alexa Ayers, the tall, slender, long-haired girl who works in another branch of accounting and feels the same way about the company that I do. I often come across her in the hallway between our cubicle rows, and it was through these meetings that we began joking (and, if I'm not mistaken, occasionally flirting) about the barren and uninspiring atmosphere of the company that alienates us. When Alexa laughs I forget the way the company wants me to think and can once again see its shortcomings for what they are. (I just needed to know I wasn't alone.) Seeing that upbeat look on her face makes me want to wrap my arms around her shoulders in her lavender work blazer and kiss her against the hard blue fuzz of a cube wall. One scenario I fantasize about involves me coming across her one night when we're both working overtime, since it's only after we've escaped from the stifling atmosphere of the daytime into a world where we can be ourselves that I could ever hope to engage her on a more honest (and carnal) level.

I think about Alexa often in both a romantic and an emotional way and realize that what's drawn us together is both our subtly critical attitudes toward the company and our mutual reluctance to leave it, since we're both young and lack the skills to obtain much in the way of other jobs. I'd definitely ask her out on a date were she not already in a relationship with Rodney Sean, an upper-tier member of my data-processing team whose chief achievement has been winning several Employee of the Month awards that he keeps hung on his cube wall where anyone walking in can see them. One of his campaign ideas was recently deemed worthy enough to be picked up by our marketing team, and though the campaign itself was as bland and uninspired as all of our others, its being selected was enough to earn him a disproportionate level of respect among our department, though I still can't understand why.

I hate Rodney not just because he's in a committed relationship with Alexa (this is actually the second reason) or because he's achieved more than I have (this is the third), but because of the condescending way he treats everyone around him, especially those whose ways of looking at the world differ from his own (as mine does), causing him to talk down to others with an arrogance not quite direct enough to call him out on, but one subtly relayed through his lack of eye contact and the authoritative manner in which he presents his opinions as statements of fact. I wonder how heavily this habit carries into his relationship with Alexa, and it repulses me to imagine him taking her for granted as if she were one of his data entry projects. In an ideal world I'd be able to somehow steal her away so she could be with someone whose worldview resonates with hers, or better yet I'd be able to show the entire office how idiotic Rodney and the rest of them are by coming up with a marketing campaign that'll surpass all of theirs, and if that campaign were new and innovative enough then the people above Harding would definitely give me a promotion and a new office that would earn me the respect of everyone, especially Alexa, who'd then want to—

45

"At long last," Stark began with an exaggerated clearing of his throat, "we're going to talk one more time about Flip's novel, which I must say has come a long way." He turned to the clipped packet in front of him to signal that his introduction had finished. "Does anyone have any thoughts?"

Across the table Kendall sat staring at Flip with a look of menace, his cold eyes blank and expressionless and his manuscript copy in front of him covered with notes.

Flip felt the sweat drip down the back of his neck as a strained gurgle churned in his stomach. How long had it been since he'd last eaten? A slow, unsettled surge of fear crept over him as he considered dashing out of the classroom and away from the English building and the entire campus forever.

An uncharacteristically thoughtful silence had fallen over the room. Craig moved his restless knee up and down as he looked over Flip's packet, Lawrence scratched the side of his neck with a blank look, Melvin's face held an expression carefully calculated to suggest deep consideration, and Brad rubbed his chin as he watched each of the others. Only Jackson sat relaxed, his eyes darting around the room as he twirled an uncapped pen between his fingers.

It was Kendall who finally spoke in an upbeat tone of exaggerated distinction. "I, for one, would like to applaud Phil on the impressive changes he's made to this over the semester," he said with a glance at Stark. "If nothing else, these pages feel more fine-tuned, without all that extended monologuing that plagued the first draft."

Flip watched as Brad and Melvin nodded their heads.

"I feel like for the first time I actually understand what the main character *wants*," Kendall continued with a tightening of his fist. "All that muddy rambling from the first draft's been eliminated, and in its place we finally have some sort of direction the novel's moving in."

"Oh, definitely," Lawrence said.

"The problem is, though," Kendall said, ignoring the interruption as a tense, disparaging tone entered his voice, "is that I'm still seeing a completely unsympathetic protagonist who complains about everything around him to the point where I just want him to shut up and do his job like everybody else." He aimed his cold, vaguely threatening eyes in Flip's direction. "I thought about this question with the first draft, but it feels even more important now: What makes this character so special to believe that he's so much better than the people around him?"

Flip felt his vision grow fuzzy again.

"That's an excellent point, and I'm glad Kendall brought it up," Melvin said, leaning forward with a commanding air. "I also couldn't quite sympathize with the narrator here and kept asking myself why this guy isn't off running his own company somewhere if he's so smart and talented. Since I haven't actually seen him do anything worthwhile, I keep getting the impression that he's just talking big."

Flip looked to Jackson for help, though as expected Jackson sat slouched in his chair watching the others.

"That's exactly what I was about to say," Kendall said, speaking slightly louder than before. "I find myself questioning the narrator's reliability here since his perspective on the world seems so idealized and isn't based on actual experience." Without warning he focused his eyes squarely on Flip's. "And probably the biggest example of this is his irrational hatred for the Rodney character, who doesn't seem to have done much to the narrator besides offend him with his Employee of the Month awards. The intended effect seems to be for me to hate the Rodney character as much as the narrator does, but because we never actually see this Rodney guy doing anything arrogant, instead I start to think that the narrator is just being petty since I've already heard his other condescending views about the people around him."

Flip's heart slammed forcefully against his ribcage as he fought back the urge to vomit.

"It seems to me," Kendall continued, "that the narrator can't quite be trusted here, and that the Rodney character's actually a hardworking, competent employee who's done everything right at his job and come up with some effective campaigns, so why should we hate him for being successful?" He let the question hang unanswered as he stared Flip down again.

No one said anything, and Flip wondered whether he'd been condemned and sentenced without need for further workshop.

Then, someone else spoke.

"I don't know, man," Craig said, bouncing his restless knee up and down under the table. "People do passive-aggressive shit all the time, so I totally took the narrator's word for it that this Rodney guy's super-arrogant even though he has to be all sly and backdoor about it so people can't call him out."

"I was also struck by the Employee of the Month awards," Stark said as he shuffled vaguely through his manuscript. "I got the sense through what the narrator's told us about this world that it's not socially acceptable for people to brag openly about their achievements, but since the Rodney character wants people to think he's important he's developed sneakier ways of flaunting his accomplishments." He gave a brief but visible shudder. "Plus, I always found those awards pointless anyway."

Flip felt most of his vision return but struggled to catch his breath as Kendall jumped back in. "That's a good point, but even if the Rodney character wants to covertly show off, we're still getting the very real impression that the narrator's just bitter at not having won the awards himself, which leads to his resenting the Rodney character for being better at his job than he is."

"I thought that too, actually," Lawrence said quickly. When it became clear that Kendall was going to let him speak, he continued. "I definitely sensed some resentment on the narrator's part, but then I realized that it's perfectly natural to resent people who've beaten us at things, and I thought Flip captured that really well. Maybe what we're seeing between Rodney and the narrator is actually a natural butting of heads that happens whenever a group of people are all vying for the same few opportunities, which is what seems to be going on here."

"That's funny you mention that," Brad said, "because I was also thinking that this Rodney guy was ignoring everybody else in his quest for the top." He gave a merry but uncharacteristically grim chuckle. "And you know—I kind of found myself wanting to see him fail!"

"I don't think so," Kendall said at once. "I think we've seen too much of this narrator's hyperbole to trust his opinions about the world around him, especially when it comes to his lusting after Rodney's girlfriend, which no matter how you look at it is a despicable thing to do." He turned his packet to a dog-eared page obscured almost completely by black pen marks. "I mean, he comes right out and says on page thirty-nine that it's wrong to want to be with her and that he should be going after other girls besides the Alexa coworker, but then two pages later he goes right back to wanting to steal her away. That not only shows me that he doesn't care about anyone but himself, but also that he's not even brave enough to try dating girls he actually has a chance with."

"I'm going to respectfully disagree with everything you just said," Craig called out from the other end of the table. "This plan of his to steal the girl is the best thing the book has going for it. We've all seen that office romance shit before, but this thing with the Alexa girl is bigger than all that because this guy's trapped in his office park all day long working in a cubicle the size of a port-o-potty, and he needs to get laid bad. This girl's the one person in that hell hole who sees things the way he does, and that's deep shit— they have this real connection. This girl could be the most ordinary girl in the world, or maybe she's even ass-ugly or has a horrible facial scar or something, but none of that matters because she's this guy's fucking oasis against the monotony of his stupid job, so of course he's going to fall for her."

Stark raised his eyebrows in what seemed like genuine surprise. "I hadn't thought of that, but it makes a lot of sense. I was going to add that by trying to prove himself a better romantic partner than the Rodney character, the narrator's really acting out an unconscious urge to get revenge on this office world that's treated him cruelly. So in a way, wanting to sleep with Alexa is his way of giving the middle finger not only to Rodney, but to the entire company."

Flip had become gradually aware that something that had never happened before was happening around him now, and with it came equal parts reward at having provoked a thoughtful discussion and terror at having so blatantly exposed his own motives.

"That's what I kind of liked about it," Lawrence said, "that there's this place with so much tension and hidden hate where nobody has a real chance at getting a promotion but everyone's still trying to get ahead of everyone else, so it makes sense that the narrator would feel bitter and defeated about the whole thing."

"But that doesn't make the narrator right," Kendall said. "It actually makes him worse because stealing a girl just because you hate the guy she's dating is about the most superficial reason I can think of to want to sleep with someone."

"I'll agree with Lawrence, actually, and just want to add one thing," Melvin said. "We're all products of our environment, and we always start acting like the people we spend the most time around. If everybody in that office is acting all phony and business-like, then the narrator's either going to become completely entrenched in that world like the others or he's going to go crazy and reject it all."

"*Crazy*'s a strong word," Jackson said, speaking for the first time. "In a lot of ways the world we live in is pretty fucked up, and while most people just shrug that off, there's a certain kind of person who can't bring themselves to accept the status quo, especially when it doesn't make sense or restricts our basic needs for freedom and self-expression. If that person's smart enough to realize that they can't actually change their surroundings, they're probably just going to put on a cheerful disguise and start living in their own world to shield themselves from the bullshit."

"Right," Melvin said immediately. "That's what I meant."

"I wouldn't say that justifies his wanting to sleep with the Alexa character," Kendall said again, "since you can't just use the excuse that material conditions make it acceptable to do bad things."

In what was unquestionably the most thoughtful, concisely expressed statement Flip had ever heard him utter, Melvin said, "But he hasn't slept with her yet."

"But he's thought about it!" Kendall answered, a tremor of anger flaring into his voice and barely repressed fury leaping from his eyes. "He goes off on this elaborate fantasy on page fifty-four about wanting to perform oral sex on her next to the break room microwave!"

"Oh man," Craig said. "That was my favorite part."

"I'm sure it was," Kendall said with annoyance, "but the graphic nature of the fantasy, which I took to be overly detailed and borderline misogynistic, is so repulsive that it makes the narrator out to be some depraved sex maniac."

Here there came a pause until Stark himself spoke. "I didn't think the oral sex fantasy was that graphic—I actually thought it stood out from the blandness that's conveyed in the rest of the pages since that's the first moment when we really find a release from the office world, and until I got to that scene I hadn't quite realized how restricted I was feeling."

"So why not put in more of that?" Craig said. "More fantasies, more passion, more eating girls out—and I was thinking, what if the book *started* with him eating the Alexa girl out for real?"

"I think that would feel even cruder than what's already there," Kendall said coldly.

"I agree with Kendall," Brad said. "Starting the book with oral sex would feel too obvious a ploy for the reader's attention. But I do want to talk about how Flip shows us all these outlandish characters from the very first chapter."

"Mmmmmm," Lawrence murmured. "There are a lot of characters."

"Maybe too many," Brad said. "I have trouble keeping track of them all, and I'm not sure exactly what their function is in the story beyond adding atmosphere. Even now I'm getting the impression that the side characters aren't crucial to the story and that this is really a novel about the narrator-Alexa-Rodney love triangle."

Kendall sat heavily in his seat, his control over the discussion lost.

"And what was the deal with that Timothy guy?" Lawrence asked suddenly. "The one who blindly believes everything the company tells him. Is he learning disabled or something?"

Jackson snickered and spoke again. "No—the narrator suggests at one point that he's too afraid to imagine life outside the company, so he's wrapping himself in the fantasy that it's going to provide him a stable future and ignoring all evidence to the contrary."

"Jackson makes an excellent point," Stark said. "I'm sensing one of the novel's themes is that everyone in this office faces an uncertain future and is afraid the people around them are doing better than they are. That's led to this overly competitive atmosphere that's made even the narrator desperate to create his own successful marketing idea and win over the girlfriend of this co-worker he doesn't like. The co-worker characters, though, seem to have responded to the pressure by playing to these dryer, no-nonsense versions of themselves that Flip portrays in an exaggerated manner so readers can easily recognize them." He paused, both to let this sink in and because he seemed to actually consider it himself. "The interesting part is that while we know the narrator's aware of what's going on, we're never really sure whether the other characters secretly think the way the narrator does and just aren't saying so, or whether they've actually become the oblivious caricatures we're seeing on the page."

It was the most beautiful summation of his writing Flip had ever heard, and he knew in that moment that the novel was working—it wasn't entirely where it needed to be yet, but it had pushed the others past unfocused criticism into actual discourse. It was the thing literature could do better than any other kind of art, and as the angst of having his inner secrets exposed began to settle, he felt his muscles unclench and his mouth finally moisten. That he'd made this happen with his own work, even on this imperfect level, felt astounding.

It was then that Kendall, with his teeth clenched and his eyes still narrowed behind his rimless glasses, spoke even louder than before. "Oh come on now—I can't believe you don't see it. Sure the whole thing's disguised a bit, but Phil hasn't written a novel about office life at all—he's written one about grad school life, and he hasn't been very subtle about it because all he did was change the names and a few background details." He held up a page covered in black pen. "William, look at page thirty-three when he makes fun of his boss for speaking with all those unnecessary pauses." He pointed at Melvin, Craig, Lawrence, and Brad in succession, his words pouring out with more vehemence. "Or look at the one who chatters on about nothing all the time, the crazy one with restless leg syndrome, or the clueless one who writes all of his reports using the same syntax, not to mention the one who's keeping account opportunities secret so he can steal them for himself! Phil clearly thinks academia's a sham and that we're all a bunch of self-serving drones too blind to understand the system, but he's too cowardly to say that to our faces so he's chosen to mock us in his fiction instead. I'm surprised he had the audacity to even show this unless he thought we were all too stupid to notice so he could have a good laugh, or maybe he was so desperate to show off how clever he is that he didn't care. I'm half inclined to believe this is some bizarre social experiment, but I personally think this twisted worldview is how he actually thinks and he's just spilling it on the page as a form of cheap therapy."

He hurled Flip's pages across the table with a clatter. "But that's not the way things fucking work. You don't make fun of real-life people in your fiction, you don't make fun of grad school in your fiction, you don't interrupt when someone's escorting the visiting writer, and you definitely don't fucking try to steal people's girlfriends." His hate-filled eyes stared directly into Flip's. "You can't do that. NO ONE does that. And if you're such an amazing writer who understands the goddamn system so well, why the fuck are you still sitting in workshop with all us peons?"

The silence that filled the room was deafening. For what seemed like hours the only sounds were the hum of the fluorescent lights and the slow turning of pages as the rest of them checked whether Kendall was right.

Jackson, his face blank, drummed his fingers on the desk and stared at the ceiling. Stark's eyes met Flip's with a disappointed look that Flip was too frightened to turn away from.

It was finally Craig who said, "Fuck, man, I don't really sound like that, do I?"

That was when Flip knew that even though he'd clinched some key victories, it was Kendall who'd won the war.

46

"YOU DIDN'T actually think that would work, did you?" Jackson asked when they were alone in his office after Stark had suggested they all leave an hour early. "Just like it's not so easy to make someone fall for you when they're dating someone else."

"How was I supposed to know that?" Flip demanded because he knew as always that Jackson was right. He tried to pace around the cramped, broom-closet-like office that Jackson had somehow gotten to himself but found he didn't have enough room to move and stood by the desk with his fists clenched. "It just felt like everything was going to work out."

Next to him a single window looked out over a dirt pit behind an orange construction fence.

"Of course it did," Jackson said as he tossed a stack of Cormac McCarthy novels into his bag. "There's plenty of things that feel right but never work out in real life, even though we'd all be a lot happier if they did. Things would be way less screwed-up if the genuine world always won out over the materialistic world, but unfortunately the ideal outcome isn't always the one that wins. Novels are full of meaningful stories that enrich our understanding of the world, but after we put our books down we've got to deal with real-life stuff like bills and jobs and relationships. Sometimes people have bigger things to worry about than the truth."

"Why didn't you tell me that before?" Flip asked with his palms gripping the air.

"Because I couldn't destroy your natural impulse to try," Jackson said. "There's enough people out there who've resigned themselves to the materialistic world, and it's rare that people actually go after something bigger. At the end of the day you have to decide whether you want to write something genuine or whether you want to go after the fabulous prizes—but that's only if you see them as prizes at all."

Flip closed his eyes and ran both hands over his face.

"Anyway, Albert Camus has this great essay in *The Myth of Sisyphus* where he talks about art as a coping mechanism for helping us overcome our personal phantoms," Jackson went on. "You just have to be careful how you do it. No one likes seeing their own flaws held up to a fun-house mirror on the page—you remember what happened in *Harriet the Spy* when the other kids found her spy notebook, don't you?" He picked up copies of *Of Human Bondage* and *The Razor's Edge* as he stood to leave. "But let's not worry about that—how about we head back to my place and I'll make you the best Monte Cristo you've ever had?"

"I don't want a Monte Cristo!" Flip shouted because he no longer cared who heard him. "I wanted Derzen to leave Kendall but clearly that's never going to happen, and I wanted to wow people with a meaningful novel, so now I have to go home and figure out another way to write one."

Jackson nodded as he opened the door. "If that's what you want, then you should go for it. Just don't forget the Faustian contract in reverse."

"Don't worry," Flip said. "I won't."

A Brand-New MFA Thesis Novel That Shows People the Empty Truth Inherent in Human Interaction in Such a Way That None of My Former Coworkers or the Other Grad Students Will Realize It's Really About Them

a novel by Flip Montcalm

In the evening I fall victim to a dull foreboding that how the fuck am I going to write a fucking I hate this fucking place fuck fuck FUCK fuckfuckfuckfuck-fuckfuckfuckfuckfuckfuckfuckfuckbqhke rlfgbqerrlkvbqelkuuhq3iguh135p58 9ty19t8gb135g!!!!!!!!!!!!#%^^^#%^GFKTUFI^VLUKY^F&ICVLF^&FF^%F O*^FO*^F BNVDFR<L:?<>MBHJDXF>MNBHUJLKJHFX&$%^7t8o7ihr p8fhhq er9r98grvbffviddafuv eqrgip3h7go873hgp3g?L;'m

With a scream of fury Flip threw himself away from the laptop and beat the carpeted floor with his fists.

The next day he wrote a final paper for the Great Plains Studies class on the role of the sod house in *My Antonia*. Then he wrote one for the Critical Theory class on Foucault's distributions of power.

from: William Stark, M.F.A.
to: Flip Montcalm
date: Fri, Dec 1 at 4:32 PM
subject:

Hi Flip,

Seeing as how the semester's almost over, it's probably better if we hold off meeting until after the break to discuss your novel. I also think it's better if you take some time to decide what you really want to write about, and then we'll go from there.

Also, sorry about the three-word replies.

Will

When the semester ended, Flip flew back to the town he'd grown up in, where there were mountains and lakes and he could play Splendor with his friends who wanted to hear all about grad school and what it was like in such a different place. Some days he went for walks through the woods on the old snowmobile trails or sat on the guardrail by the town's covered bridge watching the river flow onward.

When he came back after the break he spent a lot of time lying around the apartment thinking. The weather had turned unbelievably dry and the harsh winds whipped at his face whenever he went out. One freezing cold morning the Honda refused to start and he had to pay to have its battery replaced.

Everything just seemed so empty, somehow.

Then one day something happened:

Derzen Draskovich

That's awesome! I'm really happy for you

Thanks

Anyway, I should probably get back to work. I still have a bunch of reading to do and a paper I should be working on

Yeah, me too! Good luck with the rest of your work

Thanks. You too

Monday, Feb 19 · 3:48 PM

Hey! Sorry I've been so out of it after everything last semester. You want to grab coffee later this week?

Feb 19, 3:48 PM

 Type a Message

47

Derzen Draskovich's poetry has appeared or is forthcoming in The Westchester Review, Pilotwing, Spherical Outliers, Moreover, *and* The Avocado Sundry Review. *She's excited to announce that after finishing her MFA she'll be continuing on to a PhD in creative writing.*

"THE WHOLE thing really came as a surprise," Derzen said with both hands wrapped around her coffee mug. "The department doesn't usually fund people moving from MFA to PhD since they want us to establish connections at other universities instead of just working in the same place. But my letter said they're increasing annual funding by four hundred dollars and giving new PhDs a one-two teaching load their first year to help them get settled, so the extra time should really help me start prepping for comps. And did I tell you I finished my MFA collection?"

"No," Flip said. Aside from the two of them, the coffee shop was nearly empty since the forecast had called for steady snowfall with accumulation into the evening. Outside a thin layer of wet snow had already begun to coat the sidewalks and the roofs of the cars parked throughout the old downtown. Behind Derzen sat the shop's only other patron, a twenty-something girl with dreadlocks and a nose ring who was cutting images out of magazines, and Flip occasionally stole glances at her as she leafed through pages before stopping to snip an image and place it in a cigar box.

"It came out really well," Derzen went on, "and my committee wants me to start sending it out right away because if I can get it published I'll have a much better chance at getting a longer collection looked at, and if I can somehow get two books out then I'll be a much stronger candidate if I want to go on the job market after only three years. I know everyone says you should take the full five years for the PhD since you've got the funding, but the sooner I'm out of here the sooner I can move on to something better, you know?"

"That's true," Flip said. Such agreeable responses were the only ones he'd found himself able to utter in the half hour since they'd sat down. How shocking had it been to get Derzen's text, which had caused him to put down his phone and lie down on the air mattress he'd finally managed to repair. He'd felt no anger at her over what had happened, only a lingering sense of curiosity mixed with traces of fondness that had dwindled as the weather grew colder.

"It's really not as rough out there as people think," Derzen said, and then corrected herself. "I mean, it's rough, but it's still possible for people who are good enough to get jobs. I'm already planning to meet up with Jennifer Vallencourt and Wendy Nottingham at this year's Association of Creative Writers Conference, and we're hoping to put together a panel on Marianne Moore for next year, so if that goes well I'm thinking they'll be willing to at least write me a back-cover blurb."

Flip wondered whether Derzen would continue talking in this tone if a man engulfed in flames were to hurl himself through the coffee shop window. "What did Kendall say when you told him the news?" he asked.

Derzen seemed to relax as her fingers loosened their death grip on the coffee mug. "He was happy, of course, and he talked about staying on an extra year as a lecturer until I finish, and then both of us going on the job market and seeing if we can't get into the same place, or at least somewhere close. In any case, we'll see what happens."

Flip wondered exactly what their conversation had sounded like and which ideas had been suggested by which parties. "He didn't have to convince you to send the PhD applications, did he?"

Derzen's face grew more serious. "No. I decided to send them myself because I needed to keep my options open."

"That's good," Flip said. "No one should feel forced into making that kind of decision."

"No," Derzen said. "It's horrible when people feel forced."

They fell into a silence that wasn't quite awkward but also wasn't quite the Uma-Thurman-*Pulp-Fiction* kind until Flip said, "Kendall also told me you never wanted to see me again, but I wasn't sure whether that was him talking or you."

Derzen took a sip of her coffee and nodded. "I know. It was a crazy time and I had all these things bouncing around my head and I let myself get carried away that night. But our friendship is still important to me because you understand what really matters. I guess it just seemed better to let things lie for a while."

"That's part of why I've been spending less time on campus lately," Flip said. "Kendall was pretty angry, especially combined with that whole mess about my novel, so it's probably better that he decided not to take workshop this term. It's pretty empty now that he's gone and Craig's switched to poetry, but it's nice that the rest of us can talk more."

Derzen nodded again, and Flip wondered how much Kendall had told her about the novel. "I think that was the best thing for everybody," she said.

"He still won't make eye contact when I see him in the hallway, though."

Derzen looked away for an instant. "Oh, he's like that with everyone. He told me there's no hard feelings on his end."

"Really?"

She nodded. "Yeah."

"So he must know you're having coffee with me right now?" Flip asked.

"I didn't tell him specifically," Derzen said, "but I will if he asks. I'm free to meet the people I want to meet, and when I texted you the other day it was because I missed our talks and I didn't want to see our friendship die." She shifted her feet under the table. "I'm sure Kendall would prefer it if I hadn't texted you, but being jealous never did anyone any good, and we're really just sitting here talking about grad school stuff. In a different world things might have worked out some other way, but that's just how things are."

"Yes," Flip said. "That's just how things are."

Another of those responses that led to silence, and Flip took the opportunity to remove a small object from his jacket pocket. "Anyway, I didn't get a chance to give you this after Thanksgiving, but I thought you might like it now."

She stared at it with her brow wrinkled and turned it around, studying its stem and curved base until she finally asked, "What is it?"

"It's a fig," Flip said. "Like from Sylvia Plath's fig tree."

When he said this Derzen looked away with an amused, embarrassed smile, then glanced around the coffee shop struggling to keep from laughing until she turned to Flip again. "Where did you find this?"

"From the Sylvia Plath gift shop at Smith," Flip said. "They also sell Easy-Bake Ovens and Ted Hughes action figures."

This time Derzen laughed a tremulous, open laugh and covered her mouth with both hands. "That's the worst thing I've ever heard! It's like you're tearing my adolescence apart." She looked back at the fig. "You know, until now I wasn't even sure what figs looked like. I always imagined they were purple, like plums."

"Me too," Flip said. "I also finally read *The Bell Jar* over break and liked it a lot."

"Isn't it great?" Derzen said. "I know it's melodramatic and overdone and we're not supposed to hold it on a pedestal, but a certain part of me will always love it."

Outside the sky had grown dimmer as the snow continued to fall, and they put on their jackets while the girl with the dreadlocks continued snipping pictures at her table. They walked side by side down the coffee shop stairs and across the sidewalk leaving footprints in the snow until Derzen stopped beside an expensive-looking late-model hatchback with blinkers on its side mirrors and a dealership's plastic ring encasing its license plate.

"I decided to drive instead of walking," she said as she pulled open the door. "Do you want a ride?"

Flip looked inside the car, which was very clean and looked as if it still retained its new car smell. He wondered what Derzen would have thought of the duct tape holding the Honda's driver's seat together if she'd chosen to run away with him.

"No thanks," he said. "The snow's nice, so I think I'll walk."

When he said this Derzen's cheery look faded and a distinct but faint trace of concern crept into her eyes. "Are you sure?" she asked.

Flip nodded. "It's no problem."

"I feel bad because I didn't even ask about your novel," Derzen said. "Are you going to rewrite it or work on something new?"

"I haven't decided yet," Flip said. "For now I'm just bringing old short stories into workshop while I figure out what to pitch to Stark for an MFA thesis."

Derzen nodded again with the same concerned look. "Just don't work too hard, okay? And you know you're always welcome to come out for drinks with us if you need a break."

Flip nodded too and said, "I know." He realized he'd forgotten something and said, "I'm sure you'll do great in the PhD program."

Derzen's expression remained unchanged. "Thanks."

They faced each other for what seemed like a long time, the snow slowly clinging to their clothes and hair in a moment that felt like a gross parody of their last goodbye under the tree. "I guess we can always meet for coffee again," Derzen finally said.

"Of course," Flip said, though he now felt certain that they wouldn't. "And we'll see each other around."

"Of course." She pulled the car door all the way open. "Don't be a stranger, okay?"

"I won't," Flip said.

As Derzen drove away he walked off through the snow watching the flakes fall against the billowing clouds. He walked this way past the ancient corn and cattle feed warehouses and the scrap metal storage yard to where the alphabet streets again became residential, turning every so often at a corner to watch the buildings of the old downtown and the snowflakes twisting against the immense gray sky. When he reached the apartment he removed his jacket and pulled open the blinds to let the soft light into the living room where there still wasn't any furniture, then stood staring out the window. The snow was falling faintly over the university, the Prairie Fire stadium, the office buildings of the city, and further westward, over the dark and empty farmer's fields, faintly falling like in James Joyce's "The Dead" all over the Midwest. It was falling, too, upon every part of the duplex with the low porch where Kendall had waited for Derzen's return.

He stood thinking about a great many things until he turned away from the window, sat down at the folding table, pushed aside the books for his Nineteenth Century Lit class, and opened a new notebook.

Acknowledgements

I always joke that the surest way to tell a recent book from an old one is to look at the length of its Acknowledgments, though rather than fall into another academic pitfall, I'll try to limit this one to people who helped in the creation of this book specifically.

First off, many thanks to Jessica Bell of Vine Leaves Press for reaching into the slush pile to take a chance on this book, and to my awesome editor Melanie Faith, who, in addition to her expert writing eye, shares both my fondness for *Daria* and my cluelessness about sports. Thanks also to Amie McCracken of VLP for doing the hard work shuttling this book to publication.

I also owe major thanks to everyone who read and gave feedback on the manuscript from its early to near-finished stages, including Jack Hill, Josh Bresslin, Piper Tallis, Tristen Rogers, and others I've probably forgotten. Thanks to Mike Rushia and Stu Keenan for lending their handwriting to chapter one, and to the Toyama Writing Group: William Leroux, Lindsey Henderson, and Leilani Rapaport, who offered their insights over Gusto's fries and free drink bar refills.

Thanks to Joe and Sara Face for giving me a place to stay while I edited the rough draft of the manuscript, and to Paul Hanson Clark, Daniel Robotham, and Hugo and Katherine Rodriguez, who were there during a difficult time. Special thanks to Joanne Tulonen, Teresita Fiset, Annabel Davis-Goff, Christopher Miller, and the late Steven Bach, excellent teachers who introduced me to more than a few of the novels that inspired the structure of this book. I also owe thanks to the University of Nebraska-Lincoln English department, including Jonis Agee, Tim Schaffert, and visiting writer Sean Doolittle, for introducing me to the writing world and helping me hone a different novel that started out in much rougher shape than Flip's.

Finally, I'd like to thank my parents, for giving me the freedom to pursue the life I've wanted.

Vine Leaves Press

Enjoyed this book?
Go to *vineleavespress.com* to find more.